I0547604

Vienna

and

Choice

Two Novels by E. L. Schoeman

Schoe Box Books Publishing 2022

2022/12/19

This work is a work of fiction.

Font Garamond and font size 12

Cover art and design by Ellen Schoeman Photography

Photography by Ellen Schoeman Photography

ISBN 978-0-9948999-0-3

Choice

1

The Survivor

"Everything will be fine," she told herself. "I will not let you die so easily."

Her washed-out jeans felt heavy on her legs. The bottoms were soaked from the downpour an hour ago. It wasn't raining now, but the after smell reminded her of her father's advice. 'Marriage is like a steak dinner,' he'd said the day he'd come up with a husband for her, a thunderstorm raging on outside. 'Some people ruin it by adding condiments. Some people overcook it. Some people cook it just right but add all the wrong sides. And some people throw away everything else and just eat the steak.'

'What does that have to do with your not giving me a choice? You forgot to add that some people ruin marriage by getting married.'

'I don't know what I mean,' he admitted, walking away as if that settled it. 'But now I really want a steak.'

She swung her crossbow into her steady hands, knocking open the ratty excuse for a door, and entering through the back of the warehouse. There was a musty, vomit-like, unwashed smell along with the darkness that had to remain darkness because any light would give her away. If the lights went on things would come out or things would go running.

Her army boots were exceptionally silent as she moved, listening for noise above the scurrying of rats. If she was lucky, it wouldn't be done eating. If she was luckier, it hadn't started at all, but she was never that lucky.

She'd never saved anyone before.

For months she'd been trailing it all over the country. Staying in hotels, buying overpriced gas, sending late night texts to her father to tell him she'd lived another day. He never responded, not unless she said she was on her way home, and he decided he wanted her to pick up something for him. Can you believe that? Not even a 'glad you weren't eaten, honey. Have a good night.' All she got was, 'I'm out of bread. Pick some up on your way through.'

She was trained to move through darkness: to close her eyes and see then what her open eyes missed. Fear wasn't an option, even when it was there, tasting dry and like she hadn't brushed her teeth in days. But there wasn't room for fear now, listening to the shuffles up ahead as she crept around boxes and shelves, careful with the placement of her feet, the crossbow light in her hands.

It was here.

She fired once before flinging herself to the side, missing its quick attack. Her back hit a light switch. Blinding her, the place lit up. Being tackled to the ground sucked. Having the crossbow knocked out of her hands sucked more, but wrestling with the thing on top of her sucked the most. Struggling free, she kicked it in the head, and headed for the crossbow with it laughing behind her.

She turned, ready for the second act.

He looked the same from when she'd seen him last except that his eyes were black with white, upside down crosses for irises. Blood was running from the sides of his eyes. But he was the same well-set, darkened skinned beauty her father set up as her fiancé.

There wasn't time for horror or shock. Because how was she to know her husband to be had turned into a crazed monster? There was only time to act and she hoisted another arrow and let it fly. Another, another, and another arrow flew, all avoided by the slightest tips of his head.

"The Master of the World commands me to kill." Her fiancé looked at the limp body of his victim adjacent him. "So I'll kill."

"Fate?" He didn't seem to recognize his name. Was he this mounds of crazy when he'd taken her hand, promising he'd protect her, that they would want for nothing? Did it matter? She hadn't cared then. She didn't care that she'd have to kill him now. "What's your Master's name?"

His gaze held her, blood now streaming from the sides of his mouth. "The Master," was his answer.

"How lame," was hers, and she took the handgun she'd been hiding behind her back and double tapped him in the chest. He fell back. Not dead, he scrambled to his feet. Hissing with fury, he rushed at her.

"How lame," was her response, pulling the blade from her belt and cutting off his head, watching as it bounced along the floor until it rolled against the wall. The rest of him twitched to nothing.

She walked over to the head and took it into her left hand. Collecting her equipment, she started away until the body shifted. Freezing, she turned back slowly. The victim she'd thought was dead was trying to push itself up.

It was worse than having the creature resurrect itself.

The victim took in the scene. "Is it dead?"

She raised the head in her hand. "You're a boy?"

"Yeah."

Man, he looked like a girl. "But I heard a woman screaming."

She could make out his blush under the blood and warehouse dirt as he sat there, unsure of what to say.

"Never mind then, it was only you." She took a few steps back, trying to leave, but unsure how to do so. This was just all around awkward. I mean, what was she supposed to say to this guy? "So you're a doctor, huh?"

"How do you know that?"

Because those creatures are only killing medics... "Well..." She'd never had a survivor before. Ever. She wasn't trained how to deal with those, she was only trained how to deal with *things*. "Later."

"Wait." He was up and following her. "What's your name?"

Walking faster, she didn't turn around. "None of your damn business."

"Can I call you 'NYDB' for short?"

No response.

"I'm Deacon."

No response.

"You can't just leave me here!"

"You need a lift or something?"

"I mean, you can't just expect me to..."

"To what?"

"To forget about you. To let you disappear."

She vaguely looked back at his scrawny form: bony and delicate. His Asian features and wild, frightened eyes. "You look like the type that should be used to it."

"That's what I mean. I get the chance to latch on to a crossbow slinging girl like you, I better make sure she's the one that doesn't miss out on a guy like me."

"Not interested in useless luggage."

7

"Think about this. Really think about it. I'm a medic. You're a badass, don't get me wrong, but that *thing* ripped your arm open, and you've got a bloody lip. I can heal you quicker than you can heal yourself, unless you've been to med school…"

"I haven't."

"Great. I mean, great for me."

"I know what you meant."

They were out of the warehouse, and he was taking her lime green hot rod in with wonderment. Not that she blamed him. These days it was all horses and horse shit, and the roads were a bloody mess.

Tossing the head into the trunk, she got into the car and rolled down the passenger side window. He stood on the sidewalk, a blood-soaked forgotten puppy. "What are you waiting for? Get into the fucking car!"

2

The League of Dragons

He'd been quiet. He'd been quiet until he started tending to her arm. He told her that she might want to pull over, but she drove without twitching from the pain.

"Where are you going anyway?"

"The job's not finished," was her answer. Traffic was bad, but traffic was always bad. She'd like to think it was easier outside of this horse-and-carriage-new-age. When gas prices weren't scaring cars and trucks off the road and throwing their lot in with four-legged creatures that didn't need insurance. Carriages needed to be insured, though. What was up with that?

"But that thing's dead."

It was awkward, having him touching her. But it was mostly awkward because he looked so awkward doing it. "You ask too many questions."

"I've only asked one so far." He went back to focusing on his work, having reason to hesitate because with talking he wasn't doing a very good job with patching her up. He thought of everything that had passed. Working all day with a cancer patient. Walking out of the hospital at closing time, only to have a man standing in front of him, blood oozing from his eyes, making him scream like a girl when he tried to bite him. "You knew I was a doctor."

There really wasn't anything else to do but talk when driving. She could turn on the music. But it would just come in and out, mashing up different songs and old shows together because there wasn't much for radio around here or anywhere except maybe in Red. They were in Yellow: not much for electronics. She was amazed they even had gas stations. But that didn't make it any easier getting used to company while driving. "Fit the trend."

"What does that even mean?"

She fought a sigh. "You were its third victim this week alone."

"We're extra juicy, I guess."

"I took down one just like it beginning of the year. All medics, too. That's how I caught this one's scent. They're raking in the body count."

"I guess I'm lucky to be alive."

"That goes without saying."

"So, what? Vampires?"

She thought he'd be quiet after the whole 'I'm lucky to be alive' thing. But no. "What about vampires?"

"Was it them?"

Vampires were more common in the Green District, and they didn't have eyes like that. "No."

"Werewolves?"

"Professional guesser, are you?"

"I take it you have some idea, then?"

The truth was, it wasn't a typical case. She'd never seen a creature like it before, and creatures generally don't have preferences based on job descriptions. They kill to eat, they kill to kill. They don't usually target like this. And why doctors?

"Are you, like, a goddess?"

She gave him an 'I could kill you, you know?' look. "What does that even mean?"

He decided not to say anything about how pretty she was. Her fierce, purposeful, determined features. Her blue eyes had a great deal of depth, although they were buggy (probably from lack of sleep and too much caffeine). "It means there's got to be something twisted about you for hunting instead of being hunted."

"What's so great about being hunted? Why would I join that team?"

"You're taking that head somewhere. You're going *somewhere*. Wouldn't it be easier to let me in on who you are?"

She decided he might shut up if she just told him. "I was raised a Dragon."

"A Dragon? As in the League of Dragons: warriors, slayers, and oh my gods!"

She sighed. It didn't shut him up. "What are you babbling about?"

"Have you ever seen him?"

"Who?"

"Who? *The* Dragon." He gasped. "Don't tell me. He's your father!"

"He's not my father."

He exhaled loudly in disappointment. "Oh, because that would have been –"

"He protects my father."

10

Deacon jumped about in his seat. "Holy crap! Who's your father?"

"That's classified information," she said, annoyed. She didn't even know why her father was important. She'd never seen him do *anything*.

Deacon rubbed his arms as if protecting himself. "I'm a little bit scared of you now."

"I need to stop for bread," was what she said before turning up the music, knowing it would come in and out, but also knowing that it would drown out everything else.

3

The Nest

The lime green hot rod passed through the silver gates. The barbed wire fences (that were more like barbed wire fences on steroids) loomed above them, caging in brilliant stables, mansions, and well-designed combat training areas.

Some kids got milk and cookies, teddy bear kind of homes. She got swords, arrows, and the whip marks on her back. Friendly sparring and not so friendly punishment.

It had hard edges, but it was home.

White wolves swarmed the car before she shifted into park, growling and snarling, jumping up and trying to scratch the paint off her car.

Deacon's nails were trying to rip apart the passenger's seat.

Boy not big on puppies?

"Stay here," she ordered, but judging by his reaction to the wolves, the order was unnecessary. He wasn't about to move.

The pups growled. Growling back in German, they made a path for her, parting as she made her way to the trunk and then to the front door. A loaf of bread was in one hand and a severed head in the other.

A butler, who looked like he walked out of an Egyptian temple, opened the door. His arms, chest, neck and face were beautifully designed with thick black charcoal. To touch him would smudge and ruin the artwork.

He wore baggy black pants. The fabric was silent against him as he moved, stepping out of her way.

She didn't address him, walking by him and toward her father, his arms crossed behind his back, wearing the same sharp, intellectual expression he always wore.

His taste in style and décor was a cross between Medieval, class, and the twenties. Clashing nicely with the peculiar people he employed and the army of warriors that were housed here.

She threw the head of her fiancé down at her father's feet. "Don't ever try to set me up again."

Nothing shocked her father, and this was no different. He bent down, taking the head of her fiancé in his hands, and carefully examined it.

"Bread in the kitchen, please," was all he said.

Chucking the bread onto the counter in the next room, she went back to stand, arms crossed, in the doorway.

"How unfortunate..." he said under his breath.

"Low blow trying to set me up with a monster whose idea of a snack is raw human flesh."

"That reminds me, there's coconut cream pie in the fridge if you're hungry."

"I'm not." Although she forgot to mention to Deacon that there were cupcakes in the backseat if he was hungry, and he probably was. "I assume you're not completely senile and can tell the difference between monster and monster. So, what, Fate was turned by something? I assume he was some important Dragon kind of prince to you since you tried to set him up with me."

There was no response.

"Something big is starting. This new kind of *thing* is a *thing* I've never seen before. Look at its eyes, as dead as they are, those irises still pierce into you. And if Fate was a Dragon, *this whatever-it-is* can get to us. Was Fate a Dragon?"

There was no response from her father.

"Whatever. I'm taking the pie with me." She went to turn back into the kitchen.

"Fate wasn't a Dragon. But even so, the fact that he's now in this state is inconceivable."

"So something big *is* going on?"

There was no response from her father.

"I wasn't kidding about taking that whole pie with me," she warned him that he had better start talking.

"Your case file is on the stool."

She looked to her right where a yellow envelope waited, her name written on it. "You're putting me on a different case?"

There was no response from her father because, obviously, the answer was yes.

"You can't expect me to accept this," she said, angrily.

13

"I expect you to follow the rules of the League of Dragons or you will face punishment."

Thanks, dad. Thanks a lot.

"You'll get fat if you eat that whole pie," he told her.

"I wasn't going to take the damn pie, relax." She snatched the envelope off the stool and ripped it open. A quick skim told her that this was bullshit. "It's a basic haunting."

"Consider it a vacation."

"Dad!"

"Parental concern: you're overtaxing yourself."

"Dad!" She fought to keep back the growl in her voice.

"I'm only worried about your health. I do this because I love you."

"I'll do this bullshit haunting, but then I'm going right back to figuring out why Fate was found munching on some doctor kid." It was out of her mouth, and there was nothing she could do about it. But in all honesty, she didn't think *the* Dragon would step out of the shadows that he haunts as he follows her father's every footstep. The fact that he'd appeared was a warning.

Her father didn't look away from the severed head. "Have a nice, easy week, my dear. Let daddy worry about the rest of it."

Fat chance.

If the envelope could have a neck, she'd have already wrung it before heading out the door. She glanced at her Master, *the* Dragon. His heavy gaze was fixed on her, and she fought a shiver before growling in German for the pack of white wolves to stop jumping all over her car.

The Dragon's gaze was lethal, and she knew that he knew that she wasn't going to leave anything about this alone.

4

Home

Her apartment was six hours away from what living with her father had to offer her. But as the sun came up over the Grey District, her hot rod parked in a stall in the stable next door, her mouth was already filled with the taste of peaches (even if she did decide to take Deacon home with her). What else was she supposed to do with him?

The Grey District was an early Victorian London crossed with the circus: all tailored coats, top hats, walking sticks, buckle shoes and tall boots. Tigers were on leashes instead of dogs. The smell of candied apples was always in the air. Carousels were around every other corner, and a giant Ferris wheel went around and around in the heart of the district. Baked sweet potato and crepe stands were outside her door. Cupcake stands were in every district, but they were the best here.

A sinister dislike crept over the fact that she was opening her apartment door, letting someone in that she'd never let in, ever, in her wildest of dreams. The first floor was an easy escape if something was ever to follow her home, and an even better deal not having to climb floor after floor, having every other tenant wondering if Deacon was here for a different reason other than having nowhere else to go.

She didn't know if it was what he expected. Wall to wall with books. Dusty. No pictures on the walls except for the odd posters of manga characters, ancient, unopened bottles of wine, and candled chandeliers.

"There are cupcakes in the fridge if you're hungry," she said aggressively because the guy that never shut up took this opportunity to do so. "They're not stale or anything…"

"I'm not hungry."

"Okay, well…" She held up the envelope, indicating that she needed to work.

"You're not going to sleep?"

"Never did sleep much."

He nodded, following her to the couch and watching as she dumped the contents of the envelope onto the wooden table in front of her. She had gotten up to make a fire, but other than that, she set to reading what new danger she would be up against.

"What does any of this mean? Appearing and disappearing objects. Loud noises at midnight. Unexplained scratching during all hours of the day. Flickering lights…?" Deacon continued to read over her shoulder, a confused expression on his face.

"Generally, I'd have to see the place to get a read of what I'm up against." But this was so easy it was almost sickening. "How are you with haunted houses?"

"I tend to scream like a girl, remember?"

At least he was honest. "I'm leaving first thing in the morning. You can come if you want, I guess. Or you can get the hell out. Or you can stay and eat everything in the fridge before it goes bad."

"What else is in the fridge other than cupcakes?"

"Cupcakes."

"I'm going with you."

She felt her body stiffen. He really would be useless, annoying luggage. It would be easier on her if he'd just get the hell away from her. "You're in my personal space."

"What?"

"Stop reading over my shoulder," she hissed.

"My bad."

She sighed. He sat beside her, which wasn't much better. "I'm going to make some tea. Make your own."

He followed her to the kitchen.

"You like wine?" He nervously flicked at the many bottles around them.

"No. I hate wine."

"Then what's with all of it?"

"I just sort of collect them," she admitted, wishing he'd go fall asleep somewhere or stand in a corner, out of her way.

He fidgeted as if he wanted to say something else.

"What is it?"

"Don't Dragons Nest in the same place? Wasn't that the Nest we were just at? This is a nice apartment. How can you afford this place? How do they let you live so far away from the Nest? And you asked, so don't say I ask too many questions."

16

It was true, Dragon's don't get paid. The leaders set them up at the 'Nest.' That was true, too. She had her ways of paying for her independence, but that didn't mean she had to share that information with him or any piece of information with him.

She set down the container with the tea leaves in front of him before collecting everything that was in the envelope, marching to her room, and locking the door behind her.

5

The Warning

They drove for four hours without saying a word. She was still furious, having thought she'd escape early without him, but instead found him wide awake, sitting on her couch, reading her latest manuscript, his face full of shock.

"This is you, isn't it, NYDB? Scarlett Chances is your pen name..." he'd said to her, and the last thing he'd said to her as she ripped the manuscript out of his hands, her teeth bared and temper flaring.

They had a forty-hour drive ahead of them, and she was fine with the silence and the marinating in anger. Because, so what? Yes, she wrote dirty books for cash. No, he didn't need to snoop. No, he didn't need to make a big deal about it.

"Are your books...?" Deacon finally asked after thinking about it for four hours. "Are they all like that? Guy on guy..."

"Most of them," she admitted because she might as well admit it. "Why? You not into kissing boys and liking it?"

"No."

She glanced over at him, raising her eyebrows. "I find that hard to believe."

"I'm sorry I read it," he told her, sincerely. "After I read it, I was really sorry I'd read it. But mostly, I'm sorry because I should have asked permission, whether I thought permission would be given. I was just trying to find out who you are."

She might as well cut him some slack. Asking questions was getting him nowhere. "Fine. Whatever. Just get over it."

"So where are we going?"

They weren't out of the Grey District yet. The districts were made up of roads, hearts, and sides, all of which were controlled by Carin, the selected council. They needed to drive through the Purple District: one of the many districts that took its colour *too* seriously. The building, houses, and cupcake stands were all purple. The trees – bark, leaves, and all – grew purple. Purple roses lined the engraved roads whose words were written in purple ink that told a story about knights and dragons, all in Latin so most people couldn't read it, even if they wanted to take the time to. She'd been to the Purple District before when she was too young to remember how to get there.

"I need to stop for directions," she said, pulling into one of the existing gas stations. By the absent look on Deacon's face, she guessed he didn't know how to fill a car up with gas. Once she was finished, she asked the owner, "What's the best way to get out of here?"

"Where you headed?" the man with the skull tattooed on his face asked her.

"Purple District." She noticed Deacon had come to stand at her side.

"Just stay on that road." He pointed to the way they'd been going. "It'll take you right out. Not the fastest way, but it's the safest."

Her mouth went dry as if she'd been sucking on salt. It didn't feel safe. The taste tried to stick to her throat, so she asked, "Got another way?"

"The fastest way is to stay between the Purple and Blue Districts, driving along the sides."

"Why isn't it safe?" Deacon braved to ask.

"That's voodoo territory," the gas station owner responded. "The sides of districts are filled with voodoo tramps."

Her mouth lit up with a warm peach taste. "Thanks."

They started away, Deacon glancing back at the man with the skull tattoo, his red hair spiked and ratty about his head, eyeing them as they went.

"We staying on this road?" Deacon asked her.

They got into the car. "Nope." She started the engine. "Blue District? That's the hospital highlight of the Great Districts, isn't it?"

Deacon nodded, relaxing, his look of concern vanishing. "It's mostly a district dedicated to universities. But, yes, the best hospitals in the Great Districts are there. I went to school in Blue, but I'm originally from the Purple District. I've never seen anything voodoo related there." The car picked up speed. "The Purple District's a clean place. Pretty. You know? A lot of forests and bridges."

"A lot of clinics there, too, right?" She gripped the steering wheel.

"Other than Blue, it has the best health care of all the districts." Deacon agreed, slowly nodding because he was slowly catching on. "You're not asking me because of what I think you're asking me? Are you?"

19

She smiled. Her father had missed the most important fact of her last case: the doctors.

"Why are you driving so fast? If you're right, we're heading straight into doom!" Deacon complained.

There was a dry taste coming in her mouth, slowly it was forming, telling her there wasn't much time. "There's only so much hope left."

"What is hope like?"

She wondered about that as the world blazed by, having an answer, wondering if he'd understand. Sometimes it was easier not to respond, but she said, "I don't know. But it tastes like peaches."

He crossed his arms in front of him and she noticed, though he hadn't complained, that he'd been in scrubs since he'd been on a monster's takeout menu. She made a mental note to stop for supplies for both of them. Interrupting her mental note, he said, "I don't think I believe in hope. I thought it was hopeless when I was taken to that warehouse. I thought that no matter what I did, I was going to die. And then you showed up." He paused, catching that blush again. "I think if hope for me exists, I think if it has a taste, I think it lives in you."

"I'm not interested in dating, marrying or having your babies." She made things quite clear.

He blinked and blinked again. "Seriously? I give you a compliment and you think I want to see your panties?"

"There's no hope for that either."

He sighed, frustrated. "I didn't mean... Forget it. How much longer anyway?"

It turned out being a forty-two-hour drive with stopping for gas and supplies: food, clothing, and toothpaste. That dry taste was getting stronger, but a thin line of peach still hung in her mouth, telling her that no matter how dangerous it was, they had to go this way. There was something this way, something that she couldn't explain, but she needed to know, have, or see.

The backseat was filled with cupcakes, and she was eating one. Deacon was asking her how she stayed so thin when all she ate were those little things, when a man appeared on the road, walking toward the speeding car.

Slamming on the brakes, she knew as the taste in her mouth flickered stronger that he was who she was searching for. But the flickering came and went as she sat there: came and went, came and went, making her slam the door behind her as she marched forward, crossbow aimed. Deacon stepped out but stayed close to the car without her having to order him to.

His white hair was spiked and tipped with gold. His eyes were blood red slits, his lips cracked and bloody, and his teeth were sharp and threatening. In black, a tattoo ran down his face, spelling, 'Words.' He was shirtless, showing her that along the left side of his body read, 'This is Me and Fate.' And on his back, along his shoulders, read, 'When Death Saves Your Life.'

They circled each other, and then she circled him before they both stood. He'd decided all he needed to know about her, where she was still deciding if this encounter was going to lead to bloodshed.

He extended his arm, his palm toward her, empty, and then a peach appeared, making her jump, because how had he known? This couldn't be a coincidence.

He waited, and finally, she accepted what he was offering, listening now to what he had to say.

"I waited for you," he told her, his voice snake-like: hissy and low. "But you're too late, little Dragon."

"You know who I am?"

"I waited for you, little Dragon." The Voodoo Priest stepped closer to her, pushing her long hair behind her ear, and cupping her face. "But I cannot fight for something that's already been destroyed. I should never have appeared here, leading you here. Not when you need to run now, little Dragon. It's too late."

"You're telling me to flee?" She tried to see by him, but he was controlling her gaze. "What is waiting for us up ahead?"

"Only death," he answered, already disappearing into the air.

"Wait!" she ordered, moving to hold on to his arms, but they were fading, disappearing before her. "Who are you? Why would you try to lead me here? What is it that you want? What's happening?"

But he was already gone.

Deacon timidly came up and put a hand on her shoulder. "And you say I ask a lot of questions," he tried to say gently. Adding, "What do we do now?"

Her mouth was so dry she wanted to vomit. Salt clung to her throat, making it impossible to swallow, to speak, to breathe. But she had to. If there was death up ahead it was for her to face. "We're going to find out what the hell's going on."

That was what being a Dragon was all about.

6

The Demon Responsible

Smoke filled the air, rising from the waste, from the destruction, from the once was: because there was nothing left. Nothing, but rivers of ash. Nothing, but how hundreds and hundreds of thousands of people were wiped away, two districts cleaned from this earth, lost.

"I don't understand," she whispered. They'd driven until the shock sank in and they had no other choice but to pull over and step into the disaster themselves.

"You killed that creature, right? It couldn't have been him." Deacon thought for a moment. He was quietly talking out loud, trying to work it all out, trying to figure out how to make sense of this. "No. You said you'd seen another like it, right? How many would it take to do something like this? God, I have no idea. That *thing* that came at me wanted to eat, not burn. This is way beyond that. This is way beyond insanity." He kept close to her, his shoulder hitting her shoulder as they walked. "This couldn't be voodoo men, right? Why would it be, right?" Dismissing all of that, he rested on: "It can't be a coincidence. Something's killing doctors, and here the heart of them is destroyed."

"The Dragons were created to protect us from this," her voice came out soft, timid, and unlike her.

"You tried…" He spread his arms as if to say, 'What could we have done?'

"No. My brothers should be here."

"NYDB!" Deacon was running, and now that he was, she saw what he was running toward. A boy of – what looked to be – seventeen was strapped to a post that was left untouched. The only things that were left in this once flourishing place.

She turned the boy's limp hands palm up to see the familiar crest. "He's a Dragon." She dropped his hands, clawing at the ropes he was strung up by. "Cut him down," she told herself, grabbing the knife from her belt. "Cut him down!"

"There's nothing you can do for him," Deacon whispered, long finished with checking his pulse. "He's dead." Tears filled his eyes, watching as she lay the body on the ash-land's grave beneath their feet. "We should have just checked out that haunting, avoided all of this. I wish you didn't have to face something like this."

"Me? This is your home district." Did he have family here? She was scared to ask.

"I know." His voice almost gave out on him. Looking uncomfortable in his white shirt, tailored vest with its fancy buttons and dress pants. Looking uncomfortable in his skin. Looking uncomfortable to be standing instead of crawling through the ash, begging for mercy, begging for none of this to be true. "I'm trying not to cry in front of you."

"Men who cry…" He came up behind them. Three arrows were in his arm, and he began pulling them out one by one. "Such a turn on."

"Deacon, run!" Choice screamed, the *thing's* hands were slashed up and battered, but that didn't stop him from taking her by the neck, her feet lifting off the ground as he raised her up to get a better look at her, disregarding Deacon as he fled.

"This job is never without its perks," he purred. Black rings hugged his black eyes. A collar made of bone and blood dug into his neck as if he were a dog let off his leash. "I don't get to introduce myself to girls very often, especially to such a *fine* looking *Dragon*."

"Who are you?"

"You've never seen a demon before?" He rolled his shoulders back, his red button-up shirt moving with the action. He was wearing jeans when she thought she was the only one in the world who still wore them. "That's cute."

"You did this?" He'd have to be a ridiculously powerful demon. The kind of monster even she'd never be able to defend herself against.

"Enough talk." He lowered her to her feet, making her flinch as he moved his hands down her arms and waist. "There's no need to talk about how you're going to die."

An arrow whizzed past his head, making them both look up to see Deacon steadying another arrow, her crossbow in his hands.

"He's trembling. I knew he was the bedwetting type." Without touching her, the demon brought her down to lie on what was left of the earth.

24

Coming too close to her, he whispered, "Hold that thought. I'm going to kill your boyfriend first."

"He's not my boyfriend," was all she could bark back.

"Touchy," the demon commented. Straightening up and cracking his neck, he told them both, "It's always best to stretch first," before stretching his arms and legs and then cracking his knuckles. He spread his arms open, smiling at Deacon as he said, "Make my day, sweetheart. Put in your best effort."

Deacon chucked the crossbow toward her, and she reached up, catching it as it flew through the air, and fired, hitting the demon right between the eyes. He fell back, hitting the ground.

Bouncing to her feet, she grabbed Deacon's arm and pulled him toward the car. "Run," she chanted before turning her head to look back. The demon was gone, reappearing right in front of them.

She let go of Deacon's hand, pushing him to the side so that she alone slid into the demon's arms. He took the crossbow from her, holding it above his head, before kicking her feet out from under her, and then breaking the crossbow over his knee. "I think under any other circumstances, we could have lived happily ever after. You know, if you weren't thinking about killing me, and I wasn't about to kill you?"

"What's with all the smartass guys lately?" she whispered, her nails digging into his ankle as he rested his foot on her neck.

"I hate to think we're all the same. I just killed all the purple people. The blue people, too. That makes me one of a kind, I think," the demon boasted.

"So you did do this?"

"Surprise." He shrugged, taking a bag of coffee beans out of his pocket. "You want one?" he offered.

"I prefer tea to coffee."

"That's sick." The demon scowled. "Now I won't feel bad killing you."

"Why haven't you yet?"

He shrugged again. "Boredom, mostly. I'm waiting to see what you do next. You're a Dragon. You can't be this disappointing..."

"I'm not!" She sunk her knife into his ankle, releasing it and twisting his leg with both hands, spinning herself up and around until he was face down with her on top of him, stabbing him until there was so much blood she couldn't tell where she was stabbing anymore.

25

She stood up, vaguely taking in Deacon's astonishment. There wasn't time to be concerned about if he wanted to throw up, so long as he didn't do it in the car because they still needed to make it to the car.

"He won't be down for long." She urged him forward. "A few stab wounds won't make much of a difference to him. He's too much for me to take down alone."

"I think you got him," Deacon corrected.

"No, I didn't." She pulled him to a stop because the demon was cracking his back, smirking, appearing and disappearing all around them, whistling as he went.

"Why are we still alive?" she yelled at the shadowed air. "Killing hundreds of thousands just enough for you?"

"You have to swoop in for the masses," the demon whispered into her ear, wrapping his arms around her waist. "Only one let himself get singled out. Your brother, was he? Put up a decent fight, too." He breathed her in and she could smell the coffee beans on him. "Big displays get so boring. It's the little things that stick with you, the one-on-one battles that bring a smile to the day."

"Who's your Master?"

"Don't bring him up. He's not a very nice guy."

"So someone is controlling you."

"Were you sick on Demon Day in Dragon School?"

No. She knew demons couldn't enter the world without being summoned, and that there wasn't supposed to be anyone alive with the ability to summon them. She knew that demons couldn't be destroyed, only sent back, but she didn't know any exorcisms strong enough. She'd need, like, six more Dragons to get that kind of heavy job done.

Plan A of today's survival method was to keep the demon entertained until she thought up something better.

Her arms cut through his hold on her, slamming the back of her head into his face. She turned with just enough time to lash out, her fingers pulling his right eye out of its socket before he stumbled back enough that she could breathe a little easier.

The feeling didn't last long.

"What cruelty." He appeared beside her, snatching his right eye back and shoving it back into proper place. "The person I'm possessing is still alive, you know?"

26

Never having survivors made her not so interested in them.

"I don't mind. Oddities like you make being here worth it: the ones that don't fret about punching me in this face." A sword appeared at his side. He drew it forth. "All right, Dragon. Pick your weapon. I'll wait."

He'll wait? She wasn't sure if he was trying to be the nicest demon from Hell or the craziest. "Who are you?"

"I can't tell you my real name. Do you know the damage you could do with that?" He flicked his sword, indicating for her to get a move on. "Call me Wolf, if you really need to whisper something as you die."

Wolf: because you're someone's dog. Cute.

True to his word, he waited while she walked to the car and opened the trunk. He waited while Deacon frantically asked her what she was planning to do. And he waited while she positioned herself in front of him, sword at the ready.

His blade was black and jagged with glittery, red-eyed jewels: a demon's blade. It could cut apart a normal sword like it was nothing. But she didn't have a regular sword, either. The tips and edges were blue, the entire sword engraved with roaring dragons and protection spells. It would not kill him, but it would not let her down so easily.

"Let's go at your pace, shall we? It will be over too quickly if we go at mine."

That was probably true.

Did she have any regrets? She couldn't think about that: what she'd done or hadn't done.

Her life depended on her focus. Deacon's life depended on her.

She lunged forward, attacking him while digging her blade along the ground, slashing, moving drastically and with perfect, needed precision. His arm began to catch fire, and he flew into the air, flipping out of the pentagram just before it was completed.

She kicked out, sending his sword soaring while he was still in the air. And because he wasn't an idiot, Deacon grabbed the sword and ran into the center of the pentagram, safe from the demon.

If the demon could have been caught in there, he would have been burned alive and sent back to Hell.

"I guess we're not playing nice anymore." Wolf patted out the flames on his left arm. "If that's the way you want it…"

She swallowed hard. She hadn't expected the pentagram to fail, and she didn't think the same trick would work twice.

It wouldn't.

His black eyes were there. He was nose-to-nose with her. "You've made me so very *hungry*."

Choice shivered.

His mouth was on hers and she felt her life force leaving her. She heard her heartbeat slowing as it pounded in her ears. Her eyes were fluttering. Blood was in her mouth, streaming down the sides of her face as the demon fed.

"Give me the sword!" someone screamed. Was it in her head? But then her eyes fluttered open as the demon paused, his mouth gaping, spilling her blood that he hadn't yet swallowed. He looked down at his own black blade that was sticking out the other side of him.

Beyond the taste of her own blood, was the taste of peaches.

Deacon?

Latin words were being chanted by a voice she didn't know. The demon began to cough and choke. Pulling at his collar, and then at the slick braids along his head that pulled back his long blond hair: trying to fight off the exorcism. Trying to reach around to grab a hold of whoever had him trapped by his own demon blade.

She didn't recognize the chant, but she knew the words meant 'destroy,' and the demon gave a high-pitched bit of agony before falling to the ground, showing just how many times he'd been stabbed by her, showing that the man who'd been possessed wasn't about to get back up.

The intruder pulled out the demon sword, and as Choice swayed, watching him, she wondered how his being there was possible. No normal human could have survived what happened here. No normal human could have performed an exorcism like that. No basic-skilled Dragon could have sent that demon back to Hell.

But this man did...

Dressed in classic black with deep purple buttons and highlights, he looked like a snobby aristocrat except for the weapons belt around his waist. A black rose was pinned to his jacket. The way he was dressed set off his well-set shoulders and the way she could tell that he was all hardened muscle underneath.

He started toward her. His expression fatal, his features strong, and his every step precise. He grabbed a hold of the front of her shirt to keep her from falling. "Can you hear me?"

She staggered. Deacon was voicing his worry in the background, but the intruder didn't seem to care. She nodded, the action making her lose her footing, and she started to tumble to the ground – would have – if he didn't scoop her into his arms.

"What's your name?"

The demon wasn't wrong. Names were powerful things, especially with magic. But peaches were in her mouth, severely, and she let her eyes close, soaking in the taste, the smell, and the feeling.

"My name is Choice," she answered him before she fell unconscious.

7

Infected

When she awoke, her eyes adjusting to the darkness of the old dungeon, she was chained to a wall. Deacon was chained in front of her, far enough away that if she whispered, he'd never be able to hear her. Between them, standing with his arms crossed, his eyes down, once in a while checking his pocket watch as if he was waiting for something, was the man who saved their lives.

"How did we get here?" Choice asked Deacon, who was wide awake, glaring at the man between them.

"He drove your car," was Deacon's answer.

She didn't like that. Not one bit. Even if the taste of peaches was so strong in her mouth, she felt like it was going to boil on out of her. "Has he said anything?"

"Except for stepping into that design you made and ripping that sword out of my hands, we haven't bonded, no."

The fact that he could move safely in, out, and around the pentagram meant he was in no way a monster. But why did he have them chained? What was he waiting for?

Would he speak to her?

"It's called a pentagram," he said. His brown eyes were specked with gold. His dark brown hair was jagged and floppy at the sides of his face. A style that didn't seem to suit the fact that he had the ability to kick major ass. He was tall and looked thin although he was very well-built.

"What are you waiting for?" she asked him.

He slowly took her in, the gold specks in his brown eyes a dominant thing. "I'd rather you didn't speak, Choice. I might have to kill you in a few hours."

"Hold on a second..." Deacon yelped.

"You were both exposed. If you have the infection, I'll know within twenty-two hours."

"What do you mean, infection?" Deacon asked before she could.

"That demon destroyed two districts, but that's not all it's done," he spoke to Choice, even though Deacon was the one who asked the question. "I've been hunting it for months as it goes around mixing its blood with humans, creating a rabid cross between human and demon. Monsters with upside down crosses for irises."

"I've taken those down before," Choice confessed, not thinking about the fact that she was strapped to the wall because she might turn into one of the monsters she hunts. "The last one said, 'the Master of the World commands me to kill.' Was he talking about the demon?"

"Is that how you got here? Did it say something to lead you here?"

"No. I followed the pattern."

"Pattern?"

"They're killing doctors. Where better to go than hospital central?"

"How old are you? Seventeen?" he asked her. "You should have stuck to the haunting case, Choice."

"I'm eighteen, and how do you know about that?"

He checked his watch. They ended up waiting four extra hours, just to be sure, before he decided they were safe. He unchained Deacon first and then came for Choice.

She lashed out as soon as she was free, trying to punch him in the face, trying to grab his arms to push him down or throw him into a dungeon wall. But he avoided each of her attacks with ease.

She tried again to take hold of him.

"Are you looking for these?" Palms forward, the Dragon crest was there.

He was a Dragon.

"You're a little young to be exercising that level of demon alone, aren't you?" she asked, suspiciously.

"I'm twenty-four. I've got a few years on you, Choice." His jagged hair fell into his eyes. "And if *the* Dragon finds out you were here, you'll be imprisoned. Three years for disobeying."

"You guys needed help out there." We lost two districts: mission failed.

"That's not your call."

He caught her fist when she tried to punch him in the face.

"Fine." She gave in. But he didn't let her go. "What's our next move?"

"Excuse me?"

"We have to find out what that demon was planning, don't we?"

31

He smirked: something between being impressed and annoyed. He shook his head. "You've got a haunting to clean up." He let her fist fall and started walking out of the dungeon. "I assume you can find your own way out. You look like vaguely intelligent beings."

"Wait!" she persisted, and he hesitated. "Where can we find you again?"

"You don't," he promised, continuing into shadows.

"What's your name?" She didn't want him to leave. The taste of peaches was leaving with him, but Deacon put a hand on her shoulder, keeping her back.

Because he was already gone.

8

Searching

The dungeon had been built underground. Both Choice and Deacon were shielding their eyes when they climbed their way out. Relief filled her, throwing her arms around her car and kissing the hood. She'd been worried about the other Dragon's driving, but her car didn't seem in worse shape than when they started their journey.

Exhausted, hungry, and in a desperate need to pee, they stretched and did all that was necessary after being forced to sit in one spot for twenty-six hours. Choice expected to be stiff and in pain from the battle with the demon. But it was clear that someone took the time to heal her when she'd been passed out. She had barely a scratch now, and since Deacon was chained right along with her, it could only have been the other Dragon.

They got into the car and she turned the key. Where were they going to go from here?

"What do we do now?"

He was always asking her that, and how was she supposed to know? Except that she did. She was going home to break into her father's study, read a bunch of secret files and see if she could find answers. Whatever was going on, it was bigger than she originally imagined.

"You're thinking about that guy, aren't you?"

Of course she was thinking about him. He'd saved their lives and then disappeared.

Thinking about him was perfectly normal at this point.

She drove on in silence. Deacon didn't stop asking questions she didn't respond to as they passed scenery washed-out by their exhaustion. Away from the ashes, they had to stop while herds of sheep crossed the road, passing fields of bay horses that raced the car as they drove by. The Brown District was horse country: the best stables, the best trainers, and the only place to buy horses, not that she ever would. It was the next over from Orange. A few hours from Purple. Orange was where her haunting case was located, generally having to cross Purple to get there, but she figured she might as well search for a map and find a new way around at dad's.

While she was searching for answers to why a demon would spread an infection or why those infected were hunting doctors.

It was easy to tell when she drove into a different district. The street signs were the colour of the district's name. Not that they noticed, passing through the silver gaits of home, and getting surrounded by white wolves that were set loose to greet them. Deacon complained because the entire ride she had them listening to whatever music they could get. Turning out to be Korean rap and hip-hop. Not that Korea existed anymore. Neither did Germany. Although, she growled for the wolves to stay off her car in German. There was only the Great Districts now. The world ruled by the selected council. One government: Carin. And they were probably swarming the ashes of the Purple and Blue Districts right about now.

She told Deacon to stay in the car.

A butler, the same Egyptian inspired one as before, opened the door for her before she'd even thought to reach out for the handle. She didn't address him as she walked by. No 'thank you' or 'nice to see you' as she started into the mansion.

"Your father asks that you wait in the drawing room," he said to her, bowing. He gestured to the room to the right, where she was deemed to take a seat and wait.

Choice waited for the butler to leave the room.

She walked out of the drawing room, past the strong scent of tea coming from the kitchen, mixed about with brandy. She passed endless rooms with closed doors until she heard voices coming from one of them. It was her father's tone that told her Carin was here and Choice frowned because even though Carin was the government, they were still outsiders and outsiders didn't belong here.

"Dragon Princess..." The butler came up beside her. "Please return with me to the drawing room, as I've prepared tea with a bit of brandy to help you sleep. I take it you'll be spending the night? I assure you that would please your father."

"I'm not staying, but tea with brandy sounds great." She started back with him because she had no other choice.

"I beg you to reconsider. I'm sure the pet you've left in your car will be fine there." He gestured once again for her to sit and to remain seated.

"I'm sure he would be." Why would she take offence? She wasn't about to invite anyone in here that didn't belong, and her useless luggage didn't belong. "Stay with me a moment," she demanded when the butler was going to wait outside the door after serving her tea.

"That's not permitted of me."

"Why is Carin here? How many members are polluting our Nest?"

He couldn't help but smile because he too didn't agree with letting outsiders in where the Dragons were safe. "Your father's been very busy with them since you brought that severed head here."

He answered without answering, which was perfect because Choice figured it out. Scowling, she said, "Fate was a son of Carin? Disgusting. Why would my father set me up with anything other than a Dragon?"

"That's not my place, I assure you," he answered without answering, but he couldn't keep his agreement out of his eyes. Dragons were born for Dragons. That was all there was.

"Excuse me, Princess." The butler bowed again. "I must see our guests out now."

With his leaving the room, Choice took the first sip of her tea, listening to the voices in the hall, bits of arguing and bits of compassion, before the door closed behind the members of government who dared to enter the Nest of the Dragons, all because she'd been stupid enough to bring Fate's head here.

Fate: a dead son of Carin. And now with two districts destroyed, the government probably wasn't looking too kindly on the organization that they felt didn't exist unless they needed someone to blame or fix their problems for them.

Her father entered the room and took in Choice's appearance. "You should have texted me. I need baking powder." He sat down in the chair opposite her. "How'd the haunting go?"

She took another sip of her tea. "I haven't taken care of it yet."

"Why not?"

"I'm on vacation hours, remember?" She set her cup down, her insides warming, and she only realized now how tired she was. "I heard something's happened. Two districts…"

"Yes." Her father set his hands behind his head. "Everyone died, including our stationed Dragon. No one survived."

He didn't look impressed that she'd came all the way back (task not completed) to talk shop, and he really didn't look impressed that she'd missed the chance to pick him up some baking powder. But she narrowed her eyes at him, not for that, but because he had to be mistaken. "You didn't get even one report?"

He sighed. "I just told you."

She was there, but wasn't supposed to be, so there was no way she could have sent a report in, telling them what happened. But one Dragon had lived; had saved her life. Unless he too wasn't supposed to be there... Two Dragons disobeying at the same time? It had to be a record of what has never happened before.

"I have to pee," she informed them. Her father nodded. The butler tried to hide his astonishment of her behaviour that he really should have been used to by now. She got up and started out of the room.

"There's blueberry pie in the fridge if you're hungry," her father informed her. "You know where your room is if you're tired."

She caught the butler's eye, the words 'I assure you that it would please your father' hung in the air. "Sorry, I've got perishables in the car." They didn't comment because they knew she had someone with a heartbeat stashed in there. "And since when are we pie people?"

"I've been in a weird mood lately," her father admitted, making her shrug and head to the bathroom. Making sure eyes weren't on her, she skipped the bathroom and let herself into her father's study.

The wooden walls and cabinets weren't something she was used to seeing as a child. The antique weapons encased in glass were new to her eyes, having only seen them once or twice before. She'd never been allowed in here, and certainly not without her father.

Not being an idiot, she knew everything would be locked and probably booby-trapped, but since he'd just been in here, the door was unlocked and files were still open on his desk.

"Who are you, father?" she wondered, not for the first time in her life, as she sat in his desk chair, searching through pages printed with Latin words. Useless, they were all of Fate. His description, his rank, the last case he was on, his climbing position in Carin. He truly was a prince to them, and the perfect marriage candidate apparently for her, until she killed him.

Underneath Fate's file was one with her name on it. She hurried to open it, seeing her newest case, the haunting, haunting her, describing why it was perfect for her. That description read, 'with Choice out of the way.'

"What does that even mean?" she whispered, flipping through pictures of the severed head she'd tossed at her father's feet, and then holding up a piece of paper with a list of names. Fate's was the last one on the list. Pictures and descriptions, and why they'd be a perfect cross with her, ability wise.

A list of potential suitors.

"Oh, gross..." She couldn't believe her father had a list like this. Like his own daughter was breeding stock or something. The shock increased with seeing a familiar face. Gasping, she shut the file harder than she'd intended to, creating a 'bang' she knew someone would soon come to investigate.

There was no more time, answers or no answers, she had to retreat.

Slipping out of the study and into the bathroom to flush the unused toilet, she walked out just as the butler was locking the study door, looking at her curiously.

"I just had the best pee of my life," she told him, watching his cheeks fight to redden, her rudeness throwing off suspicion, and she walked back to the drawing room where her father still sat.

"You look flushed, my daughter." He stared at the wall in front of him. "Did you find yourself into something you shouldn't have?"

"How do I get to the Orange District without going through Purple?" She wasn't going anywhere Carin was crawling around. It would take forever, and it was already a forever kind of drive.

"I'll have Sebastian draw you a map on your way out." He didn't press his last comment, knowing perfectly well that she knew that he knew she was snooping into things she wasn't supposed to be snooping in.

"Okay," she said. He looked tired, but it was probably because she was a horrible daughter.

Sebastian was there, handing her a map. "Should I see you out, Princess?"

Her father flicked his hand at her twice, dismissing her.

She nodded. "Sure..." But she still wasn't closer to anything.

9

The Haunting

It was a five day drive to the Orange District, and as the sun began to set, the orange-tinted bulbs of the streetlights came on. Deacon was sleeping, his head against the window, bumping and rolling about when the car drove over uneven ground.

When they had to sleep, they slept in the car. But now that they were here, Choice was desperate to find a place to spend the night. Somewhere with pillows. Somewhere with a bath because the boy beside her smelt a lot like boy, and she smelt a lot like dried, rotted demon blood.

The road was busy, even at this hour, giving her a chance to reacquaint herself. Here it was all black suits and orange bow ties; black breeches and orange riding boots; white dresses with orange stripes, carried by chestnut horses with orange jeweled tack, travelling down marigold and pumpkin-lined roads. The entire town had a ginger, spicy smell from the cupcake stands selling spiced orange cupcakes with pumpkin pie icing, and tiger cupcakes with peanut butter swirls. Flavors only to be found here.

Mirrors walled the buildings because once you were a regular here, it was next to impossible to leave. The lore around the pubs was that the mirrors were placed to trap the spirits of the residents inside when they died, so that even in death they could never leave.

Mostly Choice had always thought the mirrors were a vanity thing, and that was why it was also known as 'The Two-Faced Town.' But the Orange District did have more than triple the ghost trouble than any other district, so the local pub lore was probably true.

She started rolling down the passenger's window, rolling it back up, rolling it down, and rolling it back up again until Deacon shifted awake. He groaned, and then rested his head back against the window until she rolled it down completely, his eyes snapping open and then snapping at her.

"Look who's not so sweet after all," she commented.

"Look who can be a brat after all." He stretched his back and then took a great deal of time rubbing his neck. "It fits you like a baggy shirt."

They passed an inn, and doubling back, she slammed on the brakes, throwing Deacon flying forward. "They have a new cupcake!" she squealed like the fangirl she was as she passed a cupcake stand.

"That's why you tried to send me through the windshield?"

"Honey and Orange! I've never had one before. Do you want one?"

Wide-eyed, he said, "I'm good, but thanks..."

She jumped out of the car, rushing to buy a dozen. "There's *nothing* wrong with dinner," she told the salesman with black stars covering his face, wearing a black and orange striped suit. She glanced back at Deacon, proud of herself. "I'm such a good provider," she whispered. Then setting to business, she asked the salesman, "You get a lot of ghosts down the streets at this hour?"

He shrugged. "It's The Two-Faced Town: because it's more than the living you'll face here."

She breathed in the honesty and the cupcakes. "The Orange-Eyed Theater still running or is it shut down now?"

He shrugged again. "Biggest playhouse in the district: busy, crowded, impossible to get tickets, impossible to get in. You're not from around here, are you?"

She shook her head. "Thanks."

Skipping to the car, she ignored Deacon's worry for her sanity, and continued back to the Show House Inn where a large busted woman with bangs in long stringy braids, wearing devil horns, handed them a room key.

The inn's walls were wallpapered, each with a black and white picture of some old movie star. Choice particularly liked the ones with guys in jeans and leather jackets leaning against their cars. It reminded her that at one point in history she would have fit in somewhere better than she did now.

Caged robins were singing at the end of every hall, looking out of the windows their cages were hanging beside. Deacon hummed one of the Korean hip-hop songs they'd listened to on the way here as he walked down the hall beside her, looking for their room.

First floor and room number nine.

Choice took her time putting up wards and packing salt against the walls, in every corner, and on every windowsill, while Deacon headed straight for the shower. When she was finished, and Deacon returned, smelling like the lilac shampoo the Show House Inn provided for them, she started flipping through her uncompleted manuscript.

"Working at this hour?"

It was the way he said it: like her novels were something other than what they were. Like her being able to write in general was something other than what it was. "Don't act like the fact that I write is cute. It's my job. And it's as honest as I get." Books were just as much a part of her as demon slaying and ghost hunting. She watched him nod, and drawing back from snapping at him, she recoiled, saying, "Go get some sleep. Tomorrow I'm going to teach you how to kill a ghost."

He sighed, hardly looking forward to it. Curling up on the couch beside her, he fell right to sleep even though they'd asked for a room with two beds. But Choice stayed awake, manuscript pushed aside, pen in hand and fresh paper before her. Thinking of what to write because Deacon had been correct. She couldn't stop thinking about the twenty-four-year-old boy that had saved her life. She'd never been saved before. She'd never had to be. So it was no wonder she was filled with an overwhelming desire to punch him in the face.

Deacon fell asleep on the drive to the haunted playhouse. She could tell he was having a nightmare, so she stuck a pen up his nose and poked him awake while she drove. He jumped, his hands flailing, snatching up the pen. Taking in what she'd done, he shook his head while she fought hysterical laughter. Nightmares were a bad sign. She knew she generally thought of him as useless, but he was stronger than she thought he'd be. He never complained, not about slaying demons or hunting ghosts or seeing where he'd grown up fall to ash. But nightmares were bad. They meant he wasn't handling everything as well as he was trying to.

Not that she could blame him…

"Very funny." His face changed to pure horror, pure panic. "NYDB!" He pointed out the window, his voice coming out frantic. "It's one of them! It's one of them, there!"

"Where?" Choice carefully scanned where he was pointing. Nothing was there. Was he seeing things because he'd just had a nightmare? Or was the creature just as fast as she'd remembered them capable of being? "You're sure?"

"I was almost eaten by one. I know what they look like!"

He wasn't faking. She could tell he really did believe he saw one of the infected. Would she ever forget the way their eyes pierced into her, like they were seeing through shades of perfect sin, like they could taste all the horrible things she'd ever done in her blood if they could only have a taste.

She stopped the car and got out, searching, and scanning the area without getting too far away from Deacon. But she found nothing. Excitement tingled down her back. If one *was* here, what was it here for? If one was here, could she trap it and interrogate it? If one was here, would she finally get answers?

She walked back to the car, Deacon sliding back in his seat, waiting and watching to see what she was going to do next. But what could she do? It was gone now, if it was there at all. "Have a cupcake. Cupcakes make everything better."

"I'll be fine as long as I stay with her." He chanted under his breath, talking about her as if she couldn't hear him. "She won't let us die."

At least not so easily, she thought as they drove, but the same roads seemed to appear over and over again. The same large rocks in front of street signs, the same street signs down different streets, and all the while they passed themselves in the mirrored walls of the buildings. Frustrated, she pulled out Sebastian's map. She didn't know how he knew, but her father's butler knew where he was going perfectly well around the Orange District.

"Does everything seem the same to you?" Deacon asked her before she decided to pull over to study the map. "Like we've been here before? Like we're going around in circles?"

"It's just the way Orange is. They don't like people leaving." She made sure to take care with reading every word Sebastian wrote. His handwriting was better than hers. His Latin and spelling better than hers, too, and she dared to call herself a writer.

"Good place for an infection." Deacon looked out his window, trying to see if monsters were following them. So far so good. "No one can go for help."

"Yeah, and creatures follow the scent of blood, so they'll have no problem finding their way out." She started to catch on to what he was thinking. There was no stopping the infection from getting in. But everything was stopping victims from getting out.

A word hung on the air, but neither of them said it.

Massacre.

"Let's get to the theater," Deacon insisted, already ready to leave the Orange District behind them.

"Sure thing."

The Orange-Eyed Theater didn't take long to get to once she listened to Sebastian's directions. It was the little things she had to look for: the paw prints littering the sidewalk down the original O Street; the engravings of full bloomed trees in the road driving down the new O Street. Each letter in the word 'orange' was a street name, and there were original and new streets for all of them without telling drivers which were new and which were original or which were just the colour orange, when they decided to add them in too.

Eventually she took original O Street, staying straight until she got to Main Street and into the heart of the district.

The Orange-Eyed Theater was the first building they saw.

Down Main Street the trees were engraved with bleeding hearts and watchful eyes beside benches and water fountains. Poems and ancient skeletons were encased in glass. Posters advertising plays about ghosts that spent their time killing little children didn't make Deacon any more thrilled to be there or that they were there to find a ghost.

Already, even at this early hour, the theater was packed.

Parking, they waited for carriages and horseback riders to go by before they crossed the road, dreading the lineup to get in. Luckily for them, Choice was a Dragon, and had been urged to be there.

Deacon followed her as she ignored the line and walked up to the front doors where a snooty woman with long orange gloves and a feathered headdress judged them and said, "Back of the line."

"I'm not here to see the play," Choice informed her.

"Then you've come to the wrong place, not that you could get in anyway," said the woman, her giant high heels *too* orange, even for this district.

Choice held her hands up for her to see, palms out. "I'm here to kick some ass."

Swallowing hard, she took a step back as if dragon fire might blaze from Choice's palms and kill her. Timidly, she waved them inside. "I'll text my manager to let him know you're waiting for him."

"You do that." Choice walked past the woman, not stopping to see her shiver with fear.

Deacon was right on her heels.

"That was awesome!" he said to her. "I can't believe I'm saying this, but I've got to be careful on how seriously I take your awesomeness. I might forget you're only human."

A scrawny man with one black star on his right cheek walked down a flight of orange-carpeted stairs to greet them, holding a wild lily out for her, but she didn't take it. He smelt of pepper and chocolate. His jacket was over a shirt with a picture of an open book with two orange eyes on its pages.

"We're awfully busy today, but I didn't want to keep you waiting," he said, his voice deeper than she thought it would be, the top hat on his head tilted to the side. "I'll show you to the third floor: where we've been having the problem. I'm Forgotten, by the way. No honorific necessary, please." He hesitated, glancing at Deacon, and then he extended his hand to Choice. "I can take your things up for you, of course. There's no need for you to carry such a heavy looking bag with two capable men beside you."

Choice felt the weight of the pack on her back. It was filled with everything she might need to take down a ghost: the easy way or the hard way. She started up the stairs. Third floor, was it? "No need, gentlemen. I only ever rely on one capable woman."

Forgotten's gaze darkened at Deacon as if he couldn't believe he wasn't insisting on taking some of the weight for her. "Very well then," he gave up, and they made their way through the crowded theater.

She knew the ghost was haunting the third floor. It had said in the file. She knew. Although, ghosts don't tend to like noisy, busy places. The third floor was occupied by women's dressing rooms, and half- naked women fluttered about, rushing to get make-up on and off, throwing costumes on and throwing them off.

Deacon lowered his eyes, fighting that blush of his.

"I suppose I can't kick everyone out, huh?" Choice asked Forgotten. It might be easy for her to shoot and miss in here, even though she'd never fired her gun and not shot her target.

"Things will die down in fifteen minutes. They're all going on stage."

Deacon seemed happier to hear that than she was. Probably because he was having a hard time seeing where he was going with all the naked ladies he was trying not to be rude to.

They waited fifteen minutes and within that time they listened to the actresses complain about anything and everything. 'My boyfriend did this.' 'My dress is doing that.' 'Breakfast was awful.' 'Yesterday's performance went *too* well.' 'My stomach hurts.' 'My head aches.' 'I can't remember what I did an hour ago.' Whispers went through them, wondering who Forgotten had brought into their dressing room, deciding among them that she was here to fix their ghost problem.

A woman wearing a fluffy pink bra and fluffy pink panties confronted Choice, asking, "You're a Dragon, aren't you? Is that right? Can you cure memory loss?"

"That has nothing to do with a ghost." Choice dismissed her assumed condition of stupidity. "If you think you're dying, you should see a doctor."

The ladies cleared their throats, fidgeted, and fell silent, most of them tearing up, before one of them finally admitted, "I'm afraid that would be impossible."

Even Forgotten was in a state of distress over the subject, and Deacon and Choice exchanged glances.

"Why?" Choice asked the woman in front of her.

"All the doctors in Orange have disappeared."

Choice didn't flinch. They could go to a clinic in Purple or a hospital in Blue, but those have disappeared too.

"Everyone around here isn't doing so well, actually," the woman in fluffy pink admitted, rushing now that all the other actresses were leaving the room. "Without doctors, even the simplest of illnesses are life-threatening."

With that, the actress rushed after the rest of them, disappearing from sight, leaving the room empty except for three.

"What are we going to do now?" Deacon whispered to her. He was talking about the doctors.

"Two women died here within the last month, correct? One whose husband was the murder suspect, and another who died on stage in a fluke

44

accident?" Choice searched for clarification from Forgotten, ignoring Deacon.

He nodded. "Obviously we assume it is Mary, the woman murdered, supposedly by her husband. The ladies say she won't rest until her husband is dragged into death with her, but who is to know what a dead person is really thinking."

"I'm going to find out." Choice opened her backpack, pulling out everything she would need to summon the spirit here. She couldn't get rid of the ghost unless she knew who it was, because unless she could find out how she died or where she was buried, she couldn't purify her death and send her to rest.

"I must remain, but I'm going to sit down over there," Forgotten told them, wiping sweat from his brow. "I've been rather tired lately. All this madness, you know? It's been a busy season."

Or he was afraid to see the ghost close up? It wasn't an uncommon reaction.

Choice dimmed the lights. Smoke from the herbs she was burning lightly filled the room. Lighting the candles lining the circle she made with salt, she spoke in Latin for the spirit trapped in this room to come forth.

A woman appeared in the center of the circle. Her long blond hair fell at her waist, over the costume of the Shakespearean damsel she was wearing the day she died.

"Why are you here?" Choice kindly asked her.

"Bitch, you summoned me," the ghost replied, not so kindly.

"I *mean* –" Choice fought to keep back her temper and impatience, "why aren't you at rest? Are you Mary?"

"My name is Liza."

So she wasn't the murder victim. "You died in an accident?"

"Slipped and broke my neck on a prop." Liza frowned. "An accident, but it still sucks."

"Why are you still here?"

"I'm protecting them."

Choice fell into the intrigue, leaning forward with the suspense. "Protecting who?"

"My pearls," the ghost explained. "I hid them in here before I died, and I'll be damn if I'll let any of those snotty bitches get their dainty hands on them!"

45

"Your pearls?" Choice felt her insides die a little. This was why she'd been dragged here? Because some actress didn't want to leave her jewellery behind?

"My eldest sister gave them to me before she died. She was the only family I had, and those pearls were the only thing I had left of her. They mean everything to me."

Apparently. "Fine. I'll go bury them with you. With them in your grave, you should find peace."

"No. Someone will dig me up for them." The ghost took a moment to think things through. "You're one of those Dragons, you said, right? No one will try to take them from you. Please. Please accept them."

Choice shook her head. "I don't want a creepy dead woman's jewellery."

Liza put her hands on her hips. "I'm not resting until you put them on, and every second you wait is one more second you have to deal with *me*."

She had a point. "Where are the bloody things?"

Liza jerked her head toward one of the wardrobes. "There's a loose board behind that. They're in there."

Sighing, Choice struggled to push the heavy wardrobe filled with heavy costumes out of the way, reaching over to tap the boards on the wall behind it until one tumbled loose. True to her word, a velvet black box was hidden inside. Choice opened it to see the woman's pearl earrings and an elegant pearl necklace.

"Put them on so I know you'll keep them," Liza ordered, and Choice obeyed. "Thank you." Liza was already starting to fade away. "By the way," were her last words, "you might want to start running."

"That's why I hate hauntings." Choice touched the pearls around her neck. "Ghosts always have such stupid reasons for sticking around."

Wait, what did she say?

"NYBD…" Deacon stuttered, pointing to where Forgotten had been sitting. Choice turned on the lights to see Forgotten on his hands and knees, fighting to breathe. His body was twitching. Blood rushed from his mouth. And when he stood, when he finally found his feet, blood seeped from his black eyes: white upside down crosses replacing his irises.

Choice didn't hesitate. She flung her backpack at him, knocking him off balance and pulled Deacon out the door, slamming it behind them, and locking the creature inside.

The playhouse was a mess of noise. The actresses tumbled up the stairs, clawing and coughing, slowly turning into something *else*.

"They're infected!"

"They're all infected," Choice corrected Deacon, taking a second to look out the window to see the people on the streets falling to their hands and knees, crawling along the ground, blood streaming from their mouths and eyes.

They needed to get to the car. Now!

"Kill them!" Deacon ordered.

"With what?" Choice barked. She'd flown her backpack at the one banging on the door beside them, and she didn't have anything in there that could cause these guys any sort of damage. "I was hunting a ghost!"

She took Deacon by the arm and started up the stairs toward the next floor, feeling a warm peach taste in the sides of her mouth, and then she slid to a stop.

On the stairs in front of them was a three-foot doll with buttons for eyes. In a dress printed with flying black crows, it pointed for them to go left.

"Scary doll!" Deacon screamed, taking a step back, but the actresses were starting to get to their feet. "Scary doll!"

"Relax. It's here to help." Choice dragged him forward, braving past the mysterious doll because hope came with the taste of peaches, and they could really use all they could get right now.

When they passed it, it reappeared, showing them the way out. Throwing open a balcony door, they stepped out and onto a lift for window washers that took them all the way down, and onto the street. They looked up, the doll watched them watching it, and then it vanished with blue flames.

"Scary doll," Deacon couldn't stop chanting over and over again, but there was no time for that. Taking him by the hand, Choice crept forward, stopping at the edge of the building, peeking around the side to see how much time they had.

The civilians of Orange, every last one of them, were turning into monsters. But they weren't *turned* yet.

"Come on." Choice pushed them forward, making a dash for the car. Chucking Deacon toward the passenger's side, she jumped in, fumbling with the keys while the lineup that had been waiting to enter the theater twitched, getting up from the ground, their heads tilting, taking in Choice's fumbling.

She planted her foot on the gas, squealing out of there and flying down the roads that all looked the same. The infected followed them, chasing them, throwing themselves on the car, holding onto the roof, and flying off with every sharp turn.

But all the roads were the same!

"Where's Sebastian's map?" Choice didn't mean to scream the question, but it came out in screams. She hadn't had time to get anything out of the trunk. If this car stopped now, they were goners.

"Go that way!" Deacon panicked, and since Choice was a little panicked herself, she obeyed.

Because Deacon would know where he's going, right?

They drove straight, and into a dead end.

"Why would you listen to me?" Deacon cried just before Choice was going to tell him that she was never going to listen to him ever again if they lived through this.

If they lived through this: because more than thirty of the infected had followed them here.

"Stay here!" Choice ordered, kicking open her car door, and running to the trunk as the infected ran toward her, spitting out blood and laughing as they came.

She reached the trunk, her mouth suddenly blazing with peaches, just as something flew through the air.

From the building above, he rode an infected down, slamming onto the car hood. He stood up, shotgun already firing.

It gave her the time she needed. She strapped on a belt of blades and bullets, taking pistols into each hand. She turned toward the battle and never missed a shot.

The battle between thirty-five didn't last long. It was nothing: not for two Dragons. He turned his shotgun on her. "You infected?"

But her pistols already had him in their sights. "You infected?"

"Did one of those things bite you?" he demanded to know.

"Did any of those things bite you?" she demanded to know, but she knew he wasn't infected. The taste of peaches was so strong in her mouth she could smell it. It was so strong she thought she might pass out with happiness.

They were alive.

They were alive because he'd saved their lives, again.

At some point Deacon scrambled out of the car, holding onto the open car door as Choice and the intruder took each other in. He was dressed similar to the way she'd seen him last: all black fabrics with dark purple inlay, except that he looked like he'd slashed his way in here, slashed his way around, and was getting ready to slash his way out. His hair was slicked back, out of his face, showing off his lethally cut features, deceivingly making him look thinner than his muscles should have allowed him to look. And, even though he saved their lives, Deacon was glaring at him.

"What are you doing here, Choice?" His brown eyes were all gold from the rush of the battle.

"The haunting. My father sent me here," she explained, keeping her guns locked on him while she considered her own words. *My father wanted me to come here?* "My father sent me here, what, to die?"

The corners of his mouth twitched with the absurdity of the thought. "The haunting? You were supposed to be long gone from here before any of this happened."

"Are you saying the Dragons knew this was going to happen?" All this asking of questions almost made her forget that this wasn't the time or place to be stopping to chat, but she had to run with it while she got it.

"Whispers show up, just like any other case." He seemed to think taking a moment to catch up was about as stupid as she did. "They got one of us here, though."

Another Dragon's dead? "Bullshit. It would take more than those infected snots to take down a Dragon."

"Yes. It took four hundred of those infected to take down a Dragon." He pulled out his pocket watch. "I don't have time for this." He withdrew his shotgun and started walking away.

"Wait!" she demanded, and he hesitated. "Where are you going?"

He turned back. "I'm going to trap one of those creatures and have a more prudent conversation with it than this one. They have a telepathic connection to their Master, so you can see how that's more interesting than you, Choice."

"I can help you!" she urged because with every step he took away from her, the taste of peaches followed.

He took his pocket watch back out. "In ten minutes you won't be able to even help yourself. The Carin boys are about to swoop in and save the day."

"What does that even mean?"

"This entire district is infected." He put his watch away and started off again. "They're going to make sure nothing gets out. I'd drive fast, if I were you."

Carin's going to wipe Orange off the map...

"Deacon get in the car!" Choice screamed, throwing herself backward and toward the driver's seat. "Wait!" She clutched her car door, watching as the other Dragon hesitated. "What's your name?"

He didn't turn back, ignoring her question. He raised his shotgun and threw himself back into the fray as Choice slammed the door shut and drove out in reverse. She didn't see him as they flew out, racing along the roads, Sebastian's map now in her hands, and running over any infected that dared to get in their way. But they didn't need the map. At every corner, a three-foot doll pointed the way, bringing back the taste of hope she'd thought she'd lost when the other Dragon walked away from her.

They were fifteen minutes out of Orange before they heard the explosion; before they saw the flames and the smoke; before they heard the screams of the infected burning inside.

10

Like

Here homes were built into the hills and the mountains. She knew where to go because she'd read his whereabouts in the file, but he wanted her to find him. He had to because three-foot dolls appeared along the roadside, pointing the way for them, freaking Deacon out.

They hadn't said much to each other the whole twelve hours they'd been in the car so far, making it an uncomfortable drive for him and a comfortable drive for her. They'd passed a few expensive inns and even more expensive cupcake stands, Choice telling her passenger, "I can afford it," when he'd sneered at the price, preferring not to stop, to keep driving. "I just sent three more novels to the publisher, so I've got the cash."

"That worries me," was the last thing he'd said before silence ensued.

They drove another four hours, covering ground at an impressive pace, before the dolls pointed off the road, toward a wooden door in a grassy hill, vines, and wildflowers abundant over logs, saplings, and elder trees.

A grey horse with a black mane and tail grazed beside a boy sitting on one of the logs, the creature's reins hooked in his hands. The footprints outside the wooden door indicated he'd been pacing before he took a seat. His floppy hair was resting jagged at the sides of his face.

Choice got out of the car, drawing forth the gun she'd had beside her the entire drive here, and pointed it at the other Dragon.

He narrowed his eyes in confusion and wonderment. "What are you doing here?"

"What are *you* doing here?" Choice asked back.

Deacon got out of the car.

He was fully armoured, with guns attached to the chains draped down the front of him, pistols hidden inside his jacket, bullets and knives strapped inside. If he wanted to damage them, it wouldn't take him long. But instead, he humoured her, saying, "I finally caught up to a Voodoo Priest."

Deacon snorted. "Why would you want to catch up to one?"

"They know things." He had a bruise on the left side of his face, just under his eye, making him look more sinister than he'd looked before, and although he answered Deacon he never adverted his eyes from Choice. "I need to know what he knows."

"We're here for the same reason," she informed Deacon, making him choke because he'd had no idea what they were really here for, and it was hard to imagine that a place so peaceful could be the heart of voodoo territory.

"You're wasting your time," the other Dragon told her, sincerely. "He won't let me in, no matter what I offer as payment."

Choice lowered her gun and walked to the wooden door, trying to seek him out with her mind. *I'm here,* she thought, opening herself up; clearing her thoughts. *I have no payment. I've brought with me only my constant searching for answers.* When nothing happened, she wondered, *should I knock?*

The wooden door crept open, and a man stepped out. His hands were covered in blue flames, threatening, telling them to stay back. His white hair was spiked and tipped with gold. His eyes were blood red slits, his lips cracked and bloody, and his teeth sharp and threatening. Wearing forest green and a long velvet coat, the black of the tattoo that ran down the side of his face, spelling 'Words,' stood out as well as his white hair.

The two boys moved forward.

The flames on his hands grew stronger. "Only Choice," the Voodoo Priest said, letting her walk past him, shutting the door behind them without turning his back on those left outside the door.

When the door closed, he watched as Choice took in her surroundings. His house was lined with dolls: stitched faces, button eyes, and thinly drawn mouths. She recognized a few of them, being led here and saved by them back in Orange.

The place was crawling with quills and bottles of ink, leather bound books, and jars of bones, teeth, insects, and blood. A grey stone fireplace centered the room they were in, and although there was enough light to see, shadows were painted on the wooden walls. Framed, old newspaper articles of a falling world were hung, as well as the pages of books someone else ripped out that he now kept safe.

"Why?" Choice turned on him, his defenses limiting, his blue flames extinguished. "Why only me?"

"For too many reasons," he said, his voice low and naturally mysterious. "Do you not yet understand: to be careful who you trust?"

"And yet you trust me?"

"I know you," his snake-like voice announced.

"You do?" She felt cold, and a shiver went to travel through her, but the Voodoo Priest was faster.

Draping his coat over her shoulders, he promised her, hissing, "You're never safer than when you have me beside you. Nothing can harm you here."

She looked up at him. He was taller than she was, but she could see the beautiful script on the back of his neck. 'My Choice,' it read, and somehow she knew that perhaps they had met before the infection started to spread.

He led the way into the next room, the floors covered with the drippings of wax and the drops of blood: left over bits of recently cast spells. Motioning for her to sit down, the table was covered with the feathers of a crow. Behind her, a leather jacket was draped beside bushels of drying flowers, odd strings of ribbon, and the skins of snakes.

"You know me?" she repeated, glancing at the many maps of worlds she'd never heard of.

He remained standing. "Not ten years ago, Dragons and Voodoo Priest were allies."

"Why did that change?"

"Life changes. The world didn't like my kind increasing our already significant power."

"You'd think they'd want magic on the front lines."

"Yes. But not in the position to rule." He showed her clips of memories, opening his mind to her in ways she'd never be able to. Showing her what life was like when the Dragons were the government. Showing her what life was like when Voodoo Priests were allowed to have a say in the world because the Dragons had been kind to every creature under their protection. "Carin took over the system the Dragons originally created, taking control of the government."

But the world didn't want Dragons ruling, either. They feared their power, just as they still feared the Voodoo Priests. "It's happier with Carin." It was true. There was nothing wrong with the way Carin ran things. "Unless Carin is the one spreading the infection," she asked. But no. There was no need for them to do that, and they didn't have that kind of connection to the supernatural.

"You do not remember me?" He said it like a question, but he was hoping it didn't have to be. When she seemed confused, he explained, "You and I have met, when our fathers were arranging our futures for us, and I told you that no matter how careless your father would become with our lives, I would take everything you are seriously. Including the care of your heart. Since you were eight-years-old, I have been watching over you."

"I don't even remember you." But she knew they'd been engaged, only finding out recently when she'd snuck into her father's study and saw the list and photos of people she'd been promised to over the years.

"Yes. It turns out it wasn't your heart your father was careless with. It was mine." He set his hand down on the chair beside him. "I was fifteen." He didn't look away. "You don't even know my name."

She'd read it in the file. "Is that why you trust me? Because you still feel attachment to an eight-year-old bride?"

"I trust no one. The necromancer is half human, making it impossible for me to sense him." Behind him were jars of needles and buttons, fabrics and threads. "You're a female, and I know you, having guarded you most of your life."

"The necromancer?"

He beheld her in a way she'd never experienced before: with pity. "Are you sure you want to know, Choice? Once you know, there's no going back."

There was never any going back, but there was always precaution. "If you're going to tell me, you better tell me now what you want in return."

"You fail to trust me."

"What do you want as payment?" Because she didn't want to be trapped here if he decided that he wanted her body or soul, just failing to mention it beforehand.

"Only for you to call me by my name."

If someone knew what to do with the natural power in names, they could use it to cast spells and drain them for black magic properties. Being a magic man, it was dangerous to give away his name so easily. It was dangerous for her to say it, but this felt like a bargain without tricks. "Have it your way then, Like." She breathed in, glad nothing had happened to her, and bid him to continue.

He remained standing, glancing at the spiders tapping on their cages, before finding the words. "Throughout the world's history, two brothers have been reborn. Immortal, they return carrying with them the memories, desires, and ambitions of all their lives past. The one uses his powers for peace, and the other for domination. Necromancers: no spell is too strong for them, no demon unbreakable. But only one is truly human. The Wielder of Light keeps his true human soul: aging naturally, giving in to time, and dying as mortals die. The other is half demon: living longer, his powers stronger, with the ability to hide from even my eyes.

"They pass through history battling each other, both with a demon protector at their sides, sending them to do their wills, creating armies: Dragons and Knights."

Deciding to believe what he had to say, she asked, "The brothers have returned? They live again?"

"One will kill the other: depending on whom lives will course the future."

"Who usually wins?"

"Darkness has and can never meet triumph."

"That actually surprises me," Choice admitted. "I thought you said he was stronger?"

"Throughout history he has focused on controlling great numbers of demons. They want blood, yes, but they want their Master's blood just as much. Where his brother controls only one demon, using him to turn humans into soldiers, creating an army that's loyal, honest, and prepared." The surety in him was intense. "In the dark brother's previous lives, he seeks ruling. Now he seeks to destroy." He crossed his arms in front of him. "He's using his protector to spread a demonic virus. The infected do not question, they do not fight their Master's will. They do not think what he hasn't thought for them. He's created a perfect, loyal, and obedient monster. They're sent for our doctors first, killing them or infecting them, so that nothing can heal his desired burning world."

Choice fidgeted in her seat, excitement filling her, gripped by the story. "The Purple and Blue District?"

"Led by the protector, the army of Knights took away the heart of our healers first."

"That's not very nice." But now, disregarding the infection, even the simplest of ailments were fatal. She made a mental note not to catch a cold. "This demon...?"

"Leviathan," he named him, "a Prince of Hell."

"You know his name?"

"I can't do anything with it. I'm not powerful enough to overthrow a necromancer's hold on his demon."

It was a lot to take in and a lot to believe, and yet, in the world she knew today, it wasn't hard to believe at all. It meant there was an army coming, and it meant they needed to prepare for it. "Does my father know about this?"

"Your father is a necromancer: the Wielder of Light, and it's not the first time *the* Dragon, his demon protector, has met Leviathan, as Leviathan is *the* Dragon's brother."

"My father's a necromancer?" And what's worse? "I was raised by a demon!"

He beheld her with that look of pity again. "He's still your father, Choice."

My father's a necromancer...

"Does that mean I'm...?"

Like shook his head. "No. Like with voodoo, our abilities carry on through to male lines only."

Misogynistic blood! "I thought in fairy tales the dragons were the bad guys and the knights slay the dragons?"

"This is your life, Choice. Only you can decide what side you're on."

Did she really have a choice to be a Knight or a Dragon? She weighed her options. She could accept the fact that everything she knew came from people who avoided telling her that everything she knew came from a demon and carry on. Or she could willingly get bitten by an infected and turn into a crazed monster that wants to bite people. Hmm...

A grey and white cat jumped from one of the shelves and onto Like's shoulders. The silver collar told her the cat's name was Swagger.

"What do we do now," Choice wondered aloud, "apart from finding the good for nothing necromancer and wasting him?"

"Nothing is that easy." Like reached up to scratch the cat's head. Its purr was loud and affectionate. "Life changes. They've only ever had the bonds of hatred they've owned for each other, but now their desires have differed. He's never wanted to destroy everything before. Your father's never fallen in love, has never had anything but his brother, until this life. He's never had a child. The love he's had for you has never existed in history before. He's never had that weakness."

She didn't take offense. But there was something else she wanted to know. "I was never told what happened to my mother."

Like nodded. The cat jumped down from his shoulders and onto the table, feathers slightly moving with his quick landing. "Leviathan killed her."

She couldn't be upset about it. Not really. She'd never known her mother. "You have no idea who the necromancer controlling him is?"

The necromancer...

Like sighed: a hissy, unnatural sounding thing coming from him. "Don't expect him to be like your father just because your father's a necromancer reborn. Other than being male and half demon, he can be of any age. He could be anyone." He picked up a feather and then let it fall from his hands. "The only thing we know for sure is that in the end he's going to send his army after your father. That is his true and only target."

How did she expect to act after learning a massive monster army is coming to kill her father? She didn't get scared. "What do I do?"

"It will come down to a battle between Knights and Dragons," Like explained. "If Light prevails, we'll have stopped the army, killed the necromancer, and protected your father. If we fail, darkness will spread, the world will burn, humanity will be forgotten, and the necromancer will stand above it all." He said, "As you can see, there's a great deal to be done."

"You're not going to tell me to sit this out? That it's too dangerous?"

"We're too few for you to be slacking off."

Choice smiled. Maybe she could have married this guy.

"Remember: trust no one," Like insisted. "The necromancer could be anyone. He could even be me."

Choice raised her eyebrows, but he was perfectly serious. "On that note..." She stood, preparing to leave, unhooking the green, velvet coat from her person and holding it out for him to take back.

"Keep it." He disregarded her outstretched hand. "It's a cold path you're about to take. A little warmth will do you good."

She hesitated, but then threw on the coat, deciding it was better to accept the gift than to argue about it, especially with a Voodoo Priest. She didn't think he was the necromancer, though. Why would he tell her everything there was to know about the Dark Wielder if he was him? To gloat? She didn't think it was him, not when the taste of peaches was a sweet warm thing nestled in her cheeks when she was around him.

The taste of hope didn't lie.

The grey and white cat batted at her feet as she walked, and bending down to pet the creature, it purred and swatted at her fingers.

"Swagger likes you," Like commented.

She let a noise of agreement sound in her throat before preparing to leave. Looking back, she nodded once, saying, "See you on the Dragon's side, Like," and stepping out of the house, the wooden door closed and faded behind her until there was nothing there at all but a green, grassy hill.

It was true. There was no finding a Voodoo Priest, not unless he wanted to be found. She didn't interact with the boys glaring at each other, perhaps who'd exchanged hard spoken words or whatever. She was too busy to care about what they'd been doing and if they'd been getting along. Although, with how thrilled Deacon was to see her, she didn't need to guess that they weren't.

"Choice." The other Dragon's tone was severe, seeing now that there was no hope of his having an audience with the Voodoo Priest. "I need to know what he told you."

Ignoring him, she got into her car. He didn't want her help before, and now she didn't need his.

Deacon followed her, smugly.

"You can't hide from me, Choice," the Dragon warned her. "I will find you."

Choice didn't spare a glance in her rear view mirror as she sped away.

11

Break Down

The sky was painted with stars, casting dreamy starlight, singing them to sleep as the moon hung overhead. Choice fought to keep her eyes open, her hands moving over the steering wheel, dreading the hours of driving ahead.

It was no wonder, then, that she took a wrong turn, and then another.

Lost, she drove with the map on the wheel, her eyes fighting to focus, and Deacon sleeping beside her. It took five hours before she finally got back on the correct road, the stars still twinkling in that consuming way they did, trying to draw her eyes closed. She gave herself a brilliant slap in the face, but the best tasting cupcakes waited for her in her dreams. Her dreams were a world where she was a little girl, rushing into her father's arms, him spinning her around, carefree and safe.

That was when the car broke down. Dying in her hands, it stopped and refused to move any further.

She sent her fists into the steering wheel over and over again before getting out of the car and slamming the door behind her. Deacon rushed out after her.

"My car!" Choice threw her arms over the hood, and then spinning around, she started shrieking at the cruel heavens for doing what they'd done to it. "My car! This can't be! This can't be happening!"

"Really?" Deacon took in her freak out from a safe distance. "After everything that's happened to us, your car breaking down is what you decide is unbearable?" He exhaled sadly. "This wouldn't have happened if we had horses. Who is dumb enough to own a car these days, anyway?"

She'd never been able to ride those damn things, and her car breaking down *was* unbearable and she stomped off the road and into the valley beside them. Pulling her hair out wasn't helping. Cursing and screaming wasn't helping either. She needed to cool off.

"Where are you going?" Deacon called after her.

"I need a minute!" she angered, her army boots coming down hard on the soft earth as she went, walking until she decided that if she went any farther, she wouldn't be able to find her way back.

The world around her was a forest with great gaudy bows hugging the trees. Massive vines of giant blue daisies towered above her head, along with other giant flowers she could walk under and not touch the tops of. The ground was a mess of grass and fog with imprints of black hearts that she stepped over as she walked.

The waterfall was flowing with numbers, ticking with the passing time, and Choice wrapped her green, velvet coat around herself to keep out the chill from the mist. But it was too beautiful to stay away from, and she sat down by the water's edge, soaking in this odd, calm moment in time.

She braided her long hair before Deacon took a seat beside her.

"My father's in danger," she told him because it wouldn't be polite to let him get too comfortable, too relaxed. There was danger, and she was heading into it. He didn't have to.

"Again: and you freak out over the car?" was his response.

"There's an army coming for him. I don't know when. If you want out, you know I've never wanted you around anyway."

"I know." But they both knew there was no way she was getting rid of him. "What are we going to do now?"

He was always asking her questions like that, and how was she to know? Except she did. "I'm going to fix my car."

12

The Stupid Plan

The lime green hot rod purred, its exhaustion rectified. With the maps out of the way, no longer needed, Choice sighed as they drove into the next district, slowing down because of all the horse-related traffic.

It was as good as bliss as bliss could get: hot on a case, her car running smoothly, pulling into a hotel with a hot meal in mind.

Things would get complicated after that.

"This is a stupid plan," Deacon complained.

"You got a better one?"

"How about we don't do this? Hide in the mountains or something until someone else figures this mess out sounds good to me."

"Hiding's never been my style."

"This is a really stupid plan."

She had to admit, it wasn't the soundest, but it had to be done. The infected so far had attacked them. Now she was going out to punch back.

Okay, it was a really stupid plan. But what else was she supposed to do?

"Just remember what I told you," was her way of assuring him everything was going to be fine.

"I'm not planning on letting you down. You don't have to worry. I've been caught by one before."

She figured that was as close to being a trooper as she could expect him to be, and she pulled into the hotel, having time to eat, but neither of them did. Watching as the Red District continued on as best it could.

News travelled fast from district to district, and with three districts destroyed, everyone was wondering which one would be next. Naturally, security was tight, but the guard remembered how his dad used to have a car just like hers and let her and Deacon in Red without problems.

The Red District was littered with skyscrapers, old prisons that had been reconstructed into museums; walls with painted or written stories about old wars. Poppies lined the roadsides, and every wall of every building was red.

To them, getting in wasn't the issue. It was what to do with the people inside.

"Come on." Throwing a few coins on the table for the tea they didn't drink, Choice led the way out of the hotel's restaurant.

Standing on the roof of a seven-storey building, she waited. She could see her hot rod, trunk lid open, parked below her. Deacon was fidgeting a short distance from it.

She'd triple-checked everything: the nets, the ropes that would be keeping her from smashing into the ground, her loaded guns, and Deacon's remembering of the plan.

There was no keeping the infection out, no matter how hard anyone tried. It was here. It was everywhere, and she was going to bag one of the *things*, trap it, and see if it could be interrogated.

Okay, it was a really stupid plan. But what else was she supposed to do?

The view, soaked in the glowing sunset, was enchanting. The lights, the architecture, the life. It was impossible to think that all of this could be lost so easily. Red flags moved about in the night air. Shadows danced off buildings as Deacon waited below. The bait in the illustrious evening.

So far, everything was going according to plan.

Except now...

Spinning around, her fingers were on the triggers of the guns she was holding, but she didn't fire.

His long coat was restless around him as he held his shotgun over his shoulder. The waning light darkened his features, yet, at the same time, granted him a look of grace. His eyes were like gold, brought on by the accomplishment of finding her so quickly.

Choice couldn't afford to react, to give away her feelings of dread. She was here to fight a monster, not a Dragon.

"You shouldn't be surprised," he said to her, taking a step forward.

There was something about the way he walked, something about how his shoulders were set, how they moved with his strides that made her think about what it might be like to run her hands over them.

62

"I told you I would find you," he said.

Did she look surprised? Glancing down, she made sure Deacon was still okay.

"I need to know what the Voodoo Priest knows."

"This isn't a good time."

"Why?" The other Dragon was beside her now, seeing what she was seeing. "Maybe I didn't find you soon enough. What are you doing?" But he didn't need her to respond. "I've interrogated dozens: there's nothing to get out of them."

"That was you. This is me."

"Do you have any idea how stupid this is? One wrong move, one loose knot, one untied string will lead to you getting bitten, and you being just like them."

"Why do you care? What am I to you?"

"I need to know what the Voodoo Priest told you."

No. She shook her head. "If I tell you, you'll just leave."

"Why do you care? What am I to you?"

Choice turned away, but she couldn't help absorbing the taste of peaches. Why did he alone seem to bring so much hope?

"Did you ask him any questions?" he started his interrogation, and it *did* feel like an interrogation. "Where are they hitting next? Where are they harbouring? What are they waiting for?"

True, those were really good questions she'd never asked. Those were really good questions she'd never asked while she was busy being overwhelmed at the time.

"Or were you out of your depth?" he asked, meaning it as an insult and she took it as one. When she didn't respond, instead, watching Deacon like the hawk she was supposed to be watching him like, he tried to control his frustration, saying, "The Voodoo Priest was our only shot."

"Our?" She snorted. "Suddenly we're a team now?"

"I need to know what the Voodoo Priest told you."

"Yeah, you keep saying that. Why?"

"Because –"

"Because my father's in danger?"

"Yes." His gaze was the most intense thing she'd had to handle yet. "If you want to protect your father –"

"I have every intention on protecting my father."

63

If he was shocked by her dismissing the subject, he didn't show it. "You plan to do that alone?"

No. She knew there was nothing about any of this that she could do alone. But that didn't mean she wanted his help.

"Are you planning to take the army down yourself, too, Choice?" He inhaled, studying her like their age difference was incredibly far apart. "We need the other Dragons. If we head back to the Nest —"

"We? Don't be simple." She looked right back at him as if he were the child he was seeing through his eyes. "*The* Dragon knows what's going on. It's *we* that have to catch up with *him* if we want to be a part of this fight." Since he was here looking for answers right along with her, she guessed the higher-ups wanted him stuck on some lame haunting case too. *Sorry, dad, there's no hiding from this. It's everywhere.* "Besides, why would I go back to the Nest at this point? I'm not supposed to be here. I never went back for orders. That's disobeying. I can't afford to take a three-year-load-off right now."

"So you do this?" He took another look down at the dumbest plan there was. "This is going to get you killed, Choice."

"If you believe that," she said, though she would miss that peach taste if he walked away. "If you *really* believe that, then don't stick around to watch."

He studied her, seeing her anew and seeing her through new shades of annoyance. Exhaling, he weighed his options, and then decided. "You forgot to calculate something into your plan, Choice."

She made a disrespectful sound in her throat. He had some nerve thinking himself superior. "What's that?"

He took a step toward her. His eyes, a sharp shade of gold, took in their surroundings. "That, to the infected, everyone is bait."

He rushed at her, making her gasp, her arms flying out as he slammed into her, flinging them both off the seven-storey building.

He held her, and she could feel the weight of him, his arms strapped around her, unconcerned about falling through the air, the intensity of his gaze locked on her.

The rope pulled, held, and then snapped with the weight of both of them, letting them land on their feet, breathless, but unharmed.

"What the?" she demanded to know why he chucked them both off a building, but he was already shouting orders for them to get into the car.

Choice looked up. A man was flapping through the air, following after them.

No, not a man. An infected.

Had he just saved her life? Again?

"Damn it!" Choice hissed, aiming and firing, but without a solid headshot, she couldn't kill it, and she didn't *want* to kill it. She wanted it alive.

"Choice!" the other Dragon yelled, but she stood her ground, trying to force the infected flying through the air toward one of the traps they'd set up just for him.

With his arms and legs spread out, a giant smile on his face, the infected caught her every bullet without reaction.

"Kill!" he overjoyed, preparing to bite her, going to land right on top of her.

"Choice!" the other Dragon pushed her out of the way to get bitten in her stead, but the infected belly-flopped onto the pavement. The other Dragon took hold of her shoulders. "It won't be worth it if you're dead!"

She slapped him away. "Nothing will be worth it if I fail!"

He shook his head at her madness. "There are other things we can do."

She didn't have time for this, and she pushed away from him. The infected peeled himself off the ground and got to his feet. Choice ripped apart a net from one of the set traps and flung it at him to slow him down. Unhooking the whip from her belt, she lashed out, letting it string around the infected, pinning his arms to him. Unhooking the second whip, she took away his legs.

The infected tumbled to the ground, snarling.

Choice sighed. They'd set up half a dozen traps around this area and didn't use any of them.

All it took was a net and two whips. For some reason that disappointed her.

Shivering at the thought of touching the infected in order to stuff him into the trunk, she decided it would be safer to find a hook, pulley him up, back the car up, and drop him into the trunk.

"Allow me," the other Dragon interrupted her thoughts, kicking the infected over, grabbing his legs, dragging, and tossing him into the trunk and slamming the lid.

He turned to Choice with an outstretched hand. "Keys."

"Who said you could drive my car? Who said you were coming with us? Where's your horse?"

"Unavailable," he said, glaring at the one in the car now because there was no way Deacon was going to give up the front seat. Warning them, "You're going to need help getting that out of the trunk."

Because how *were* they going to get it out of the trunk? Because how *were* they going to get it out of the trunk if the infected managed to untie himself? Yeah, he had a point.

"Then get in the back!" Choice hissed, piling in, and speeding off.

13

The Loyalty of the Knights

She lined the cell with plastic in case things got messy. It had been difficult to break in, even with her skills as a Dragon. The least they could do was clean up afterward as the prison was spotless, unoccupied, and retired into a museum. The halls were filled with the distant screams of memories, and the museum creaked with the satisfaction of being used for its original purpose once again.

Deacon stood out of the way, keeping the creature that was gnawing on the prison bars a significant distance away from him. While the other Dragon stood, arms crossed and leaning against the wall with one foot up behind him, resting, planning on being a whole lot of no help.

The gentled, reborn prison was all marble floors, polished up, framed, encased in glass, with stretched out diagrams, and torture equipment put out on grand displays. With the major equipment out in the open, the place was perfectly set up for her to cause someone incredible damage. But this was *something*, and the rest of these particular *things* she'd come in to contact with seemed to be beyond the rules pain set up to be obliged and obeyed.

She hadn't been sure if they'd make it into the prison with *it*, wondering if he'd untied himself when he was in the trunk bashing around. But they'd gotten him into the cell, locked it behind them, and had an extra fifteen minutes to spare before the infected managed to release himself. Not that she'd wanted to get close enough to torture him anyway. But now there was no hope of trying to see if torture would work on him.

Coming to stand in front of the cage, the creature tilted its head, taking her in like the cell was about to open and he was about to launch forward. She tried not to think about the way he was looking at her, piercing into her with his black eyes like he could read sin in her blood: the blood he wanted to taste. Talking to him was probably a waste of time, but she wanted to see what talking to him would accomplish. Her hopes weren't high, but there wasn't much else she could do at this point.

"Do you remember anything about who you were before this happened to you?" she asked. It wasn't one of her more pressing questions, but it was still something a decent human being might take into consideration.

Was there hope for turning it back into something vaguely human?

And should they be feeling guilty when having to kill the infected?

"I want to kill you." The creature tilted its head to the opposite side. "I *want* to kill you."

"This isn't going to get you very far," the other Dragon commented from the background.

Choice ignored him, observing her caged monster that didn't look so good from throwing himself off a building and landing face first. "You'd like being tortured, wouldn't you?"

"Please." The infected gripped the bars. "Please spill my blood. Let it pour onto the floor. Slip and slide in it, let yourself get the feel of it until it becomes like your own."

Yeah, torture wasn't about to work on these things.

"My Master commands me to kill. I want to kill for my Master. I can't wait to kill you," the creature began to say over and over again. "I can't wait to kill you. My Master commands me to kill."

"You're all like this, huh? Lame." Choice crossed her arms, getting ready for business – to get serious. "I think it might be true that you have a telepathic connection to your Master. Your creator: that demon."

"I sent that demon back to Hell," the other Dragon said from the shadows. "It would be hard to shout orders from there, making him not our problem anymore, but the damage was done. He spread the infection, and now it's spreading itself."

Choice ignored him. Controlled by a necromancer that demon surely hasn't sweated Hell for very long, and from the way the creature was unconcerned, she'd say she was right.

But let's see what happens when I do this. "Leviathan."

The infected cowered. "How do you dare to know my Master's name?"

"You know his name?" the other Dragon came off the wall to stand beside her. Impressed, hopeful, and twitching with controlling his excitement. Twitching with controlling his anger. "I spent five months hunting that demon. You can't tell me he's had a short vacation."

"The demon Leviathan is leading you, controlling you." Choice had to turn her voice into thunder as the infected threw himself at the cage, snarling to get at her, damning her for knowing – for saying – his Master's name. "Who is controlling Leviathan? I want a name!"

"The Master commands me to kill. I want to kill for the Master!" The creature reached out for her, furious. "I will kill you."

"Have you even seen your Master?" Choice stood her ground, unflinching from the rage before her. "Can you hear his voice inside your head right now?" He continued to reach out for her. "Where is his army hiding? When are they going to strike?"

"You will burn!" the creature snarled. "He will burn you, Dragon!"

"Because he's Leviathan," Choice offered. "General of the Knights?"

The infected stopped. Gripping the bars, his lowered head rising to grin at her.

"You're a Knight, aren't you?" Choice continued, knowing now that everything Like had told her could not be doubted. "And you seek to kill Dragons, don't you?"

"Not *the* Dragon."

The Dragon? Because he and Leviathan are brothers? Could she dare ask him if he knew *the* Dragon's real name? Could she chance asking something like that in front of another Dragon, who surely didn't know that everything he knew was taught to him by the kind of monster he'd spent his life destroying? "Because Knights kill Dragons."

"He will burn you."

"Leviathan will burn the world – the world of the Dragons," she corrected herself, assuring him that she got the message. "Your Master *is* leading the Knights."

"My Master will burn you," the infected didn't disagree.

"Son of a –" the other Dragon cursed under his breath, kicking the side of the wall as he stormed out of the prison. Choice couldn't watch him go, couldn't be sure if she'd ever see him again, except the taste of peaches wasn't leaving with him. She had to focus on her prisoner.

Not that she could blame the other Dragon for being upset. He'd sent that demon back to Hell, and now it was clear that the pesky creature was, again, running amok.

"I just thought of something," she said out loud. Shockingly, the creature seemed curious. "If you can hear your Master's thoughts, can he hear yours? Does he know you've given me this information?"

She hummed in her throat, dismissing the thought. There were too many of the infected to keep track of them that way. The demon couldn't have the time to listen to them all or care about what they'd have to say. It was more likely they were listening to some kind of recording playing over and over again, controlling them with that until he had something better to say to them.

But the infected didn't dismiss the thought of betraying his Master, and with a heart stopping cry, he lodged his hands into himself and began thrusting out his insides, ripping out his intestines, throwing down his heart, and peeling away his ribcage.

"Choice..." Deacon was paralyzed, he'd slid down against the wall because *this – this –* used to be human. It was because of that that Deacon whimpered for its mercy.

Choice raised her pistol and fired, blowing its head clean off. Lowering her gun, she whispered, "Interrogation over." Sickened, because whoever this necromancer was, Leviathan got him what he'd always wanted and what, according to Like, he'd never had before: loyalty.

14

The Next Stupid Plan

She stepped out of the prison and onto the red road, the night a quiet, resting beast. She'd rolled up the plastic, clearing the cell of any traces of a monster being there, and stuffing the evidence in a competent bin that could withstand being, and was getting ready to be, lit on fire.

With his shotgun over his knees, the other Dragon sat on the prison steps, soaking in the melancholy moonlight. "Five months I hunted him…" His dark hair fell into his face, thinking about the demon, Leviathan.

Deacon was still inside, making sure they were leaving everything the way they'd found it, as Choice came to stand beside the sitting boy. "You're passionate, even for a Dragon." She couldn't help wondering if Leviathan had killed someone close to him, the way he obsessed over him. She couldn't help wondering in what small ways his life differed from her own. "I plan to stop Leviathan."

His eyes took her in: expectant and judging. "Why are you fighting so hard?" It was a question he didn't expect an answer to because they were all fighting for the same reason: survival. But still, the question was there, wondering in what small ways they differed from each other, if at all.

"Why are you fighting so hard?" she asked back.

"Maybe I have something to prove."

"To whom?"

"Myself." The stars overhead were smudged by the lights and the buildings, unnoticed as he thought about the demon he was obsessed with destroying. "I like a job finished and staying finished. There's no sappy story to me, only my wanting him in Hell because it's my job to want him there."

"Like I said: passionate."

"Shouldn't you be interrogating?"

Was he dismissing her? It didn't matter, she wasn't about to listen to anyone or anything she didn't feel like listening to, and generally she didn't feel like listening to him. And even if she did, there was nothing left to interrogate. "I accidentally put a thought into his head, and he started ripping himself apart."

He realized she wasn't joking. "That's the last thing I thought you'd say."

"You thought I'd say I'd given up?"

"What did you tell him?"

"I asked him if his being there would make his Master think he'd betrayed him." Red maple trees grew in abundance, as abundant as could be allowed with the crowded buildings, and the leaves sighed as the wind breathed over them. "At the very thought of betraying his Master, he destroyed himself."

That certainly was the last thing he'd expected to hear. "That's insane."

It was insane. She completely agreed. "That's what happened."

He was nodding, expectantly, sadly. As he got to his feet, swinging his shotgun over his back, he looked at her like this would be the last time he'd see her, ever, and how that might not be a bad thing. "And now that you're at the end of your last crazy plan…"

Yes, she *must* be giving up now, right? Yes, she *must* see now that she was in way over her head, right? Hardly, but she wasn't too fond of what she knew she had to say next. "I need your help."

"Excuse me?"

Was he horrified or thrilled that she'd decided there was never any giving up and going home? Neither, it seemed. There was only all around shock and it didn't look like there was much room for anything else. "You exercised Leviathan once. You're powerful – more powerful than I am."

Shock subsiding, he was starting to digest what she must have in mind. "I don't like where you're going with this, Choice."

"I want to summon Leviathan," she said. "I want you to summon him for me."

"No. That's insane, Choice."

Maybe it was, but neither of them had many options left. "You spent five months hunting him." She stood her ground, making him see how right he'd be to stand beside her in this. "Don't you want to tell him to his face that he better not get comfortable – that you're coming for him?" Her words hit something inside him, and he stopped looking at her like she was crazy.

72

Instead, agreement clouded his face, trying to strip away the rational thought he was trying to keep hold of. "Even if it turns out that I can summon him..." He shook his head, the moonlight bouncing on and off him. "I won't be able to hold him for long – if I can hold him at all. And then he'll know where we are. As soon as he breaks free, he'll kill us all."

"Then we better be prepared for that."

There were too many buildings, too much enclosed space, and too many people around that could interfere – too much chance and not enough certainty that made him admit, "I can't summon him here."

What kind of damage could a summoned demon cause with all these buildings if he could shake loose and attack them? She knew, too, that this wasn't the ideal spot to work any kind of spell. "We'll go wherever you need to go."

Something changed in him as he walked toward her. "You're insane." He touched the pearls around her neck. The gold in his eyes was remarkably overwhelming. "If this goes wrong, this will be our last day on earth. Any requests?"

"Yeah." She leaned closer to him because she couldn't help herself. "What's your name?"

"Seven. My name is Seven," he whispered, her lips catching his direct attention, pushing her hair back behind her ear before Deacon cleared his throat and he stepped away.

15

Leviathan

It turned out that Seven knew every underground dungeon there could possibly be, directing Choice to the sides of Red, that, if she didn't know were still a part of the district, she'd say they were in the middle of nowhere. Deacon refused to give up his rightful spot upfront, forcing Seven into the backseat, and since he was there and helping, Choice told the story that Like told her from the driver's seat, leaving out Like's name, her father, and that *the* Dragon was a demon.

There were some things she wasn't ready to talk about.

Getting out of the car, Seven walked, found what he was looking for, and pulled back sheets of turf to open a dungeon's door that was now at his feet. He went down first, flicked on the light switch, before Choice and Deacon followed, Deacon muttering how it was a stupid idea to trust this guy.

But the taste of hope didn't lie. Being with Seven meant there was always hope.

He was setting up everything he'd need for the summoning. Creating a barrier that looked to Deacon to be a circle with a lot of odd designs.

"What do you want us to do?" he'd asked before Choice could. "I think I can handle salting this place corner to corner or drawing those pentagram things." He glanced at Choice to see if she was impressed.

"The more dangerous it is for him, the more he'll fight against being summoned, the more I'll have to fight to summon him, draining me before he even gets here," Seven answered. Although, when he talked, he always looked at Choice as if she was the one asking the questions. "Holding him is going to take everything I've got." He clarified. "Those things have to be made if, and after, the demon breaks the limited hold I'll have on him."

"If Leviathan steps out of that circle," Choice told Deacon, "it won't help us much to hide in pentagrams, and he's not stupid enough to step in one. He'll just cave the walls of this underground dungeon in on us and walk out of here like a bear we tried to kill by poking with a stick."

"This is a really stupid plan," Deacon informed them.

"Not if I can hold him," Seven admitted.

"Can you hold him?"

"Probably not."

"So…" Deacon wrapped his arms to hug himself. "You're saying if we want a moment alone to reflect before we die, we better do it now?"

Seven straightened up, finished with creating the barrier for the demon, and started out of the dungeon, saying back to them, "I'll be outside if you decide you're still man enough to do this."

Choice didn't watch him go. It wasn't Deacon's fault he was afraid. He'd never been trained for something like this – never been prepared for something like this. He was just a doctor, and being, she guessed, around twenty-two-years-old, he was close to still being a boy.

"Do you need a minute?" she asked him, wondering if he'd prefer being alone.

"What do you want out of life, NYDB?" Deacon whispered. His arms were still wrapped around himself. His attention was set on the floor. "Do you ever think about all the things you haven't done?"

His Asian features, the sweetness in his face, the kindness in his eyes, made him appear to be so much younger than he was when he was afraid like this.

"I know it's not fair for you to be a part of this."

Deacon finally raised his head. "I don't care what you think about my not being a Dragon. But we're both human. Please don't forget that it's not fair that either of us have to be a part of this."

She didn't know what to say.

But she didn't have to say anything. Deacon exhaled, trying to smile. "Sorry, NYDB, but I think I do need a moment to myself."

Nodding, she turned, shoving herself out of the dungeon, and into the dim sunlight to see Seven sitting on the hood of her car. He, too, looked troubled.

"I can't believe I'm doing this." Seven admitted when she sat down beside him. "*If* I live through it and get back to the Nest…"

"You'll probably be imprisoned now right alongside me." Because they were following their own orders. Because what they were doing wasn't cleared by the higher-ups. And that was as good as disobeying. And she was already wanted for disobeying. "But I'll be there, too, so it won't be so bad."

75

He didn't look convinced. In fact, he looked suspicious of her; weary. "This necromancer you spoke of, the one controlling the demon, it could be anyone?"

"Yes."

"It could be you." He was serious. His shotgun was beside him. "You could be sending me into a trap: me summoning the demon, and then you letting him free, and him killing me."

She smiled lightly. At least he was thinking more highly of her now. "The Voodoo Priest said the necromancer can't be reborn a female."

"Says the female in question." But he seemed to accept that answer. "Why would the Voodoo Priest tell you this? Why you?"

"He likes the ladies, I guess." Joking was an easy answer, and yet it wasn't much of a joke. Like trusted females over males because he couldn't sense the necromancer, and then there was the whole her being engaged to him thing... She decided to change the subject. "If I were the necromancer, I would pretend to be weaker than I am. Maybe I'd even pretend to be one of the victims – someone the infected are targeting to help me get close to my enemy. I would *want* to get close to my enemy. As far as I remember, I was telling you to go on and vanish up on that rooftop." She stretched her legs out in front of her. "I actually feel bad for the necromancer."

"Why?"

"The Voodoo Priest said he'd always focused on controlling large numbers of demons, all of which wanted to kill him more than they wanted to kill for him. Can you imagine constantly being betrayed? He just wants loyalty. I can't tell you *why* he'd want to destroy the world. But being reborn and reborn, no one else remembering what you remember, except the Wielder of Light – whoever he is – and a few Voodoo Priest who keep track of our supernatural history... It's got to be lonely."

It was clear that Seven thought she was insane. "I discourage you from sympathizing with the enemy. It's not a natural reaction for a Dragon."

"What do you want out of life?"

He hesitated. "I feel like your asking me has something to do with your sympathy for the necromancer. But on the off chance you're simply making conversation before the possible demise of us both..." He sought an honest answer. "I live for the hunt: something you should understand, being a Dragon."

"I do understand, but there's more to you, isn't there?"

Unsure, his eyes flicked with mistrust of what she was asking him. "Is there more to you? We are the hunt: that's all we can be.

"There's more to me than that," she declared, but it was clear that he didn't believe Dragons could be anything but Dragons. There could be nothing but chasing whatever they were chasing. But she nodded, agreeing with her own statement, making him exhale in found frustration as he slid off the car.

"It's time we be Dragons," he told her and started back into the dungeon to start the summoning.

"I'm right behind you." She jumped down off the car and took two strides forward before being forced to disappear within herself. A man stood in the shadows of her mind, and she knew him. He didn't have to speak in order for her to understand his being there, how his being there was possible or why he'd taken this moment to find her.

"Master!" She walked inside her mind to meet him, though *the* Dragon stayed within the shadows, his figure hidden and unclear.

His being there meant she was in bigger trouble than she thought.

"I know I've disobeyed, staying on a case I was told to stay off of, and I didn't come back to the Nest after I finished with the haunting like I was supposed to, but I did send in a written report. Did you get my report?"

He didn't respond.

"I'm sure you've been tracking my thoughts for some time now, so you probably know everything I've found out about you, about my father." She swallowed nervously. Pleadingly, she said, "I can help you."

"Stay out of this fight," *the* Dragon ordered of her.

"You don't think I'm strong enough?"

"A daughter has never existed. I don't need you changing the future I plan to achieve – that I have achieved for centuries without you."

She couldn't believe this. "You think there's a chance the Dark Necromancer will win because of me? Just because I'll be there? Just because I'm alive?"

"I'm ordering you to disengage," he said, hidden by her shadowed and darkened thoughts.

"And since you're controlled by my father, my father's ordering me to disengage."

"Do I have to use force?"

77

"No." She shook her head, knowing perfectly well that in a fight with *the* Dragon, she'd never hope to win. "You've made your point quite clear."

"I hate to think one of my Dragons can't follow one simple order," he said to her before vanishing, gone from her thoughts. Leaving her with his warning, her mind focusing back onto the dimness of the morning sun and what her choices would mean to the world if she obeyed or disobeyed — and what that would mean to her.

Deacon and Seven stood on the top of the stairs, their body language telling her they'd expected her to be more capable of hurrying up with the goodbye thoughts.

Did she have any regrets?

"Are we doing this?" Deacon asked her, his fear there, but hidden well enough.

Did she have any regrets? She closed her eyes. Would she have any regrets if she walked away now?

"Yes." She stepped forward with a stronger determination. "Yes, we are."

16

War is Here

Seven chanted, his Latin beautifully spoken, creating a series of hand signs before resting them together in front of him as if he were praying. 'Open,' was the last word he said in Latin, making Choice think back on the bits of nerves and anxiety she owned before Seven took up the lead, and began the summoning.

There was no turning back now. There was no heeding *the* Dragon's warning.

Just breathe, Choice, she thought to herself.

The demon reared into view, sparking and flaming into the circle, the sides of the barrier smoking, struggling to keep that much power from escaping. He stepped forward using the same possessed body he'd taken the last time Choice had seen him, although he was neat and tidy as if he was incapable of battle. But his horrific collar was still there, scars, and the black rings around his black eyes, reminding her that the body inside the grey, fashionable suit he was wearing was all demon now.

"Well, this is awkward. Not that I don't like surprises." The demon surveyed the room. "Look, kids, I'm a good listener if you just need to talk, but you've caught me at a bad time. You see, I'm in the middle of construction for the rivers of blood I'm about to install into the earth. In fact, I was in the middle of a speech before you tickled me to come here."

Seven's hands were clamped together in front of him, focused. Choice couldn't be sure where Deacon went, but he was probably hiding somewhere. She couldn't be worried about him right now.

"Speech for what?" Choice asked him.

The demon smirked. "Aren't you guys a little late?" He raised his arms as if to say, 'what the fuck are you still doing here?' "Or did you not get an invitation?"

"Invitation for what?"

"I'll take it that your invite got lost." Sighing, he stretched his arms out in front of him, getting comfortable. "But since you invited me to your little party, I'll tell you what you're missing at mine. I'm taking you all down bloody. I haven't led the charge yet, but that was what my speech was for."

"Why would you admit that to me now?"

"Why not? You going to stop me, pretty thing? You cuties can hardly keep me in your little trap and all I'm doing is standing here. Can you imagine how screwed you'd be if I actually *tried* to get out?" He shook his head. "You'd be so screwed."

"So why haven't you?"

"I feel sorry for you."

"That's awfully nice of you."

"You think it's nice when a demon pities you? You're cute, cutie." He smirked again, checking out the one fighting to hold him in the barrier. "Hey, I know you. You're my little stalker." He took a step forward, and the circle started smoking more aggressively. "I better try not to move, huh? You'll lose me pretty quick." He stood still and the smoke calmed down. "So which one of you learned my name and decided they wanted to try caging a Prince of Hell?" He looked at Choice. "I bet it was you. It had to have been you. My stalker is too smart, and he's been stalking me for some time now and I never got any of this shit. Your bedwetting friend, I know he's in here somewhere, I can taste his fear on the air, is too much of a human. But you – my sexy little Dragon – you'd do something stupid like this." By the way Seven glanced at her, the demon got his answer. "It was you."

He reached into his pocket and pulled out a bag of coffee beans. The barrier made sizzling noises with his every action, and it was clear Seven was struggling to keep it together. "So, what do you want from me?"

"When are you striking?" Choice decided she might as well get the answers she came here for. "Where are you leading the Knights?"

"That's it? You want to know when we can fight fair and square? What's wrong? You're not having fun anymore?" He extended the bag of coffee beans to her, but she shook her head. The barrier started to spark and make a great deal of noise, making Leviathan sigh. "I'm going to end up stepping out of here just to shut that off. But then I'll be more inclined to kill you, and you're just too cute to be doing that to just yet." He said to Seven, "I'd offer you some too, but you've got your hands as full as they can get right now," before directing his attention back to Choice. "You've got nothing I want. How am I supposed to exchange things for information?" he complained. "But to have you both, my sexy little Dragon, and my very own stalker who I have come to miss, on the battlefield in front of me, waiting patiently for me to rip them apart is something I find very touching." He exhaled. "So I'll tell you."

"You will?"

"It's not much of a secret that I expect the Dragon army to show up on my doorstep sometime within the next four days." He munched on a few beans before adding, "I mean, we already worked out the details over cupcakes." He looked so happy to have mentioned how much he liked the cupcakes here. "And we decided – me and my boss that is – that since there's only one district so far that we haven't touched, we'd swarm into the Grey District and draw the epic battle there."

The Grey District... "Who's controlling you?"

"He's great. I love him. He lets me kill everything and anything I want. He's so nice." He smiled, pleased with himself for some reason or another.

"I want a name."

"Scary, scary, you've got me trembling, little Dragon. You really do." The demon rolled his eyes as he turned around, raising his hand in the air and waving goodbye. Darkness opened up, waiting for him to step into wherever the demon was planning to go back to.

"No!" Seven screamed because he couldn't hold him – there was no keeping him from leaving.

But he couldn't go yet. There were still things she needed to know.

"Leviathan!"

The darkness fell away, and the demon turned back to her, jumping with excitement. "Oh, now that you know it: say my name, say my name, say my name!" Elated, he looked as if he was swimming in ecstasy. "But you want to know *his*, right? You sure know how to make a man jealous. Say my name again, sexy thing. I'm begging you to."

"Does that collar keep you from betraying him?"

Leviathan darkened, touching the monstrosity around his neck. "This thing? This just keeps me from moving too fast too soon. Don't worry though, sweetheart. The blinders come off on race day."

"What does that mean?"

"It means we're coming to our goodbyes. I can't stay and chat forever. Any last words?"

"Yeah," Seven hissed, sweating and breathing heavily from holding the demon in check with all his strength. "Don't go ahead and let anyone kill you. Because I'm coming for you."

"Come and get me then, kids." Leviathan turned, walking into the darkness that began to swallow him whole. "Come and get me."

Seven fell to his knees, panting, as the demon disappeared. Choice came up beside him, reaching to help him back to his feet, but he grabbed her arm and threw her to the ground.

Pinning her down, his rage made it perfectly clear he wasn't bullshitting when he said, "We are *never* doing that *ever* again, Choice!"

"Okay," she said, unconcerned by his actions as he fell, exhausted beside her, both of them looking up at the dungeon ceiling. "It was a onetime thing anyway."

17

A Goodbye

Deacon was hyperventilating down in the dungeon with the relief of surviving another day while Choice walked along the velvet-carpeted ground. She was surrounded by apple trees and raspberry bushes and strawberry fields. The sun was falling, bringing on a kind of hunger because they were one more day closer to the war Leviathan promised them.

But where was Seven?

He was sitting a way's off, waiting for something, whistling and speaking to the air in a calming sort of tune that Choice had never heard of before. It struck her as odd, so she waited, unnoticed by him, to see if his waiting was waiting for something related to malice.

But then a call ran on the air: a sharp, meaningful cry. A grey horse with a black mane and tail galloped up a hill, its strong body and powerful strides allowing the creature to return to Seven's side in a very limited amount of time.

The creature danced around the boy, finally dropping its dark muzzle gently on Seven's palm when he held it up for him to touch, like a friendly hello given by a kind of brother. The horse wore a bridle without reins, but other than that, he had no tack. Choice watched Seven dig into the inside of his coat pocket and pull out a thin strand of leather, attaching it now to the bridle.

"You're leaving?" Choice stepped out of her hiding place, but Seven didn't turn around. The horse took her presence in as if she was something unremarkable.

"I have a promise to keep," he answered, speaking of his words to the demon.

"I thought since we were all going to the same place, I'd drive," Choice offered, but Seven wasn't interested. "Is it my driving? Because I'm a good driver."

He stroked his horse's shoulder. "You're driving is fine, but what is he going to do without a rider, Choice?" The horse nuzzled him. "It took him this long to find me here. If I drive on, he'll never be able to keep up."

"It's just a horse…" But there was no conviction in her voice because if that horse was to him anything like her car was to her, then it *wasn't* just any horse.

"I've had him since I was thirteen, Choice," Seven told her. "I'm not leaving Judgement behind."

"Thirteen-years-old and you name your horse Judgement?"

"His full name is Judgement's Blade." The horse struck out with one front leg, making Choice jump back. "You're scared of horses?"

"I'm not scared of them," Choice lied. "I just don't know what anyone could possibly see in them."

"You don't ride…" He raised his eyebrows. "Not at all, Choice?"

"I *drive*." She pointed to her car.

Seven admired the lime green hot rod for a moment before skilfully throwing himself up and onto his horse's back as if it was a step in a ballet dance. Choice cleared her throat. She didn't know how she was going to go on without that constant taste of hope, but it wasn't like she could force him to stay or beg to keep him beside her. Maybe they'd see each other again… On the battlefield.

"I guess this is goodbye…" Choice whispered.

His hand was in front of her face, reaching out for her to take hold of it. "Come on."

With the setting sun in her eyes, the glow was framing him. "Come on what?"

"Take my hand," Seven encouraged her.

She didn't move.

"Trust me."

With great caution she took hold of his hand, and he swung her up and behind him like she weighed absolutely nothing. Judgement snapped his mouth, biting at the bit, until Seven leaned down and whispered to him to settle.

"He doesn't like me…" Choice squeaked. She'd sworn she'd never ride a horse, ever, and now here she was, breaking a promise she'd made to herself because some boy had told her to 'trust' him. "Maybe I should get down."

Seven pushed Judgment into a walk, and like a frightened child, Choice whimpered and threw her arms around Seven. He didn't seem to mind, and after a moment of tasting nothing but peaches and breathing in the smell of his jacket – all hard work, dungeon dust, and Dragon – she calmed herself down.

"I'm going to show you how we see," Seven promised her, and before she could ask what the bloody hell he was talking about, Judgement took off into the canter. The movement of the animal was smooth, and with having a death grip around Seven, she knew she wasn't going anywhere. Slowly, the rocking movement increased and then levelled as Seven demanded more stride, and they sped along the ground at a pace that horrified Choice. Knowing that, in actuality, they probably weren't going very fast – to Seven and Judgement this speed wasn't speed at all – but to her it was too damn fast. She fought to keep her eyes open from something she hadn't experienced for a very long time: fear.

"Put your arms out!" Seven told her, tilting his head so she could catch a glimpse of a smile. Had she ever seen him smile before? When was the last time she'd smiled like that?

"No way!" He had to be insane to think she'd let go of him.

He laughed, something she wondered if she'd ever hear again, and her fear started to subside, vanishing with his boyish enjoyment of her experiencing this with him.

He slowed Judgement, bringing him back to a walk, and taking Choice back toward the car they'd left far behind them.

"Now that I know how you two *see* each other, I think you're even more insane than I'd originally thought," Choice said. Seven seemed to like that. Choice couldn't deny that the way he was when he was with horses was, well, beautiful. It was a side of him she'd never have been able to imagine. "Have you always loved horses?"

"If I wasn't doing what I'm doing, I'd be somewhere training them." He gave a nod to the animal beneath him. "I trained Judgment."

"I told you that you were something more."

Seven took her hand and helped her swing down. Leaving her beside her car, Deacon climbing out of the dungeon behind her, he leaned down to run the back of his fingers over her cheek. Shaking his head, he said to her, "Sometimes I forget how young you really are," before turning away, the taste of hope disappearing with him.

85

18

A long Drive Away

Red vines grew up the sides of fences and signs. The apple trees were covered, and the scarecrows in between the wheat and corn fields, standing guard over the crop, had bracelets of vines. They'd driven by enough scarecrows here to know they wore name tags, having signs in front of them that read, 'This Is Me Mocking You,' as if crows cared about that sort of thing. Owls flew in and out of the apple trees, breathing in the night air and then crying in agitation as the lime green hot rod blazed by.

Choice wouldn't dare stop to pick any of the apples in the apple trees or the tomatoes from the tomato plants that lined the roadway as they left the Red District. The sides of the districts, out of the heart of them, were country life, and the families of Voodoo Priests were generally farmers.

Deacon and Choice hadn't talked much, and driving for hours didn't seem to make a difference. The same thing rolled around Choice's head. *There's never been anyone but the necromancers before. There's never been a daughter…'*

"Are you okay?" Deacon asked for the hundredth time.

This time Choice answered him. "No," she said, "but I can't stay out of this fight. I've never been able to walk away from a job, especially when it's only half done. But that demon wants us in this fight. It wanted to get summoned, and it has ensured that nothing will stop me from getting there. Leading the battle to the Grey District – *my* district – knowing that I'd never be able to abandon it… Telling me when and where without a second's thought…"

"You think we'll be walking into a trap?" He wrapped his arms around himself. "So, what do we do?"

She thought about her beloved Grey District: her freedom, her independence from her father, the Nest, and the Dragons. How did Deacon feel when he had to step into an ash-filled land that was once his home? How would she feel if she got there and the Grey District was already destroyed?

A salty taste was in her mouth, and she knew it was the opposite of hope. It was there because of where they were going – because something in her instincts knew they were going to be too late. But she couldn't care about that. She had to protect what she had, and what she had left.

"We're going to go straight into the trap." And she pressed down the gas petal as far as it could go.

Deacon was biting his lips together, holding onto the car door to keep himself in place as the horrifying speed of the car jerked him about. "I care about you," were the words he was struggling to say.

Choice cleared her throat. "Sorry, but I'm just not interested."

Deacon owned that blush of his again. "I'm not talking about romance, you stupid chick. I'm saying that I worry about you."

You think we're going to die? Choice thought.

"What I really mean is…" Deacon rested his head against the window, getting used to the pace she was keeping the car going at. "I'm glad I met you."

How could that be possible? Look at how his life's been going since they met. First off, he gets abducted and almost eaten by an infected. Then his hometown gets destroyed. They fight a demon, go on a bullshit ghost hunt, have to fight off a whole district turned infected, and then they summon a demon that wanted to be summon so he could invite them into some kind of war-laced trap. Nope. She wasn't sure what there was for him to see in any of this.

"That's the dumbest thing I've ever heard."

"You're only saying that because you can't see yourself a hero." Deacon closed his eyes so he couldn't see her reaction. "But you're my hero. And you're the only hero you need."

Choice raised her eyebrows but drove on in silence as Deacon tried to be swept away by dreams. If he was able to rest, it was a good idea to do it now. War was coming, and there wouldn't be resting then. And as for the whole 'hero' thing, there was still a very long drive ahead of them.

87

19

Last Day Alive

They needed gas, but they had enough to start thinking about how much they needed gas. It was on the list: save the world, call publisher to tell them that, no, she can't come in to talk about their pressuring her into doing book signings because she's a little busy being anonymous and saving the world, and get gas.

She had a list of things to do and Deacon, trapped within himself, appeared to be listing things on his mental pad of paper with his mental pen. Making all sorts of mental squiggly notes same as she.

Choice let her hands rest comfortably on the wheel. What would Deacon be thinking about while driving headfirst toward possible doom? What should she be thinking about?

She was trying not to think about Seven, reminding herself not to think about him. That's when Deacon decided to speak up, asking her if she was okay. Of course, he'd be annoying, and 'thinking about her' was all over him. Meaning, he was thinking. Meaning, he had mountains of questions he was tasting in his mouth, sitting on the sides of his lips, hanging there.

"Pull over," he ordered, pale and squeamish.

"Why? Are you going to be sick?"

"Yes. Sure. Pull over."

"Don't you dare vomit in my car!" She slammed on the brakes, but Deacon stayed as he was. Waiting three minutes, Choice finally asked, "Are you going to hurl or what?"

"This could be our last night alive."

"So what?"

"So what? So we should do something." He stared at her as if she clearly missed the point. "Come on."

"I've got a war to get to!" Huffing, she followed out of the car. *"This could be our last night alive,"* she imitated, asking herself, "Why do boys keep saying stuff like that?"

Deacon was walking in circles, wanting to do *something* (whatever *something* was), but couldn't decide what would be significant in the middle of nowhere.

Sighing, Choice climbed onto the car's hood, resting her back on the windshield. "Come on," she instructed. She and Deacon looked up at the abundance of stars, satisfied that it was that something Deacon was looking for, and Choice had to admit, it wasn't so bad. She'd even miss it, this picture: her, her car, Deacon, and the stars.

Parked in front of a statue of an angel, said that if you stand before her and make a wish, that wish will come true, Deacon asked her: "If you could have a last meal, what would you choose? And don't say cupcakes."

Owls flew overhead, landing on the statue and soaring away. "I'd have a plate of sausages and vegetables completely smothered in gravy."

"I was expecting something smothered in chocolate."

"You said no cupcakes, I went for second best." She fingered the pearl necklace around her neck. She would wear them into battle tomorrow. "What would you have?"

"I'd have lobster quiche, I think. By our meal choices, I would say I'm probably the chick in this relationship."

"You've always been the chick in this relationship."

"Fair enough." He expressed amusement.

She kept her attention to the stars; the vastness. Was she supposed to feel small? "We're going to be fine tomorrow, you know?"

"Because you won't let me die?"

"Because you're braver than you give yourself credit for. Braver than you think I give you credit for."

"Don't think too much of me, okay? I'm depending on *you* to be saving *my* life."

"Fair enough."

"If you could do anything on your last day – I mean, if we had time to plan – what would you do?"

"I don't know." *Your last day alive?* It was all bittersweet: a dreary song with that sad ending, foreseen, but the beat and melody chasing the lyrics made it precious in its own way. *This could be your last day alive.* "I'd make sure my dad's okay: make sure he's prepared. I wouldn't leave his side. I'd protect him, more than what I'm doing to protect him now. What would you do?"

"Are you kidding? I'm sitting under the stars with the most beautiful woman there is. Waiting for the end of the world any other way isn't on a guy-like-me's list. Except, maybe, to have her interested in him. Except, maybe, if he wasn't a little bit scared of her," he said, making her smile, achieving his intention. "I'd have gone back to Purple, if Purple still existed. I'd have spent it with my family, just like you would have spent your last day with your dad."

"Your family..."

"My parents and my brother."

She closed her eyes. They had to leave. She had to leave now. There was no way she was going to let what happened to Purple happen to Grey. There was no way she was going to let what happened to his family happen to hers. Not if she could stop it.

"We can't let him win..." Deacon whispered. "I can't let you experience the pain I'm going through. I can hardly bear it. I won't be able to bear seeing what would have to be hidden, hidden in you. You're too important to me. You're... You're my best friend, I think, NYDB."

"You don't have many friends, do you?"

"Had," he corrected, his face painted with stars, "but not anymore."

20

The Battle for Grey

'Into my world,' were the words written in bone, washing away with the overflowing wreckage. The battle cries were enough to ripple fear through the best of them. The severed heads of people were scattered about along with the severed heads of black-eyed monsters

The war between Knights and Dragons had already begun.

The Dragon was in the middle of it all. He was leading Choice's brothers and sisters through the agony as they held in agony. Bloodied and shredded, the outnumbered Dragons didn't stop to count their losses or lick their wounds: there was only obeying the orders of *the* Dragon. Those orders – Choice could hear them echoing through the air – were to follow with drawn swords into the darkness he was spearheading into.

Dressed in warrior-black, *the* Dragon was almost faceless with the massive amount of scars covering him. Shadows followed him, even drenched in blood, shadows folded around him, blurring him from the vision of others. He didn't notice Choice yet, and if she could help it, she planned to keep it that way.

"We're late!" War didn't wait for them to feel sorry for themselves, for them to have a moment of quiet contemplation under the stars, and it wasn't waiting for her to get out of her car.

An infected charged at them and Choice leaned out of the window, squeezed two bullets from her pistol, and didn't watch as the remains flew everywhere, folding herself back in as the car squealed to a stop, the monster's head blown off.

Deacon got out of the car with her. "But we're not too late."

He was right. The war had begun, but hope wasn't lost (even if she couldn't taste it). The Grey District was still standing strong with the Dragons and the inhabitants of Grey defending the home that was theirs to defend.

Her home.

Choice opened the trunk, strapped weapons to herself, and threw a gun to Deacon.

He caught it with unsure hands. "What am I supposed to do with this when I've never used one before?"

Two of the infected rushed at them, Choice pulling the trigger of the gun in her hand as demonstration. But Deacon looked more like he wasn't about to go around copying her more than ever.

"Then take one of my crossbows. You know what to do with that, right?"

"Enough to know to pass it to you when you need it, yeah."

Useless luggage, Choice thought before slamming the trunk closed and stepping into the fray with Deacon on her heels, hiding behind her. She'd planned to give him the crash course on weapons, learning on the job kind of thing, but that act of kindness was destined into delay by distraction.

Like was in front of her. His hands were full of blue flames. His arms and chest, neck and face were covered in designs alight with blue. With them, he urged a pentagram, formed from his will alone, to construct itself around them.

"Be on your guard," were Like's hissed words to her, "I have yet to find the necromancer."

"Be on your guard," Choice told him back, "I have yet to win the war. Do you think the necromancer's here?"

"Your father's not, meaning there's no knowing at this point. But the demon protector may come for you, to hold you for future ransom." He took hold of her sword and laid his index finger onto the tip, the blade taking on flames of blue. "Those inscriptions on your blade will not be enough. But a sliver of my power, combining with your own, will ensure that you will withstand the battle."

Choice could feel the difference in the blade: the swiftness, the weightlessness, and the agility. "Thanks."

He stepped closer to her. Disregarding the infected that ran into the sides of the pentagram, burning alive. He took her hand and she could feel the enchantments he was designing on her body; could feel the blue flames within her skin as they painted her tongue, palms, and stomach like tattoos. Uncurling her fingers from her formed fist, he then placed a white button in her hand. "Keep this. If you find you need me, hold it tight and speak your demand. I shall appeal to it."

She looked down at the plain white button before stuffing it into her pocket, finding him gone when she raised her head. The pentagram faded away. Choice held a pistol in one hand and a sword in the other. Deacon mumbled about how screwed they were in the background, and she fired as infected came charging toward them.

And then she caught sight of him.

Leviathan stood on the top of the tallest building, his attention travelling past his valiant brother and onto her. In a light grey suit, he slicked his hands over the many braids travelling down his head, his blond hair catching the glow of the red sunset, drawing out over the battle, drawing the setting sun's shadows over his figure.

He stepped off the building, disappearing and reappearing in front of her. The infected bowed out of his way, snarling at Choice and Deacon, but waited for their Master's command.

"Deacon," Choice ordered, watching the demon watching her. "Don't be shy with that crossbow if it means saving your life."

"Hello, Princess," the demon kindly addressed her.

"You wanted me here." That was painfully obvious. He'd been waiting for her. "I'm here."

"Miss Selfish thinks my big bad plan is all about Miss Selfish." He took two steps forward, his suit made of animal skin. "Not that it matters what I'm *really* doing here. The damned are dominating."

"Doesn't matter. You're still going to lose."

"I'm glad you're here. Things were getting so dreary without you and your comedy." He tilted his head, the twenty infected coming up behind him achieving the same action. They were swarming, surrounding them, enough that the weapons they were holding wouldn't be enough if their Master turned them loose on them. There wasn't enough instruction in the world, let alone enough time for instruction right now, to teach Deacon anything about fighting. Not with an annihilating amount of infected in front of them, dooming them.

"Come now, little Dragon, tremble a little. It would be the cutest thing, watching you tremble in fear," Leviathan mocked her, and it was Deacon that reacted.

A boy that would normally be wetting his pants, held firm to the crossbow in his hands, conscious of the gun at his side that Choice had given him. He fired the first shot and the second, the arrows moving through the throat of an infected.

"That was just luck," the demon informed them, and Deacon fired again, missing. "Told you so."

The infected shot forward, toward Deacon, as Leviathan took Choice by the throat. "My lovely little Dragon." His eyes fell to her sword. "Your weapon looks different," and he gripped her wrist, forcing her to drop her blade and hold in a scream of pain. "Devastation suits you, little Dragon. Are you going to cry about my taking your sword away?"

Choice wasn't panicking. She wouldn't be a Dragon without having some sort of plan. She just hoped Deacon could hold on until she could initiate it...

"How do you like me without my collar? Sexy, right?" When she didn't say anything, he sighed in displeasure. "Where's the fight in you, Dragon? You know what? It's because you're a tea drinker. Hike up those caffeine levels, girl, it will do you some good."

She could feel the blue flames on her tongue, and she grabbed at Leviathan's neck and licked his face. It was more his own shock than the enchantment that dazed him, giving Choice time to head-butt him, kick him down, and grab her sword. The blade sparked as she spoke words she didn't know she could speak – voodoo words – and blue flames grew around them, creating a pentagram of protection. Leviathan barely made it out of the pentagram in time before it fully formed around them, listening to the infected caught inside scream, turning to ash.

Quickly, Choice glanced at Deacon. He was on the ground, motionless.

Was he infected? No. If he was, he'd be an ash-pit now too, along with the others. But was he alive?

"Deacon..." *Don't be dead,* she thought before turning back to Leviathan. "Where's your Master? Where's the necromancer?" She extended the tip of her sword toward him.

Leviathan blew her a kiss, walking forward, the blue flames flirting with his dead skin instead of destroying him.

"How is this possible?" Choice stepped back, but the demon was already stroking back her hair, had already taken away her sword.

"I will admit, getting my face licked was a bit of a shock. The Voodoo Priest gave you some very nice gifts. You must be very special to him. Although, you both didn't calculate something. Little enchantments and pentagrams will do nothing to me now." He leaned in to speak directly into her ear. "I don't have a collar on."

94

Choice went to strike him, but Leviathan had already taken hold of her hands, forcing them behind her back.

"You don't want to meet my Master, little Dragon." He kissed her cheek. "Better to just let me kill you."

There was a war inside her head, spiking the sides of her mind. Claws clawed into her brain, pulling out and opening to show ash falling between skeleton fingers. The ash rose: a clock with numbers telling her that time was running out, and before her the Grey District burned and where it didn't burn, it dripped with bodies and blood. Her father was dismembered on the ground.

Deacon was hanging from a burning building, and Seven was walking away, turning back a faceless figure, falling to his death as a demon laughed in the distance. She – Choice, her exact replica – was kneeling, twitching to her feet, her head tilting back and forth, and then turning to her. Black eyes were shining out from where her own eyes used to be.

Choice screamed, but she knew she was trapped in an illusion. She held the knife she'd pulled from her belt and sank it into her thigh, the pain bringing her back to life. She looked at the impressed demon. He pulled the knife from her thigh and flicked it away.

"I want to keep you as a pet," Leviathan said to her, adoringly, his mouth heading for hers. Her hands were released, and she moved to punch him, but he'd already slapped her in the face. She moved to swing her body, to put as much force into one solid kick as she could, but he'd already grabbed her leg, tossing her away like a doll.

"When will you learn, little Dragon?" He came over her, his body weight keeping her down as she reached out for her sword. If only she could take hold of it.

His mouth was on hers, and she felt her life force leaving her. She heard her heartbeat slowing as it pounded in her ears. Her eyes fluttered with the blood filling her mouth as the demon fed.

He took a moment to look upon her, to see her life leaving her. His own satisfaction leaving him as he asked, "Why are you smiling, Choice?"

She didn't answer.

"Why are you smiling, Choice?" Leviathan asked again.

The taste of peaches was overflowing, blood was dripping from the sides of her face, but she hungrily gobbled that peach taste down as Seven sank his blade into Leviathan's back. Judgment reared up at the infected behind them, the tip of Seven's sword nearly scratching at Choice's own flesh, before he ripped Leviathan's own demon blade out of the person he was possessing and ran the blade through him again. He began chanting, exorcising him.

"Seven! Stop!" Choice demanded, trying to force him away from the demon. The exorcism would send any demon within ten miles back to Hell.

"Why?"

"Because he's not the only demon you'll be sending back…"

Leviathan didn't try to fight. Instead, he took in Seven's expression with amusement. "You didn't know your Master was really a demon? Yikes, that's going to shove a wedge up the ass of your relationship with him."

"He's a demon?" Seven's face twisted with disgust, looking toward *the* Dragon, before continuing with the exorcism.

"Seven, stop! What are you doing?"

"He has a place where he belongs and it's not here. This is my job and it's the only thing I know, Choice." *The* Dragon continued to fight, continued to slaughter; continued to lead the Dragons against the Knights. "I'm exorcising him, and if any other demons get caught in the crossfire, then I'd call that a day we're lucky to have."

"No!"

But there was nothing she could do. Seven's words were absolute. They could hear *the* Dragon's screams, and they filled Choice in a way she'd never been filled before: tasting his rage, his panic, his ambition, and his identity slipping away, back to Hell.

Leviathan faded. The eyes of the body he was possessing were already blank when Seven finally withdrew his blade, stepping backward, out of the pentagram of protection.

An infected came up behind him. Before Choice could warn him, Seven swung his blade and chopped the creature's head off. When he turned back to Choice, he won her fist in his face.

She didn't have to tell him why she'd punched him. He knew he'd made her question what was right, and that maybe he did the right thing. He didn't need an explanation, watching her launch into the army of remaining infected.

Deacon came to stand beside him. "Maybe where she comes from that means she likes you," he said sarcastically.

"Still alive, are you?" he said, though he never took his eyes off of Choice. "She and I come from the same place. And yes, that's what it means." His expression was perfectly serious.

Disorganized now, with Leviathan destroyed, the Knights attacked without effect, giving the Dragons time to spread pentagrams along the ground. The infected, clumsy with blind rage, rushed forward, with their arms extended, into the seals, burning to ash.

As the numbers of infected began to decrease, more and more warriors circled around their Master, confusion and horror on their faces, seeing *the* Dragon fallen.

Would they ever understand what really happened here today? What really happened to him?

"After all this time tracking them –" Seven stood beside her, "did you think they would be finished so easily?"

Was this easy?

She stared at the carnage around them, the devastation, and the horror of the aftermath of war.

She didn't see Like anywhere.

"We better move," Seven informed her, looking up.

Carin had entered the war at the end of the battle, terminating the last of the infected, and the infected hadn't, at any time, tried to flee. Even when the very last infected stood, he continued to hammer away at the nails he wanted to pull out with his teeth.

"Don't worry, I'm fine guys," Deacon sarcastically informed them, knowing his well-being was the last thing on their minds.

All the while Choice knew Seven was watching her.

The taste of peaches was intoxicating.

21

What She Didn't Say

The streets were paved with carnage and devastation. Blood splashed from puddles as if it had rained as Choice walked, reaching what was left of her apartment building. The blood was the blood of her brothers and sisters – Dragon blood.

Carin was cleaning it up. Soon it would be as if the fight never existed.

"What are you thinking about?" Deacon asked her, following behind her because what else was he going to do at this point? He'd followed her through everything so far. He might as well follow through puddles of blood. "Are you...?" He hesitated. "Are you okay?"

She wasn't speaking. Seven had taken off somewhere. And she couldn't help thinking how Deacon should be sitting on a couch in a fire lit room, watching TV, his breath full of coffee and nacho cheese, thinking about a girl that wasn't her. If life was fair, his family would still be alive. If life was fair, she would be... She would be where? She'd be with whom?

The walls were smeared with splatters and lines of blood, and bloody handprints. Severed hands and bits of flesh stained and littered the hall. It seemed nothing about her home had survived the battle. But when she opened her apartment door, the lock still in place, she found that nothing was touched and nothing inside signified that a war had raged outside of it.

"How about you stay here?" Choice started back through the door.

"Where are you going?" Deacon asked, timidly, probably wondering if she'd come back or if she'd just leave him here in this one untouched room inside a city of horror.

"I'll be back." Choice gave him that little bit of encouragement, at least. But she couldn't be around him right now. She couldn't be sitting still. She needed to pace. She needed to decide if this war did feel too easy, and what was going to happen next, and if any of it mattered. Where was Like? Did he find the necromancer? Would the necromancer bring Leviathan back from Hell?

Would it start all over again: the infected, Leviathan, war, and then the countless deaths of Dragons?

Would it just start all over again?

Choice wanted to start pulling her hair out or start slamming her head against the walls that were covered with the artwork of devastation and loss.

A light was on in the stable that she'd always used as a garage and, even now, her hot rod was safely parked in there. Or so she'd thought. No one had been intruding or looking to intrude when she'd parked it.

"You're still here?" Choice walked in to see a familiar grey horse put its ears back at her. She had thought that Seven would have left the first chance he got. But there he was. And there was Judgement.

"You should be away from the threat of Carin's sight, Choice. I wouldn't want them to find me if I were you."

Because they'll do what? Kidnap me? Use me against my father? Force me into their organization? Or try to make me give up Dragon secrets? They weren't ridiculous thoughts.

"You're still here?" Choice asked again.

Seven was in the stall he was using to house his horse for the night. He kept running his hands down the horse's legs. It was an action Choice didn't understand. Perhaps he was trying to sooth the horse...

"Judgement needs to rest."

"Why are you running your hands down his legs?"

Seven narrowed his eyes at her, in an almost mocking way that made Choice feel like an idiot. "You really don't know anything about horses, do you?"

"I know cars."

"I'm feeling for heat in his legs, which would indicate weakness or injury. By running my hands down his legs, I am able to feel what I cannot see."

Choice nodded, though she didn't really understand. They'd fallen silent, so she took the moment to admire how the stable had escaped the war. Fire hadn't been set to it, blood hadn't soaked into the straw floor or designed the stone walls. No one must have tried to hide in here, and that's why the infected hadn't touched it.

Or was it strange that it wasn't touched?

Or was it strange that her apartment hadn't been touched?

"I keep feeling like something terrible is going to happen at any moment," Choice admitted. "Like the war was nothing. Like something worse is coming. You said the battle felt too easy…"

"It was." Seven straightened. He was so much taller than her. He was so much stronger. "Nothing's over. You shouldn't trust me. You shouldn't trust the Priest. Deacon, either. There's only you, Choice. Don't trust anyone, but yourself."

"What are you going to do now?" Choice asked Seven.

"I don't know. I'm deciding if there's any point going back to the Nest if I'm just going to be imprisoned. We're both going to be imprisoned, maybe even tortured a bit for good measure."

"Yes," Choice admitted. "I think I'm going to be imprisoned for a long time. I don't think there's a Dragon in history who has disobeyed as much as I have."

"It would be different if I knew Leviathan was going to stay in Hell."

"But you don't know if the necromancer is still out there," Choice agreed.

"It wouldn't be hard for him to bring him back."

"And you've disobeyed enough to make it this far." Was imprisonment wishful thinking? How long had it been since Seven went back to the Nest? Could he be looking at a death sentence? "So what will you do?" Choice asked him.

It took him a moment to decide, but finally he let himself out of Judgement's stall. Standing in front of Choice, his brown eyes specked with gold, he offered her his hand.

"What are you doing?" she asked.

"You survived a war, Choice," he explained. "You're lucky to be alive. Dragons aren't big on celebrating. I'm not big on celebrating. But I'll celebrate your being here today."

"We're going to party it up down the streets of blood and left over body parts? Not really my idea of a good time."

"I meant right here." His eyes forgot their brown colour and stayed gold. "I meant to ask you to dance."

In this stable, it was almost like there hadn't been a battle. It was almost like everything was going to be okay. She took his hand and let him lead her.

"Why do you always look at me like that?"

"Like what?"

"Like the way you're looking at me right now." Choice fought to shy away from his gaze like a *girl* might. She was a Dragon, and Dragons didn't shy away from anything, least of all the weight of a boy's golden eyes.

"If there's a difference in the way I look at you from the way I look at others, I suppose it's because I'm never quite sure what it is that you are going to do next."

She let herself smile. "There's wine in my apartment. I collect wine. I think we should go have some. Because so far we suck at celebrating."

"I don't drink wine."

"Neither do I. But it feels like the day we should, doesn't it?" She reached to take his hand. "Come on." And he allowed her to lead him, following her out where war had raged, into an apartment building where war had raged, and into a locked apartment that hadn't been touched.

It was quiet when they entered. Deacon wasn't there. Concern filled her, until she realized how hypocritical she was being. She'd left without telling him where she was going. She couldn't expect him to leave a note. Had he left for good? It would be better if he did. But still… Deacon on his own – alone – when he was so weak…

She grabbed a bottle of her best, put the record player on, and wrapped her arms around Seven's neck. "You're wondering what I'm going to do next, aren't you?"

He nodded.

"I'm going to pass you the bottle." She shoved it into his hand, both drinking while they danced too close. And when she started to get dizzy, he brought them both down onto her bed, letting her rest her head on his chest.

She knew it would be okay. That peach taste was there. She knew it would be okay, his eyes already closing, his face becoming something youthful as he fell asleep.

"Dragon," she whispered, and tried to whisper again, but she couldn't keep herself focused.

She couldn't fight off exhaustion enough to thank him for saving her life, for everything.

22

The Betrayal

She was in his arms when she awoke. She'd slept like that was the only time in her life that she'd actually slept. He was awake, but he didn't let go of her. Would they get ripped from each other by the Nest of Dragons? Would they ever see each other again, facing imprisonment?

And for Choice... What would her father say, having let a man she would never be married to touch her? Would her father understand? Would he let them remain holding each other's hand?

"Choice..." Seven whispered in her ear. There were only peaches with him. All these questions were rolling about her head, and then there were peaches. It was like, if they went back, they wouldn't be facing imprisonment at all. "Choice... We have to go back."

"I know." What else were they going to do? She had no idea where Like was. They couldn't summon Leviathan again and hope for answers on what was going to happen next. And there was no sense waiting around if the Nest already had the answers they needed. "We're too few Dragons right now to lose any to imprisonment. That's what we're hoping, right?"

He unwrapped himself from her. "Whatever happens, I want you to know –"

"It's okay." Choice figured she knew what he was going to say. "I know."

"Choice..."

Choice kissed his cheek. She got up and started collecting her things: car keys, pearls, green, velvet coat, and guns. She'd never kissed anyone before, even if it was just on the cheek...

Leaving the room, she found Deacon sleeping on the couch. He came back... What would he do if she was imprisoned? Where would he go?

"Deacon," she whispered. Watching him stir awake, she changed her mind. They weren't going back to the Nest. They were going to find Like, and together, the three of them – Like, Deacon, and herself – would find the necromancer together. But then Deacon held her gaze, and those thoughts came with a dry, salty taste.

Seven came to stand beside her. "What are you going to do with him?"

"What's going on?" Deacon sat up. "I'm going with you. Where are you going?"

Choice closed her eyes. If she was imprisoned, Deacon would go find a life somewhere. He'd meet a good girl, be in demand with being one of the few doctors left in the world, help fix the world, and then settle down with his good girl. That wasn't so bad.

He didn't need her.

"I'm not going to do anything with him," was Choice's answer before heading out the door.

Deacon can do whatever he wants.

She drove. Seven was in the backseat, like usual. The cameras at the gates knew her hot rod, but she held out her palm to them, to show her Dragon mark. The white wolves attacked her car, and she jumped out, screaming at them to stop scratching up the paint. They backed away, growling, snarling, and making Choice wonder why they were acting like this. Her whole life these wolves jumped at her and her car, and they never snarled at her like they meant it. She was the one that snarled at them...

Regardless, she started walking toward the front door. Sabastian didn't open it. Had he died in battle? Her heart sank at the thought.

Instead, she swung it open herself. "Dad? Where's Sabastian?"

Her father didn't answer.

Choice turned to shut the door. Seven was behind her.

"I feel like something's wrong," Choice admitted. "And you're supposed to use the main entrance." This was her father's house. Seven would have his own quarters to return to before he was summoned for questioning.

"The Princess of Dragons had to open her own door. Something's wrong."

"Or they're busy sorting out the chaos left over from battle."

"You're the Princess of Dragons. I wouldn't be a Dragon unless I made sure."

103

What have you done? Choice heard *the* Dragon's voice inside her head. Someone appeared, slowly approaching the Dragon Princess.

"Where's Sebastian?" Choice asked her father.

"Choice," her father said calmly and purposely. "You should have told me you were coming. We're out of milk. I see you brought a friend with you. You'd be wise to step away from him before he uses you as some kind of leverage. Although, using my daughter to get close to me is such a petty, demon thing to do. Don't you agree, brother?"

"Choice." *The* Dragon stepped out from the shadows of her father. "Get away from the Dark Necromancer."

They were in a locked, glaring battle with the boy behind her.

Choice slowly turned around. The betrayal seeping in. Her army boots were silent as they moved her body. Her filthy jeans and blood-stained shirt reminded her of him, and he was her betrayal. But how could it be? Her senses and everything she believed in had told her he was to be trusted. He was hope – tasted like hope. That peach taste had never lied – never. He'd been there – every time – to save her life. Was it all to get to this moment?

"Necromancer?" Choice fought shivering. *The* Dragon had warned her that the Dark Necromancer would try to use her against the Light Necromancer. She was the only thing that was different in this forever ongoing battle between Dark and Light. But Seven... He couldn't be.

"We'll talk about it after I kill your father," Seven – no – the Dark Necromancer answered her.

"But..." Choice closed her eyes, trying to picture the boy she knew instead of the necromancer before her here. "But you tasted like hope."

He took her hands in his and whispered, "Senses can lie, Choice."

And all at once her eyes began to sting and her mouth filled with a foul taste. Her face felt hot and her body trembled as if a spell was being lifted.

"And until you accept the truth, your senses will continue to lie." He let her hands fall and walked past her. His human, brown eyes were an unnatural, demon gold; having achieved his goal.

"I'm glad I didn't have to ask rudely for you to step away from my daughter," the Light Necromancer said. "It would have made things less enjoyable."

The Dark Necromancer smirked. "No. Although I've killed lots of little girls and boys, what's one more?"

"Voodoo Priests say you want nothing more than to destroy the world. Is that really what you want? If you were to kill me, what is it you would do next?"

The Dark Necromancer stayed poised. "What have you done, for so many years, after killing me? I don't have to wonder. History books have told tales that I have read once reborn. What do you want to hear, brother? That when I'm done killing you, I'll bring Hell to earth and create a second pit of fire? That I'll create a world of Knights – a world under one ruler? Truthfully, I haven't yet decided what I'm going to do. My one and only desire is killing you."

"All this revenge for being born half demon."

"You were the only one who believed my being born was a curse, brother."

The Light Necromancer lifted his arms and the shadows that surrounded *the* Dragon lifted. His body was of dragon scales. Smoke flowed from the sides of his mouth. His fingers were claws, and his eyes were dragon-green.

"Kill him," the Light Necromancer ordered, "demon protector."

"As you wish," *the* Dragon agreed.

But before *the* Dragon could move, Leviathan walked through the front door. His collar was off, and his spiky blond hair was soaked with blood. His face was wet with blood, and it dripped down and off his chin.

"What is my Master's command?" Leviathan stood beside Seven. "Use me for your dark will, my Master."

"I don't want anyone to interfere with this battle between necromancers. Do what you will with your brother," the Dark Necromancer ordered.

"As you wish." Leviathan already had *the* Dragon's full attention. They stepped toward each other, both taking a demon sword into their hands.

"Hello, Envy," *the* Dragon said to the other demon.

"Hello, Lust."

"Pity we've been forced to fight against each other like this."

"But it has been rather fun, hasn't it?"

"Indeed. I'll see you in the pit of fire, Prince of Hell, one way or another."

"Likewise, Prince."

Their swords flew up, attacking each other with demonic smiles on their faces.

Pleased, the Dark Necromancer stepped toward his brother.

"No!" Choice screamed, a knife in her hand.

"Choice! Stay back!" Her father ordered.

But Choice had already started running to sink the blade into the back of the boy she once knew as Seven.

Leviathan reached his hand out and, from his hand, a fiery extension of will was formed. It took hold of Choice's hair and threw her to the ground.

Seven never looked back as Choice screamed.

"Open! Book of Darkness!"

"Open!" the Light Necromancer ordered. "Book of Light!" And giant books opened behind them. Giant, glowing, transparent books that were taller than the necromancers themselves. "Come forth, Dragon of Light and Water!"

"Come forth, Dragon of Darkness and Despair!" the Dark Necromancer ordered. And two massive dragons roared. The Dragon of Light and Water soared through the air, its great wings stripping away walls and its height taking down the ceilings. The Dragon of Darkness and Despair roared. Its giant wings folded out over the demon protectors and Choice. The rubble that would have killed Choice thrown away with one easy flick of its wings.

"Dragon of Light and Water, destroy the darkness before you!" the Light Necromancer ordered.

The Dark Necromancer laughed as the Dragon of Light and Water charged. Its mouth opening, setting the room to fire and smoke.

Choice coughed helplessly. She couldn't move. She could faintly hear Deacon calling her name, probably wondering what the bloody hell was happening in here, and why it was suddenly all on fire. The demon protectors were battling by the exit. Her home was destroyed. Her father was a necromancer. Seven was a necromancer. And she didn't have any weapons...

She started running. She ran past Seven and her father, through fire and climbed over rubble. She could hear someone calling for her to come back, to stay where she was, but she wasn't sure who.

She ran past her father's destroyed study until she left the worst of the battle. Fire and noise of summoned dragons were behind her, but at least she was running down an actual path now. She made it to her bedroom – the bedroom her father kept for her. She took up the crossbow that had both her and her mother's names engraved on it, and strapped swords with dragon enchantments to her back. Armed, she ran back toward the battle.

But there was no way through. The rubble had become too much, and she was barricaded in.

She ran toward the stairs. She climbed seven floors before taking the chance to see if she could make it back toward the battle. Fire was creeping around her. Everything was smashed apart. She couldn't get close. There was only so much of the seventh floor left. She readied her crossbow. If she killed Seven, all of this would be over...

Or would it just start all over again at a different time, in another fifty to one hundred years? She took aim. "Betrayer," she whispered, and let her arrow fly.

Seven lifted his arm and caught the arrow in his hand. He looked up at Choice and smiled. She could see his mouth moving, and then a transparent bow appeared in his hand. The dragons attacked each other, and the Light Necromancer was shouting commands at his dragon. Choice was screaming, but no one heard her. Seven released the arrow. It soared through the air. And it sank into her father's human heart.

The Dragon of Light and Water disappeared. Leviathan and *the* Dragon stopped, staring from each other to the falling body of the Light Necromancer.

Choice was struggling to find a way down to get to her father.

Seven walked to his fallen brother's body. "Goodnight, Severe, Necromancer of Light. Until you are reborn again."

"Navar..." the fallen Necromancer whispered his brother's name before the Dark Necromancer detached his head from his body with the force of his boot on his neck.

"What are your orders, my Dark Master?" Leviathan asked, looking from his Master to his own demon brother. "What does your dark will command?"

The Necromancer ignored him. Instead, he addressed *the* Dragon with the demon's real name. "Asmodeus, Prince of Hell, Sin of Lust, what will you do now?"

The demon was confused.

"I'm not about to kill you, Asmodeus. Although, you may have felt some loyalty to your fallen Master, I will not force you to stand beside me. I doubt you want to stay here, in this 'Nest' of humans. What would you do if I let you loose? Or would you prefer to be sent back to Hell?"

"Are you giving me the option of being a free demon? Free from human control? To be a Prince of Hell among the human world without a collar or Master?"

"I'm asking what you would do, Asmodeus."

"I would feed as I am starving."

"And then?"

"I would continue to feed until every last human I was forced to train is raped, enslaved, and devoured by me," said the Prince of Hell.

"So be it," the Dark Necromancer released him from any hold that might have still been set upon him. "You are a free demon in the world of men. Do as you will without consequence for your actions from me." He then addressed his own demon protector. "We will be leaving, Leviathan."

Choice had climbed down from the seventh floor. She held Seven's gaze for a moment as she rushed forward, drawing her swords, but he faded away, disappearing from sight.

"We couldn't save him," Choice whispered, unable to look at her father's fallen body. "We couldn't save him…"

"I am a Prince of Hell," the demon turned to her, "and my name is Asmodeus. I have been enslaved to humans, and now I am free. You better run, little Princess. I will not harm you for lingering loyalty your father's spell forces upon me. But in an hour or two, I will be free of even that. You of all humans tempted my hunger. You don't know how many times the Prince of Lust would have devoured you. Run, little Dragon Princess. Because I'm hunting you."

Choice raised her sword to strike, but the demon had already disappeared.

Choice was left alone in the pit of fire.

23

Asmodeus

Surprise struck Choice as Asmodeus took hold of the blade of her enchanted sword with one formed fist. Taking it away from her as if it were a stick instead of a sword. She lashed out, but he was stronger. He had her throat in one hand and his lips on her lips with impossible speed. Choice could feel her life force leaving her. His hands travelled along her body, like a lover, as he fed.

When he released her, taking her in, Choice no longer saw the Demon of Lust. Seven stood over her. Her tears didn't stop his knife from taking her heart...

Choice bolted, scrambling along the ground with chaos all around her. She was outside the burning building. Her brothers and sisters were fleeing or trying to call for order or trying to put the fire out.

She was conscious of Deacon now. He was covered in ashes. His clothing was scorched, and he smelt like burning flesh. He looked terrified.

Had she passed out from the smoke? Had Deacon pulled her from the fire?

"NYDB, what happened? Where's Seven?" Deacon tried to get answers.

"I'd advise you to get as far away from me as possible," Choice told him, getting to her feet.

She scooped up her fallen weapons and headed for her car.

"Whatever you're doing, wherever you're going, I'm going with you!"

"Then we'd better get a move on," she said, Deacon already fastening his seatbelt. "I have to stop the demon who trained me from slaughtering us all. And I only have an hour at best before he starts."

The Demon of Lust was before her, stepping out of the shadows of her mind. His face full of scars and his body of dragon scales. He cupped her face in his hands. "You haven't run far enough, Princess. You're making hunting you too easy. Run faster, Princess. What would killing you mean to me if you let me kill you so easily?"

"NYDB! Look out!" Deacon snatched the wheel from Choice's hands and she shot awake. He'd saved her hot rod from smashing into a tree and saved them both from flying through the windshield.

Panting, Choice braked hard, sliding them to a stop.

"Maybe I should drive..." Deacon suggested.

"Little Princess," the Demon of Lust taunted her, walking within the shadows of her mind. Memories flashed about. Memories of the Dragon training her, pushing her into the warrior she was, whipping her when she failed, disobeyed or slacked off. He cupped her face again. His eyes were dragon-green with endless gold and swirls of fire. And in his eyes, she could see everything he wanted to do to her...

Choice gasped, threw open her car door and collapsed on the road. Turning herself over, she vomited.

"What would killing you mean, if you let me kill you so easily?"

Choice reached into her pocket.

Deacon was shouting, crying, and begging for her to get herself together.

"What would killing you mean, little Princess, if you let me kill you so easily? Are you even worth killing? Do you like what's in my eyes? Perhaps I'll keep you, and the Princess of Dragons will be mine forever..."

Choice gripped the white button in her pocket and pulled it forward. She couldn't blink. The demon was haunting her mind, waiting behind her eyes, for her to blink. "Help me," she whispered, "Please..."

Her body couldn't take it any longer – her mind giving way. Her eyes closed, and with them left her trapped in *the* Dragon's arms.

"Forever..." Asmodeus whispered.

"Like..." Choice opened her eyes. She was on the pavement, and the Voodoo Priest was watching her.

"The scary doll came first." Deacon pointed to the small doll standing on the car. "Then he did. I didn't know what to do. What should I do? Are you okay? Tell me you're okay."

Choice could see he was freaking out. She couldn't blame him. Who else did she have in the world? They were right here with her right now.

"He's strong, this presence hiding within your mind. I cannot banish him from you. His hold is too deep," Like said, his words hissing things. "But I have cast an illusion inside your head. You are safe. The illusion of you he sees is flawless."

Choice bolted up, clutching to his shoulders. "My father..."

"Your friend Deacon has informed me of what he knows," Like said. "The Dark Wielder has shown himself."

"He used me," Choice said, her voice caught on fury and desperation. "How did he know so much about me? My senses? The taste of peaches? Had he been studying me? Watching me? And for how long? Was everything, from the time I killed my first infected, a trap set up by him, to get to the moment where he killed my father? Set up so I would trust him? And what's going to happen now? Was he planning to kill me too? Why didn't he?"

"I've read every one of your books."

She fought a blush.

"How do you think I knew to hold up a peach to you on our first meeting? How do you think I knew how to lead you to me?"

"You have a crystal ball?"

"I know you," Like told her. "But you give so much of yourself away: your published books, journals, uncompleted manuscripts, your apartment, style, and vehicle. All other Dragons live secretly in a Nest with nothing where no one, no spells can enter – where no one can learn anything from or about them. If someone wanted to learn everything they wanted to learn about you, Choice, you made it easy. And if I have watched and guarded you most of your life, who's to say I was the only one watching when you never realized you were being watched by me?"

"And now my father's dead." Choice kept that same rage; that same desperation. "Now Seven's loose with Leviathan. And *the* Dragon is hunting me, and all Dragons."

Like tilted his head, curious. "The Dark Wielder did not banish your father's demon protector back to Hell?"

She shook her head. "No. *The* Dragon is free from necromancers and is the one tormenting me. Or should I say, Asmodeus."

Like filled with interest. "He told you his real name?"

Choice shrugged. "Not much good it does. I know Leviathan's name and I can't do anything about him wandering the world, now, can I?"

111

"No. He has a Master. But Asmodeus doesn't," Like said. "He must not realize we're in contact. There's no necromancer to overthrow…"

"Why do you look so happy?" Choice swallowed down her last bits of hope. "You're going to do something awesome, aren't you?"

Like smiled, his sharp teeth glistening.

24

Who Are You?

Like kissed her forehead. "Stay where you are. I'll only be away from you for a moment."

"Like…" Choice wasn't sure what to say. What was he going to do?

Deacon didn't have to be told to stay back.

He walked past the hot rod and carried on until he was sure Choice and her company wouldn't be in danger due to the summoning spell. He spoke words Choice had never heard before, in a language she didn't know. Blue flames surrounded him, and then Like became the blue flames. Within the circle of fire, Like was anew.

Within the air, a door of smoke and darkness appeared and then opened. The Demon of Lust walked forward. "Voodoo Priest?" the demon spoke, curious. "What would a Priest want with a demon, these days?"

Choice winced at her feelings of fear. She'd never known herself to wince. She really didn't get afraid. Even being trained by *the* Dragon wasn't something she'd ever feared. It was something that was honoured. But now, seeing her Master after everything he'd promised her, she found herself wanting to cover her eyes until it all went away.

Another part of her wanted to grab the crossbow out of the car and shoot him in his demon head.

"Same thing we've always wanted you for," Like humoured him. "To collar you, imprison you, to feed off your power or to send you back to Hell."

"You know my name in order to summon me." Asmodeus glanced at the blue flames caging him in. "There's only two men who've ever known my name, and you're not one of them."

"Two men, and one woman."

Asmodeus nodded. "I see. You have my little Dragon Princess somewhere. Tell me, Priest, what do you plan to do with her?"

"I have no plans for her."

"Who are you, to know her?" Asmodeus asked. "Having been hiding yourself from me? Spying on my Dragon Princess when no one's been looking? Don't tell me you're one of the many she's been promised to. Is this pathetic attempt to win her affection? You're a fool, Priest. Anyone can see she has feelings for the Dark Necromancer."

"Nothing shocks me, demon."

But Deacon froze beside Choice. Obviously, he could still be shocked.

Choice didn't know what to say.

Asmodeus took a step forward. "And what is it that you think I can do for you, Priest?"

"You're going home."

"And why would you do that?" Asmodeus took another step forward. "With all you could do with a Prince of Hell? Are you doing this for her?" He took another step forward. "Do you think she'll love you if you rid me from her life? It doesn't matter: you, the Dark Necromancer, it doesn't matter if you send me back to Hell. I'll always be the most important part of her life. She'll always belong to me. She'll always look back on me with honour and pride and loyalty. So send me back. I'll get out of Hell, one way or another, and then I'll come for her. I didn't lie to her, and I know she's listening. I can smell her. She will be mine, forever. I am her Master." He took another step forward. "If you think you're strong enough to challenge me, go ahead and try."

The demon lunged forward, in his hands appeared swords of red fire. Like blew them out as if he was blowing out a candle for the night. But the demon advanced, took Like's head in his hands, and snapped his neck.

Choice gasped, having to hold her mouth with her hands so not to scream the Voodoo Priest's name.

"Come out, little Princess." *The* Dragon paced the cage of flames he was still in. "Your Master's calling you."

Deacon was hyperventilating. "What do we do now? What do we do now? What do we do now?"

Choice shook her head. "Something's wrong."

"No shit!"

But that wasn't what Choice meant. The blue flames still held the demon in the cage created for him.

The taste of peaches was warm and vibrant.

Like's body rose behind the demon. His own hands came up to right his head, and then he began to chant.

Asmodeus turned, stunned. "Who are you?"

114

"As if I'd give you my name, demon."

The Demon of Lust roared with fury, red flames flying from his mouth as his body began to change. Caged inside the flames, the demon transformed into a fierce black and red dragon. His wings beat, but the blue flames refused to let him escape.

On its hind legs, the dragon lunged for Like.

The Voodoo Priest grinned a sharp-toothed grin as the blue flames consumed the dragon, vanishing him from sight and sending him back to Hell.

Choice stumbled to her feet. Deacon had his hands on his head, freaking out about how awesome and insane and terrifying this all was. But Choice felt lighter and free, like the burden of *the* Dragon had vanished from her. And yet, he was right, too. She felt a part of her missing. She pushed back tears. She wanted to cry out for her Master. He was her Master. He was *the* Dragon, and she'd never forget him. Everything she was, was because of him.

But more than anything, she recognized what Like had done for her.

"Thank you," she whispered as she approached him.

He pulled her in close and she could hear words on the air. Asmodeus asking, "Who are you?" And Like answering with, "As if I'd give you my name, demon."

Like whispered, "My name is Like Airell Caradoc, son of Baron Airell Caradoc, Priest of Priests, King of Voodoo."

She could feel the enchantments on her tongue, palms, and stomach blazing with new life. "I need to hunt a necromancer, King of Voodoo. Will you help me?"

"I will help you hunt the man you love."

25

The Safe House

There was no protesting against Like. Inwardly, Choice agreed that they should get off the road, rest, and start searching with fresh minds. But her stubbornness – her need to hunt Seven – kept her from agreeing.

That's when she blacked out. She remembered disagreeing. She remembered Deacon standing by her, just to stand by her. He fell first, sound asleep.

She remembered turning to Like. He was directing her fumbling into the car. "This was unnecessary," she'd slurred to him, and he kissed her forehead, sealing the sleeping spell neither one of them noticed he'd cast until it was too late.

How long had she slept? When Choice awoke, she was in a room to herself. The bed was as comfortable as her own back in Grey, but the room was unlike her own. Jars of bones and teeth and feathers littered the walls, as well as buttons, needles, and different threads. The dressers were no different, except for a few scattered pictures of Like when he was young.

The walls were full of protection wards. The room was lined with salt, and a circle of salt was around the bed, and there was a scent of sage on the air.

Like had brought them to a safe house.

She wondered if he'd carried Deacon in or if he'd left him to sleep in the car.

She didn't think about *the* Dragon or her father or Seven as she got up. She made herself not think about them. Opening the bedroom door, she wandered about in search of Like.

The safe house had many locked doors. In fact, every room except for the one she'd been in was locked.

Choice continued until she got to a kind of open common room. It was 'kind of' because most common rooms don't have bowls and jars of blood about. They don't have animal skins, bones or the remains of their slaughtered faces on shelves.

Deacon was asleep on the couch.

Like was at a desk with an assortment of voodoo items he was working with.

There weren't any chairs, and she didn't want to wake up Deacon, so Choice sat on the floor next to Like.

Without looking up from his fiddling with items, Like said, "Your sitting on the ground is an insult to you and to me."

"I don't mind."

"I do."

"So I guess this means you drove my car…" She tried not to hold his treachery against him. "Are you searching for the Dark Necromancer and his demon?" Choice tried not to think about how her father looked when he died. She tried not to think about how it was her own dragon arrow Seven had used to kill him. "I'd like to head out at soon as possible. As soon as possible being hours ago."

"You should leave the Dark Wielder to me," Like said, stopping his fiddling to look at her.

Choice shook her head. "I need to be the one. It has to be me."

"I've spent all this time hunting him. Surely, you can leave the magic to magic-men."

She felt Seven's betrayal like a living thing inside her. "I'm telling you not to touch him."

"Have you ever battled a necromancer? I believe you watched the final battle between brothers, yes? If he fights you as a necromancer, you will be slaughtered. Heart of a Dragon or no heart of a Dragon, you're not powerful enough to take on that level of magic alone or not. Because, in fact, you'd only get in my way."

"I know how he'll fight," Choice disagreed.

"You're hoping to appeal to his better nature – the better nature of the man who killed your father. You're basing everything you know on a phantom, an illusion, a trick you fell in love with. You're guessing at a phantom's actions. Choice, the man you thought you knew, isn't there. There is only the darkness."

"That's why we need a plan."

"Your plan involves attacking the Dark Wielder and his demon protector with brute force and Dragon courage. You've already failed."

"Her father was a necromancer," Deacon added, taking a seat beside Choice. Clearly he was only pretending to be sleeping when Choice had walked in. "Can't she do magic?"

"This kind of magic passes to males only." Like was getting more and more frustrated.

Deacon frowned. "Even if she tries really hard?"

"I'm not saying I don't need your help," she told Like. "I need your help."

Deacon nodded furiously. "That back there, with *the* Dragon guy. Dude, we're going to need *a lot* of that."

"We need a plan," Choice said once again.

"Exactly," Deacon agreed.

Choice turned to him. "Deacon, you should stay here."

"I'm coming!" Deacon protested.

"And how is she supposed to fight if you're captured or used as bait?" Like added.

"Probably the same way she's going to fight a necromancer without magic," Deacon said. "She'll figure it out."

Ignoring them both, Choice said, "First we'll have to find Seven and Leviathan. Since we know their names, it shouldn't be too hard to find them. Right?" Like turned away. But she knew he would cast a locator spell one way or another. "Although, my father called him something else. It wasn't Seven. Navar?"

"They call each other by the names given by their mother in their first life," Like informed them.

"So then..." Deacon wondered out loud. "Which name would we use to find him?"

"Depends on what name he truly owns in this life. Regardless, we'll search out his demon first. I'll be able to tell if the necromancer is with him," Like declared.

And then what? Choice asked herself. They'll find him, and then what will they do? Use brute force and Dragon courage? She knew it wouldn't be a fight to find them. She knew it wouldn't be a fight to get into wherever they were hiding. He wanted her to find him.

But she couldn't say that. She couldn't say how she knew.

She looked around at her companions, back to getting things prepared for the location spell.

Deacon was pestering Like.

She couldn't tell them. They'd think she was crazy.

26

This Is It

They didn't stay at the safe house for long. With Seven and Leviathan located, they loaded up the car with every weapon that might come in handy, and headed out. They weren't hard to find, although Choice didn't know the place. They were in a ruined castle not far from the Dragon's Nest.

Would there be dragon's swarming his ruined castle, creatures brought out by his Book of Darkness? Choice didn't think so. Would there be infected or higher demons guarding him like there probably should be? Choice didn't think so either.

The drive was full of awkward silence. Choice was driving, and both Deacon and Like were in the backseat. Weapons were in the seat beside her.

"I actually feel bad for the necromancer," she remembered her own words.

Choice tried not to think, but silence and all that had happened was making it impossible.

She tried to focus on the plan and the tasks ahead.

"He'd always focused on controlling large numbers of demons, all of which wanted to kill him more than they wanted to kill for him. Can you imagine constantly being betrayed?"

It had been her own arrow that pierced her father's heart.

"He just wants loyalty."

Like had reinforced the enchantments on her and added new ones for her protection. Her tongue, hands and arms, stomach and cheeks were fiercely tattooed with his blue flames. She still wore the haunting's pearl earrings and necklace as if they were lucky.

"I can't tell you why he'd want to destroy the world."

Choice searched through radio station after radio station, but it was all static. She almost wished Deacon was in a 'never stop talking' mood. But he didn't seem impressed that she'd made him sit in the back. It was only fair. Like was with them, instead of transporting himself to the ruins and battling the necromancer before she could get there. She shouldn't make him sit in the back while Deacon sat in the front...

"But being reborn and reborn, no one else remembering what you remember except the Wielder of Light – whoever he is – and a few Voodoo Priests who keep track of our supernatural history."

How would Like kill the necromancer if Choice wasn't persistent on leading? She wondered. Would he call upon his brothers and lead the Priests to the ruins? Would he be followed by an army of his doll creations? Choice looked back at him. Like was staring out the window. Or would he stand against the necromancer alone? Would he win? Would he die? Choice took a breath. Did it matter? Why think about it? Like wasn't going to fight the necromancer one way or another.

"It's got to be lonely."

And what if he killed Seven? She missed the man Seven pretended to be. She missed how she felt when she was with him. She missed how they were the same. Choice cringed at herself. She missed him as a Dragon.

"What do you want out of life?"

But he wasn't a Dragon. He was a necromancer and the man who killed her father. Like was right. She couldn't let the illusion of him stop her from protecting the people in this car – from doing what she had to do – her duty as a Dragon.

The Dragon... She dreaded her feelings of loss for him. But she couldn't help it. He was her Master. Even after everything he'd done, everything he'd been, and everything he'd promised her, she still felt his loss like her insides were in turmoil.

Her father...

Seven...

Choice parked the car and stared out at the ruins of a castle. It looked haunted and probably was. If this was any other day, she might have been sent here to clear it of its pests. If her father was still alive. If her Master was alive. In the life she'd hoped for, she would've been hunting here with Seven.

She didn't see any creatures that might have been brought out of his Book of Darkness. There weren't any dragons flying over the castle. So far, she couldn't see infected or demons or whatever else he might have had in store for someone that shouldn't be here.

She opened her door and stepped out. Her long, green, velvet coat followed behind her. She took up two flaming blue swords in her hands. Knives were hidden down her legs.

The weight of the weapons were nothing compared to the weight of what she was about to do.

"Looks like this is it," she said.

27

The Gift

Choice's wrists moved, making the swords spin in her hands. She could see Judgement in the distance, grazing away from the castle. What would happen to the animal now? Did Seven ever really care about him?

Choice started walking. First came a flight of stairs, letting her enter the courtyard. The paths were stone: the ground, the walls, the statues. It would have been beautiful once. She imagined what it would look like in the past: the gardens flourishing, the walls intact, and the magnificent home it might have been for princes and princesses.

Like was beside her. She hoped Deacon had stayed in the car like planned.

The next set of stairs took them up and toward the castle doors.

The swords moved in Choice's hands as they went, only stopping to push open the entrance doors.

The castle was full of shadows. But there was also a happiness to the castle; of being touched; of being used. There was a feeling of comfort that Choice pushed away. Other than a few broken windows, the inside seemed perfectly intact.

Choice frowned. She'd expected to see Seven as soon as she pushed through those doors. She'd expected him to be sitting on some gold throne with Leviathan standing next to him. But, apparently, it wasn't going to be that easy.

Choice readied her swords and slinked into the next room. She knew there should be booby traps. She knew there should be monsters waiting to charge at them. But everything inside her knew there wouldn't be. Like followed her into the next room, and then the next. They continued down darkened paths without even a bat flying out at them.

Choice caught sight of the demon in the corner of her eye before she moved into the next room. There were marks and designs covering his body and his face, as if warded for protection. He had a finger to his lips, as if telling her to be quiet.

He winked.

"Leviathan!" Choice warned Like before the wall closed, sealing her away.

One hand on the wall, Choice held up one of her flaming swords for its light.

"Hello, Choice." The Dark Necromancer stood in the middle of the room. Candles coming to life around them.

"Betrayer," Choice whispered back. He looked like the Seven she knew. How could she have been so wrong about him? She remembered the hope that used to come with him. But the taste of peaches didn't flood her mouth now.

"I didn't betray you, Choice, not really. That battle was destined from life to life to life. Even if I hadn't known you, I would have slain your father," the Dark Necromancer said. "But I promised you that we would speak together the last we met."

"The Priests predict that the world will burn from under you," Choice said, her swords raised. "Is that what you intend to do? Destroy the world?"

"Will I destroy the world? Will I take it over? Will I hunt down every last one of my brother's warriors and let Leviathan feed on them?" the Dark Necromancer gave an uncaring jester. "I have not decided what I'm going to do next. My only plan was to kill my brother."

"You killed my parents."

The Dark Necromancer nodded. "And yet there's still a part of me that appeals to you. Because I *was* a *Dragon* to you."

"Fight me then." Choice took a step forward. "As a Dragon."

The wall closed in, stealing Choice from Like's eyes. He could feel something pulling on his skin. It was physical, and he was conscious that it was physical. It was crawling and angry, and Like knew he'd only have so much time.

"Sorry, Priest," the demon protector came out from the shadows, "but it's a party for two in there. You and I weren't invited."

Like struck out with his thoughts, and a circle of blue flames caged the demon.

But the demon didn't flinch; as if he expected it; as if he wanted to be caged.

The human body he was possessing was butchered: all blood, torn skin, and bones. The demon seemed to be proud of the result. "She knows he's, like, her uncle, right?" the demon asked the Priest.

Like felt the pull on his skin and he fought it. He searched his mind for the destination. "We're to cancel each other out." Like understood. "You have a cage waiting for me, and I have Hell waiting for you. You seem comfortable. I take it you want to go home."

Leviathan shrugged. "It's something to do. I'm a bit bored at the moment. My Master was on such a roll, and now his creative edge has taken a downward spiral. I don't like seeing him like this. It's Hell instead of Hell for me. Demons enjoy their homeland, as you know. Vacations are nice, but home is home."

Like nodded, but otherwise couldn't move. He was in a snare created by the demon. It would transport him to the destination it was set to as soon as Like stopped fighting it. A cage was waiting for him. It looked empty. But if it had spells to keep him from transporting out, he wouldn't be able to assist Choice if she needed him.

"Shall we do this together?" Leviathan asked the Priest. "I need to banish you. There's no knowing if you can fight your way out of that snare, and I can't take any chances. I'll start. You should join in."

The demon spoke in Hell's language. Like could piece together words here and there, but it was a language of monsters that he didn't know well. Blue flames rose as Like spoke. An ancient language of Priests, and together they banished each other.

Leviathan smiled as he went.

Like's slit eyes opened to blue flames. His eyes blazed, searching the cage he was banished to. In a warrior stance, the Priest hissed with his fire. Enormous blue swords transformed within the growing fire around him and cut through the cage bars. The blue flames rose and rose until everything was consumed by the King of Voodoo.

✝

"I'm a necromancer, Choice. I'd fight you as a necromancer."

"No, you won't. You won't hurt me."

"That's wishful thinking."

"Then why didn't you kill me already? Then why was it your own dragon creature protecting me from the wreckage of the battle between necromancers? Then why was it you screaming for me to stay back when I ran off to find weapons? Why did you protect me?" And why, when the spell was lifted, did she not taste danger in her mouth when she was before him now? "You're not going to hurt me."

Seven was before her. Demon fast. He was inches from her face in the time it took Choice to blink. "I can always hurt you," he challenged her. He took hold of her hair to force her head back and then forced his mouth onto hers. The swords fell from her hands. The shock of the action paralyzed Choice, but it was a life and death mistake. She could feel her life force leaving her. Her heartbeat was pounding in her ears, slowing, and slowing.

The Dark Necromancer released her. Burned by Like's enchantments, and he hissed in pain before his body began to heal himself.

"You really are a demon..." Choice whispered, clutching at her throat. She could feel Like's fire on her tongue like a warm drink after wandering around in desert life. She could feel his fire on her face like a blush and her fingertips began to spark.

The Dark Necromancer straightened. "Your Priest has you well guarded, Princess."

"Can't take any chances with creeps like you."

"You don't even know me. You're so young, Choice."

Choice picked up a sword. "So why don't you tell me something about yourself, *Necromancer.*"

"You joke, but..." He paused before he began a tale Choice could choose to believe. "In my first birth, my true identity, I was a twin, and yet we seemed to have different fathers. We were twin boys, born seconds apart, and yet I wasn't the same as everyone else. Did my mother know I was the devil's son, born demon? I don't know. I was killed when I was ten-years-old, before I had the chance to ask her.

"But I was born again days later. I was given the same name by a second mother. A name I know you heard your father say."

"Navar."

"Yes. I was raised as a beloved son until I was fourteen-years-old. I killed a girl. She kissed me and her soul seeped into my mouth as if her lips had been a drinking glass. Before that time, I'd ignored my memories of my past life, pretending they were dreams, nightmares, something that didn't exist. I couldn't ignore them now.

"By this time, my brother had already begun his training as a necromancer. He could call upon the dead to do his bidding. He could bring people to a lifeless state and collar lower demons. He'd loved his twin brother. Our parents told him I died hunting with my father, meanwhile I'd already been hung for murder in my second life.

"My third life, Severe and I were again born from the same mother. He was the older brother by two years. By the time we were six, our memories had returned. We rejected the names this woman had given us and took up our given names: Navar and Severe. This woman understood. A single mother, she commissioned men to teach us the ways of our ancestors. I trained and otherwise stayed away from people. Until I was twenty. We'd never asked this woman how she was paying for our training. One night, I followed her. She was selling herself. Her body. Her blood for spells. Her true name so wielders could suck the magic properties from it.

"Infuriated, I turned on my teachers. I remember them laughing. Severe didn't understand what was going on. They summoned a higher demon to frighten me. They summoned him to harm me, to keep me in line. But when the demon looked upon me, he disobeyed them. Even collard, he turned on his Masters.

"'I will not harm the son of Adversary,'" he told them. This was my first year learning necromancy. I could not control such a demon, but Severe could. When our Masters abandoned their claim on him and picked up whips to beat me, Severe took entitlement over the demon and killed our Masters.

"It was after that, one asked question, that changed everything. 'Who is Adversary?' And yet, Severe didn't banish me then. It wasn't until demons, even collard, bowed to me that he found where I slept and cut my throat."

"I thought demons hated you; trying to control large numbers and them constantly betraying you and all that?" Choice baited.

"Some jealous lower demons, yes," he agreed.

"So you're some sort of Demon Prince." Choice shrugged, unimpressed. "How many years ago was that? Hundreds? Thousands?

127

Who are you in this life, *Necromancer*? Doesn't that mean anything to you? You had a mother in this life, a father! Where are they? Do they know what you've become?"

"This life?"

"We found you through the name 'Seven' not 'Navar.' You've taken hold of that name."

"You show interest in the life I've been living?"

"This is the only life that matters right now," Choice finalized. "Maybe you can't see that because you can't let go of what happened in the past – but that was the past. This is now. This is all most of us have. This life. What you do and what you've done in this life means something. It means more, and it could have meant everything if you'd let go of this circle you and my father are so fond of. Why would you live to be reborn just to kill each other instead of living in the lives you've had? Is that what my father tried to do in this life? He got married. He had a daughter. You could have followed his example and stopped this! Instead, you were jealous, weren't you? That he wasn't living his life for you anymore!"

"You think Severe was so innocent?"

"No, I think you're both horrible! You're both selfish! You think time belongs to you because you're reborn, and you strip away the lives of others without a second thought when this life is all they have. You both destroy. You've both ripped history apart when it should have been moving on to new things. You've locked us all in your past – taken away our futures! Ruined lives! You've taken away your own future – *Seven's* future!"

"Seven – *I* was born on a horse farm in Brown. When I was eighteen, your father's collared demon and a few Dragon slaves found and killed the family that raised me. Until then, I had not declared war in this life against my brother. He declared war on me."

"Bullshit! Leviathan killed my mother!"

"Your mother died when you were twelve. Six years ago, after the death of my parents."

"Do you think that matters? Do you think that makes any of this okay? Excusing yourself because he killed your parents first, so it's okay to kill mine? So it's okay to kill Deacon's?"

"I'm of demon blood, Choice. I deal in death." Seven corrected her thinking. "I'm a necromancer, Choice. I am a master in death."

Choice could taste Like's flames like they belonged to her. "If that's who you are, *Necromancer*, then I'll kill you!"

She attacked. In the back of her mind, she could picture Seven as a little boy, smiling, riding his horses through fields and streams, jumping fences and racing storms.

Growling, Choice banished them to the graves of thoughts.

A sword formed from nothing in his hands, and he blocked Choice's attack, holding her sword in place. "Son of Adversary." Choice guessed who his father really was. "You're the son of Satan?"

"Priests believe if I'm allowed to live, I will rule Hell here on earth."

"You've tried to rule before."

"I battled my brother with demons, trying to keep out the rest of the world. This time, I followed my brother's example. I made an army using people's lives. You don't think you were a tool of his? His own daughter!" He threw his weight into his sword and flung her backward into the wall.

Choice couldn't believe his strength. The strength of a demon...

"How are a bunch of Priests supposed to know what I might do if I was allowed to live, when I've never lived a full life?" he said. "You talk about living right now and my taking my own future away. This is the longest I've lived in one life!"

Choice let loose a knife from beneath her pant leg and threw it to sink into his chest. He ripped it out of his shoulder and threw it to the ground.

"Whatever happens here today, I promise you, if I have life left, I will spend it finding a way to let life move on without the two of you. It's time this world had a future of its own." Choice declared, her hand seeking one of her fallen swords. "I can see it in you. How much you want to be like me: a human." She used her sword to help herself to her feet. "Maybe you would have lived your life away from this, if you could have, like you're trying to say. Maybe you would have opened your own training stable and sold horses out of Brown. Maybe you would have been happy. Maybe, like you said, you didn't stand a chance." Choice readied herself. "I liked you better when you were pretending to be a Dragon. You suck as a villain!"

Seven caught the blade in his hand, attempting to toss it away from her. But the voodoo words seeped from Choice's lips – words she'd never spoken before. She could smell his flesh burning, and the necromancer quickly let go.

He looked at his hand, giving Choice the opportunity to strike. He used his arm to stop her blade, and somehow he deflected her blow. He disappeared, reappearing behind her with a blade to her throat. Choice used her elbow as a weapon, and he stepped back from the shock of the action. Choice turned, moving forward, but he sent his foot into her stomach, and she flew across the room.

Her head was bleeding, but she didn't care. Her warrior heart was pounding. She could feel her Master's voice inside her. She could feel the scars of her father's love, and she met Seven's blade with everything she had, and she hacked at him. Choice hacked, and hacked, and hacked and he let her. Blindly, her angry blade attacked. Was she crying?

"Choice," Seven whispered, letting her hack at him, deflecting her blade but not her fury. "I love you."

He hesitated. His words hung in the air, and Choice sunk her enchanted blade into his chest.

Horrified, Choice pulled the blade away on reflex.

Seven clutched at the wound, blood trickling from his mouth. He made a sound of undeniable pain before falling.

Choice rushed forward, abandoning her sword. Falling with his body, she caught him in her arms. He was dying. She'd made it so, and yet she was hyperventilating. He was a demon. She was a Dragon. She killed monsters, and yet... She was horrified. "You hesitated!"

"What's one more person, Choice?" Seven whispered. "What's one more person?"

"No!" Choice was screaming, shaking. "You're not using this as an excuse to come back and do what you've done all over again. Just because eighteen-year-old Choice Dunnon has killed you, does not give you the right to do to others what you did to Grey, to Deacon; to my family! Just because you hesitated! You hesitated!" She couldn't catch her breath, and how could she? He was dying in her arms.

"And you didn't. My love for you was greater than your love for me."

"I'm sorry..."

"It's too late for that now."

"NYDB?" Deacon spoke from outside the wall that was locking her inside.

"Deacon!" Choice screamed for him. "He's dying. Do something!"

130

"He's not going to heal me," Seven told her weakly. "I'm the bad guy. You're not supposed to forget that."

"I can't just let you die!"

"Good guys are supposed to."

"There's got to be something…" She fumbled in her pocket, taking out the white button the Voodoo King had given her. *Help me!* Her mind reached out. *Help me!*

A three-foot doll appeared, slowly turning its head to her, its button eyes waiting.

"Save him!" Choice pleaded.

"I don't want to be saved by some creepy doll," Seven rejected the idea.

"You *want* to die?"

"No one *wants* to die, but I'm the villain, remember? Villains are supposed to die at the end."

"End of what?"

"You write books," Seven whispered. "Doesn't this feel like the end?"

"That doll doesn't seem to think so. I don't seem to think so."

"Let me die, Choice. I don't want to suck as your villain. I'd just go back to what I was doing before: killing people, world domination, reading dirty books late into the night." He tried to smile. "Just let me die."

"You have to let him die, NYDB," Deacon said from behind the wall. "He can't be the bad guy for the rest of your life, and you can't be the good guy for the rest of his. At some point, you're going to end up back to this."

"Why did it have to be this way?" Choice was furious. "Why couldn't you change for me?"

"What are you talking about?" Seven challenged. "Why couldn't you change for me?"

"He killed your dad, and he's not even sorry about it," Deacon reminded her.

"The doll's waiting for you to make a decision," said Seven.

All those times he'd saved her. All those times he'd brought hope with him, and now, when he didn't kill her like he should have. "He saved my life…"

"Says daddy's little girl," he baited her.

She turned to the doll. "Save him, but make it hurt. Scar him from the inside out and scrape away his powers."

"Wait?" Seven blinked, trying feebly to move. "What?"

"Let's see what he'll do, how easy world domination is —" Choice said to the stitched-mouthed doll; the button she had used to summon him still clamped in her trembling hand, "when he's mortal."

The doll obeyed, placing its little hands on the dying necromancer, willing and wielding magic Choice would never will or wield.

His wounds began to heal, his drained colour returning to normal, and the failing light of his eyes began to return. The Dark Necromancer, Seven, the man that had lied about bringing so much hope, removed himself from the cradle of her arms and got to his feet.

Straightening up, he took Choice's relief in. "What do we do now?" He inspected his healed chest, shaking his head in wonderment of her. "I'm still demon. You took away my magic, my Book of Darkness, my ability to be born again. Do I get your love in return?"

"I never said I love you," was Choice's response. "You get your life in return."

He nodded. "What happens if this doesn't change anything?"

She wondered. But he was alive and right now that was the only moment that meant anything – was right here, right now. "Then I look forward to kicking your ass in the future," she promised him, because what their future actions held would have to be for the future alone.

Right now there was only them: Choice and Seven, going their separate ways. "I'll know better than to let you win next time."

"You're the one who hesitated," Choice reminded him.

"You're the one who brought me back." He knelt back down, taking her face into his hands, his thumbs moving across her cheeks, before disappearing from her life. "Everything I do from now on, all the people I could kill, would be your fault. Can you live with that? You can still kill me. Take up your sword and kill me."

"I'm still young and stupid. Maybe soon I'll grow tired of you and decide it'll be easier just to kill you."

He smiled lovingly. He smiled in a way that showed Choice all he was going to do with one full life. "And here I'll love you forever," he whispered.

"No." She shook her head. "You're mortal now."

The doll let the wall locking them in collapse around them.

"Then I'll love you for the rest of my life." Seven assured her. His eyes were full of unsaid words.

Choice pulled away from him, leaving him before he could leave her, assuring him, "As short as that may be."

28

How It Ends

They weren't far from the Dragon's Nest, and Choice decided she was going there next. She was sitting beside Deacon on the castle steps. Like's doll was watching them.

"What are you going to do now?" Deacon whispered. Was it to her or to himself? Either way, Choice answered him.

"There's Dragons out there that are in danger: from themselves, from Carin. I'm going to rebuild our home. I'm going to make an alliance with the Voodoo Priests. I'm going to battle Carin for a new government. One where we're not pushed away and forgotten, blamed and feared." She took a breath. "Did you see what happened to the Priest?" Choice asked Deacon. She tried not to say Like's name at all, not that Deacon would know what to do with it if he learned it.

Deacon shrugged. "I was trying to watch through the castle windows without being noticed. I just... I just couldn't stay in the car, you know? I saw them talking and then they disappeared."

"Did you hear what they were talking about?"

He shook his head.

Choice hoped he was all right. Would Leviathan return to Seven now if Like didn't send him back to Hell? Would Leviathan kill Seven now that she'd had his powers taken away?

"I can't believe you..." Deacon stopped himself.

"What?"

"I can't believe you let him go."

"Yes," Like said from behind them, and Choice let out a sigh of relief. "You realize you let the King of Hell's son roam free?"

"He won't be a threat anymore," Choice said, more interested in finding out what happened to him.

"Perhaps," Like's words were a hissing thing. "Or he may seek out Priests to return his power. Or demons will return his power to him. Or his father will come for him. Either way, I'll be keeping an eye on him. We'll have to. His father is waiting for him to rule Hell on earth. The son of Satan will be a target no matter where he tries to hide. You simply took his defences away, making him mortal."

"Where have you been?" Choice changed the subject. She didn't want to think about humans, Priests, demons or the King of Hell hunting Seven.

"Leviathan is in Hell. Using a similar banishing spell, he sent me to a kind of prison. He had quite the collection of dangerous creatures there."

"What happened to them?"

"Burned alive."

An explosion went off in the distance and smoke rose into the sky.

"Was that the Nest?" Deacon wondered.

Choice acted first and Deacon followed, running for the car.

Like slowly disappeared.

They sped toward the Nest. Indeed, an explosion had gone off. Fire was tearing things apart.

Dragons and Carin were in a full-blown war over the remains of the fallen Nest.

"Holy shit!" Deacon yelled.

"We're parking here." Choice unbuckled and jumped out of the driver's seat. "I don't want them fucking up my car." She went around to the trunk, tossing Deacon the crossbow and what arrows were left. "Stay here and shoot anything that doesn't look Dragon."

Choice felt the lightness of her flaming sword in her hands. She felt the weight of the Dragon sword in the other. She roared as she launched her blades into battle, hacking at Carin like she should have hacked at Seven. She hacked off limbs. She hacked off faces. Bullets rushed by her, but her eyes opened with blue flames. She felt light and powerful as she watched bullets pass in slow motion.

Her foot sank into the stomach of a Carin woman.

Like appeared beside her.

"We have to stop this fight," Choice told him. "Can you separate Carin from the Dragons?"

"Are you sure you want me to? You seemed to be enjoying the strength of my flames." They stared at each other before Like focused on the battle. Blue flames consumed everything. Like's slit eyes opened as blue fire. The blue flames put out the fire before it, and pushed groups of people to different sides, as it spread and spread.

Both groups yelled and owned confusion.

"Brothers," Choice yelled for them to hear her. Like's blue flames eased. "Carin is trying to steal our secrets, only to find there are Dragons here! I'm sure they're sorry for mistaking wreckage for weakness, but there is no weakness in a Dragon's soul. This Nest is the soul of us. We will forgive their mistake, brothers. We will forgive their mistake."

A woman of Carin stepped forward. She bowed her head slightly to the Dragon Princess before saying, "If you think you can rebuild, we will be in touch."

"Yes," Choice agreed. "There will be much to discuss. Many things are going to change."

She raised her eyebrows, but signalled for the warriors to retreat.

Uncertainty rushed through the Dragons, cries for war, and demands of explanation. Like's blue flames died away as he came to stand beside her, together, before the Dragons.

"We have been pawns in an ancient war between necromancers and demons," Choice said. "Our Master being one of them. We were created for one purpose: to destroy darkness at any cost. To that we still owe. We may have been deceived in our making, but we can stand together now. Human beings trained and raised as warriors, to continue on as Dragons. Our choice. It would be our choice. My brothers and sisters of war, I stand before you now with that choice. If you wish to remain, remain. If you wish to continue to fight as a Dragon, continue. If you wish to leave this life behind you, I give you leave to do so. But if you choose to stay, I promise you things will be different. The world cannot hide us any longer." The Dragons began to bow before their Princess once more. "Let us rebuild."

Choice wrote her story. She wrote about Seven and Like. She wrote about *the* Dragon and the necromancers. The end battle. She left out Seven's being alive. But concluded the five page summery with her first written order. It would be hung throughout the Nest, throughout history, for all to read. The Necromancer of Light will be stripped of his ability to be reborn and killed upon his return.

136

Choice had said to Like: "I promised myself I would stop the circle of death brought on by two necromancers. Brothers insistent on war; insistent on taking away lives. Can we stop my father's rebirth?"

"Only when he is reborn again, can we strip him of his powers," he had said.

"We?"

"I can't do it alone."

"Your doll took the Dark's away…"

"He was dying and willing. I doubt your father would be as agreeable. Perhaps if we found him as an infant, but we won't be sure it's him until his memories return."

"What if you use his body now to channel him, prevent his return that way?"

"We'd need his living self, Choice. If you want to put a hit on your father, we'll have to wait for his return."

"What if he doesn't return in my lifetime?"

"You're the Queen of us. It will be written throughout history. It shall be done," Like had said to her.

The Nest was now under construction, with the help of Voodoo Priests working together with Dragons. Carin sent members to help as well, eventually, once it was assured they would not be slaughtered for their actions.

"Are you sure this is what you want?" Like asked her.

Choice imagined Seven settling on a farm in Brown. She imagined him riding his horses, training them, caring for them. He'd be happy. Sometimes she imagined him waiting for her to come to him. Sometimes she imagined following him there. She imagined what his body would look like over her own…

"I was always a Dragon." Choice changed the subject. "I was never a necromancer's daughter. What does history say about them?"

"Daughters have a keen intuition, hence why I've never truly fought on the decisions you've made. They've all been noted to have the ability of prediction. Some have been said to have an extended life span. And of course, have the ability to give birth to the next generation of their kind of magic."

137

"All women give birth. All women have a sense of intuition. And women tend to live longer than men. So you're saying I'm pretty much normal."

"I fear women of magical lines feel cheated. Why must men have the ability to wield or summon magic? I believe it is because women are marvels already. Even without the ability to wield, they hold such magic within themselves. You're anything but normal, Choice. I take your lack of interest as an insult to the woman you are and have become."

"You asked me if this is what I want," Choice decided to answer him. "I want to give my people a brighter future."

As for Seven, she thought, *I hope he finds a way to live the life he wanted.*

"Did you love him, Choice?" Like asked her. "We all assumed. We all decided we knew your heart. But you didn't falter in killing him. You would have killed him. You had and have every opportunity to have a life with him, and you have chosen otherwise. Were we wrong?"

Choice didn't answer. She left Like behind her as she walked to what would soon be her office. Deacon was helping to collect what was left of files and boxes of cases.

"Hey, NYBD Princess." Deacon beamed as she walked in. He was probably just happy that he was allowed into the Nest. It had taken a lot of inner strength, but Choice had finally let him in. He was practically a brother now anyway, and the other Dragons didn't seem to mind that he was helping out. She'd have a clinic made for him soon enough and a classroom. He'd be teaching Dragons how to be medics.

Choice nodded. "NYBD Princess? Not like that nickname wasn't bad enough, now you're going to have everyone calling me that."

Deacon laughed, becoming luminous. "So, does your being the boss mean we can't go on haunting cases anymore? I don't think I'd mind getting comfortable here. Although, this place makes it kind of hard to order pizza..."

"You won't be leaving the Nest," Choice informed him. "As for me? If the Dark Necromancer somehow gets his powers back..."

"I guess he'll always be haunting your life."

Choice nodded.

It was the chance she took, to let him have his.

Vienna

CHAPTER ONE
The Suitor's Task

"Have you decided?" her father, the king of all the land, asked her. "I believe I've been very gracious."

"You have been, father," she answered while staring out the window. She was sending her dreams out, rushing them out, begging them to fling the window open and let her fly away on the wings of dreams. "Thank you."

"And?" he pressed, waiting for an answer. He was draped in ruby reds, as was his daughter. His clothes were embroidered with sleeping dragons and tulips, and hers with galloping horses and wild roses. "You asked to set a task for your admirers. However, I know it is more rather than less your plan to avoid marriage. But, as king, I could not refuse one last wish to my only daughter."

"For that, I do not love my king. I love my father," Vienna said, turning away from the window to look at the grand man, her father. His face always gave the impression that he hadn't shaved for three days.

"You had a deadline."

"I know."

"They are waiting for you."

"In the drawing room?"

"Don't be ridiculous."

Vienna's lips turned into a painful frown, as if she had tasted something dreadful. "I take it, then, they are in the courtyard?"

"Take it, darling. They've filled the courtyard."

Vienna took one last lonely look out the window, wishing her dreamed wings had come true. She wished she could stay in this room, just this room, forever. The window seat she was sitting on was a night-light blue, matching the rest of the room's blues and whites. The colors of the room were not what she loved about it, though they seemed to calm her mind a bit. It was the books the room held, old books that filled the walls built-in bookshelves that attracted her so.

Wasn't that always the case? Where dreams held fast, hiding and surviving in little, hidden corners, books might follow after them?

There were many libraries in the palace. But this one was in the highest tower, away from everything else. But this one overlooked the fields of royal horses. This one had portraits of her mother and of fiery dragons and roaring stallions. This little library, whose books were a little more wilder, a little more forbidden, was a little more to her taste.

"All right then, Your Majesty." Vienna got to her feet, her little feet holding up her little frame, with little rose shoes. Her dainty hands swept before her, dainty gloved hands that all princesses seemed to have. "I'm ready."

She followed her father out of the room, moving through the remarkable palace. She disregarded the modern and ancient items that the room had, and the modern and ancient pictures hanging on the walls. They were all so elaborate, demonstrating the best of taste, and achieved the most splendid outcomes of thought and feeling. But the princess disregarded them, as she often did.

From her father's study, or, rather, from one of her father's studies, they traveled through the curtained door and walked onto the brilliantly crafted balcony. Looking toward the courtyard, they could see that it was stained, wall-to-wall, with men. No. Not men. *Admirers.*

Trumpets cried out. Yes. Cried out. They felt like tears, maybe the only sound that knew how much Vienna hated her current situation. She felt their tearful sound as if their tears were not merely sounds, but tearful lines, already traveling down her own delicately featured face.

"King Gladness!" The announcement was made. Vienna wanted to flinch away as they announced her name. She watched as her many admirers bowed and rejoiced with her presence.

"Your princess shall speak," King Gladness addressed his subjects, although today they were more or less *her* subjects. "Hear her and know that her words are absolute. A task will be set today, and whoever conquers the task shall win her hand in marriage and become king of the land. Silence! Your princess speaks!"

The king turned to Vienna, anticipating her words to her suitors.

Instead, she whispered, "Kill me," to her father.

"Not until you're married." He kissed her forehead and bid her forward.

"I shall marry the man . . ." Her strong words filled the air. Yes. She was a princess. Even if her heart was fluttering and her cheeks felt like they would burst open, they were so warm. She carried herself with perfect poise, every word carefully placed. "I shall marry the man who brings me the diamond that best suits me."

"Well, that, at least, will get rid of the riffraff," her father said under his breath.

"Only then will I marry. Only then will one of you be king." As she spoke the last word, she turned. Her perfectly frail female form leaving the gentlemen, the princes, and the riffraff in an uproar of questions and cheers and shouts and demands. Anyone could confess their love for her, and it was her duty to hear them out, and that included the poor, and the ugly, and the shrewd.

Her father caught her arm as she walked the great hall, trying to get away from him. "I do not understand you."

"What meaning do you have, father?"

"You hate diamonds. You shriek and shrivel to wear them, calling them heavy, gaudy things unworthy of your feeble female frame. And now you're going to be swarmed with them."

"Yes." Vienna smiled a sly, wicked smile she'd learned well from being too spoiled, and too brave, and too much the princess she had been raised to be. Yes, she was a girl who wanted what she wanted and got it all the same. Thus, our clever little princess rejoiced inwardly. "And now I shall never marry!"

CHAPTER TWO
The Diamond

Being swarmed with diamonds was a reality, and not an understatement. Each day, Vienna sat on her throne, and lines of men presented her with jewels. She turned everyone away. Her father would give a nod when the suitors looked up at him, begging for someone to reconsider them, before they left, teary-eyed.

Her dainty hand worked her blue-feathered fan. Sitting for so long with so many people in one room was not only tiring, it was also drastically hot. Her darling blue gown was heavy against her skin, sticking to her, her skin dying to be released. Once upon a time, she used to gallop her horse to a secluded river, deep within the countryside. She'd strip naked and swim for hours. Her skin remembered it, and remembered it all the more as she sat, sweaty and bored.

Butterflies flew around the window frames, landing and flying, stretching, and then resting their wings as Vienna eyed the diamond presented to her. Her boredom was making her impatient and irritable.

"The largest diamond in all the land." The man opened the very large box, where, indeed, an especially large diamond was lying inside. Vienna heard her father gasp as he stood beside her. He rubbed his chin because it *was* a remarkable piece, surely the grandest they'd seen. But still the princess was unconvinced.

"This is how you see me, sir?" He was the leader of one of the larger villages in the realm, a prince, of sorts, to the kingdom.

"It is. Worth every penny."

"You flatter me, almost as much as you flatter yourself." She flicked her white-laced hand, sending him away.

He threw the diamond to the wall, outraged. The guards rushed forward and carried him away, kicking and screaming.

The next man in line came forward, offering her a small ring with a little square diamond.

A woman's cry filled the room.

Vienna looked over and saw a maiden at the palace door, trying to get in. A handkerchief was at her mouth, calling out to the man whom she so obviously loved.

Getting to her feet, Vienna pointed to the door. "Is that your wife? Is this her ring?"

The man flinched.

Oh, you are so unworthy! "Need I say more?"

And the guards came and carried him away.

Vienna sat down with a strained sigh.

Her father took her hand and kissed it as two of his advisers bowed to him. One of them came up to whisper in his ear. The king nodded, and asked his daughter, "Will you be all right if I leave for a while?"

Vienna shrugged, her fan working furiously.

"Stay with her," he ordered his advisers, who bowed, and came to stand at the sides of her gold throne. The tiara resting on her head felt too grave and heavy for her to bear. But the burden remained because another man presented a diamond, followed by another, and another.

"What is that?" Vienna asked no man in particular, objecting to no diamond in particular.

She'd had quite enough, and the passage of time was making her cruel.

"It's a diamond."

"Yes, I can see that. I've seen a great many of them today. But why do you think it's suitable to be presented to me?"

"I . . ." He couldn't answer.

"Do you have nothing to say for your diamond? Do you have nothing to say for the diamond you've chosen to represent me? Therefore, do you have nothing further to say to me?"

"I . . ." But again, he couldn't answer.

"In that case, on your way, sir."

"I . . ." He tried again, but the guards were already leading him out of the palace.

"Your Majesty . . ." One of her father's advisers spoke into her ear. She couldn't remember his name. Her father had so many advisers. He whispered, "I think it might be prudent for you to take a short break. That is, if you should wish it."

"Please!" She found herself grateful and the adviser waved away the guards. Both advisers escorted the princess away, announcing that Her

Majesty was fatigued and may not return for some time. Going into the dining hall, Vienna sat down. Water and wine and an assortment of fruits were already waiting for her.

She sighed long and low.

One of the advisers fidgeted. "Try to remain cheerful, Your Majesty. I'm sure things will get better."

Vienna looked up. It wasn't customary for her father's advisers to speak to her, and she generally had nothing to say to them. "What's your name, sir?"

He fidgeted again. "Hour." He motioned to the other adviser, who was eyeing him for his impertinence. "That's Augustus."

"Well, Hour –" Vienna took a grape and let the taste overtake her before saying, "I don't understand what you mean. Please explain it to me."

"Um . . ." Hour cringed under the other's stare. "I only mean to encourage Your Ladyship. It must seem like an ocean of endless turmoil. But I'm sure the storm will pass, and a man will show you a diamond that will end your agony."

"No, sir. That would be my agony!" the princess cried.

"I . . . I don't think I understand *you* now."

Vienna set her water goblet down. She was hunched over with laughter. She gasped, choked, covered her mouth with one hand and held her stomach with the other. She was maddened by the force of her laughter.

Startled, Hour asked, "What is it that's worthy of your amusement, Your Majesty?"

"Gentlemen!" She wiped tears out of her eyes. "This has only been the first day!"

CHAPTER THREE
The Midnight Ride

Half a year was swallowed up by the glitter and gleam of riches, all turned away, and all scorned at. The more they came, the happier Vienna was to send them away. The seasons changed, and Vienna continued to sneak out of the palace. She would bribe the stable boys with a handful of chocolates for them to saddle up her horses, and she would gallop them out, one by one, in the falling snow. Soon the whole year went by like this. At last, it came around to another winter's day, when the snow came down lightly, calling the princess to go galloping.

She held out a handful of chocolates like she always did, and the bronze-haired boy took them eagerly, stuffing them into his pocket for safe keeping.

"That's a good lad, Poem," she encouraged the boy, who was no boy. He was a few years older than her. About twenty–years–old, maybe to the day, maybe a day older . . .

The servant led her already saddled chestnut gelding to her, and they both gleamed in the cold air. The horse pawed restlessly. He was as restless as the princess, for she was also eager to run.

"There's a better lad, Poem." Vienna winked at the stable boy. He blushed despite himself, but she gave him his dignity and blamed it on the winter weather.

He held out his hand, ready to give her a leg-up. He was the only man she allowed to touch her, and that was only to help get her on the horse. In the daylight hours, she used a stool or got on from the ground. But at night, when her heart ran amok and she couldn't help but do forbidden things, she allowed one boy, the most loyal of her servants, to hold her leg and hoist her onto her horse.

"Your Majesty?" Someone entered the stable.

Poem quickly withdrew his hand.

"Hour." Vienna greeted him, unnerved because no one had interrupted her midnight riding before. Not ever.

"Alone, are you?" the king's adviser asked.

Poem's anger was clear to the princess, although Hour never once considered him. "Shall I run for help, my lady?"

He may not have considered Poem then, but he did now, while he waited for Vienna's answer.

"That's all right." She and Hour had not become friends, but they had become agreeable to each other. She wasn't sure if she trusted him, but she certainly didn't fear him. "He must have a reason for being here. Give us a moment, please, won't you?"

She sent Poem away and, as her most loyal subordinate, he obeyed without question. The stable was magnificent, with chandeliers hanging down from the ceilings. The stalls were skillfully designed with rose-sculpted bars and wood. Solid enough to keep even the most belligerent animal contained. At that hour, her most precious nickered for her and pawed eagerly for their turn, while her other loves, who admired her presence less, slept, uncaring.

Hour walked closer to her, his grey eyes and silver hair fitting well with the winter's night. He wasn't wearing a coat, although it was freezing, and his dark clothing indicated something ominous in him.

"Has my father sent for me? Has he noticed I'm missing from my chambers?" Vienna asked.

"No," Hour answered.

"That means you are here of your own accord."

His eyes gave him away.

"Don't even think about it," she told him.

"What?"

"What you're thinking about. I'm not interested in the love of a man."

"May I ask you something?"

"Only if it will please me."

"Why don't you want to be loved?"

Vienna thought about the subject, as she always did, looking like she always did when the subject weighed on her mind. "Because every woman wants that, and I don't want to be every woman."

"But maybe it will be epic."

"I'm sure it might be."

"It would be." He took hold of her hand.

"Let go of my hand, Hour," she ordered, remaining calm. She wished she hadn't sent Poem away now.

"It would be epic." He didn't let go. Instead, he slowly drew her closer to him.

He was going to kiss her! Her! Who was untouchable!

"I demand you release me!"

"Hour." A voice came from the doorway. "If you don't want me to get involved, you'll remove yourself from my princess."

Hour pulled away from her. "Augustus!" he exclaimed.

"Quickly, Hour," the man said calmly, not moving as he stared down the lesser man, "while I still find myself patient."

"Of course." Hour steadily walked away from the wide-eyed princess.

"Hour?"

"Yes?"

Augustus's tone was severe, possibly the most severe thing Vienna had ever heard. "Aren't you going to apologize to Her Majesty for being so regrettably out of sorts? Looks like you haven't been getting enough sleep. That must be it. Why don't you be off? It's late."

"Of course . . . So-sorry . . ." Hour rushed out of the stable, not meeting the other man's eyes.

"Your Majesty?" Augustus said kindly, oh so kindly, like sunlight touching skin on a welcomed afternoon.

Vienna cleared her throat. "Yes?"

"The snow is calling you. You should never have been detained." He ran his admirable gaze over her chestnut gelding. "You should be off on your midnight ride."

Clearing her throat again, she hooked her feet in her stirrups. Her fur cape snuggled about her shoulders. Her woolly long underwear nestled in her hardy socks and long, padded riding boots. Her white nightgown rustled in an unladylike manner since she was riding like a man.

Bidding her horse forward, she listened to every 'click' of her horse's hooves on the grey stone floor, before finally making her way out of the barn. She paused in front of Augustus.

"Look," he ordered. Her horse was snorting at the cool air and the questionable man. "The snow wishes to please you."

Was it snowing so perfectly before? No, not even a second ago, not until this man mentioned it, waving his hand in the air . . .

149

"Goodnight, good gentleman." Vienna didn't want to stay; didn't want to discover any more about him. In fact, he was far too interesting to be caught by her interest. She spurred her horse and left him behind. Indeed, she left all thoughts of him behind.

CHAPTER FOUR
The Warlock

Vienna sat on her throne with her father beside her, and six kittens running around the bottom of her dress, entertaining her as they jumped and swatted its many layers and ruffles. Her little crown didn't seem so unfit anymore as the lines of men slimmed. She had paid heed to all the men in the country, listening as they had tried for her hand. She had sent them away disappointed, and yet she was satisfied with herself. Her father wondered about her openly, marveling at whether she really had done it, if she really was too clever to behold.

The kittens grew. Hour stood behind the king, far from the princess and she was far too above him to grant him any attention. Finally, there was no one, and the palace was quiet; almost neglected. Vienna sat in the empty throne room, her feet up over the side of her gold throne. Her dress was unfit for court. It showed far too much skin as it was before she let it rise up to dangle her bare legs freely in the summer heat. In her hands, capturing her full attention, was a book, and it was because she was so enraptured in the novel that she didn't hear her father calling to her.

She jumped up, smoothed out her dress, and then sat perfectly still now that her father had caught her in such an unprofessional state. He wasn't alone. As the king came up to take his throne, two guards escorted a man toward them. This could only mean one thing: a suitor.

"Your Majesties." The guards and the man bowed.

"I take it you remember the palace's magic-man." One of the guards gave a nod to the trying suitor. But it was clear that both guards secretly mocked him for trying.

"Augustus?" The king seemed bewildered, but very pleased, and the magic-man bowed again.

Augustus . . . She knew him. He was an adviser for her father, and the only warlock for miles, she had learned. His eyes were emerald-green with gold and chocolate brown swirls. Yes. His eyes were very peculiar. He was slim, slimmer than her other pursuers, and though he wasn't without muscle, it was clear that he'd never drawn a sword in his life. He had kind lips, but there was a dragon-like quality about him.

Well, of course there was . . .

He bowed to her, and she gave a slight tip of her head in recognition of his presence. "You've come with a diamond?"

At first he didn't speak. He carefully – as if not to frighten her – walked forward. He stopped so that both Vienna and her father could consider him carefully, and his hand stretched out to her.

In his palm was a necklace. The chain fell through his long, slender fingers. While Vienna's other admirers had brought her great, gaudy diamond rings, he'd brought her a necklace with a well-made wooden heart.

"A wooden heart?" Vienna didn't take it. She judged it from afar, until her father's glance reminded her that she was a princess, and all people were to be respected by her. But still . . . "Is this how you see me?"

"Open it."

She took the necklace, noting that he made a point to brush his fingers against her wrist as she drew the item away. She had to admit the action wasn't entirely unpleasant. He didn't scare her, as some of the other suitors had. She could see in his face, odd as it was, considering he was a warlock, that he was exceptionally kind, and that perhaps he really did exceptionally love her.

Narrowing her blue eyes at that thought, she inspected the necklace. She didn't want to open it. She found herself pitying this man. No, in no way was she considering marrying him, but he was the first suitor that she didn't want to see damaged by her; curious because she had enjoyed damaging so many of them.

Taking the heart between her fingers, she opened it.

"You're not a diamond at all, princess."

Vienna stared in horror. There was no diamond inside.

"You're a pearl."

"Oh my god!"

"Isn't that right," the warlock whispered, knowing that he had won, "my love?"

"Oh my god!" Vienna sat, stunned, the heart lying open in her hand, the pearl taunting her.

"I see, at last." The king walked over, and inspected the pearl for himself, with a cheerful grin on his face. "Someone finally outsmarted you."

"I know it must come as a shock," the sensible warlock boy said, watching the princess. "I expected this. To imagine a princess rejoicing at the sight of a witch's son . . ."

"Don't be ridiculous, my boy." The king came up to shake his hand. "Royalty doesn't discriminate against our people. To us, all the men of Highest Guard are princes."

The warlock swallowed his nerves, eternally grateful to hear such wonderful words. "I thank you, Your Majesty."

"Please, call me dad!"

"Oh my god!" Vienna snapped closed the little, poisonous heart and its wicked pearl.

"I should warn you, son," the king said. "She's not easily pleased."

Augustus smiled warmly and lovingly. "Then I shall love her five times more than I do, ten times, a hundred times, until I can please her."

"Good man!"

Shaking, Vienna glared at her father. "How could you let this happen?"

"Me? What have I done? It was your task to set."

"You will find I am a really nice guy once you get to know me," Augustus assured her, although he was aware words from him would bring her little reassurance at this point.

"I can't accept this." Vienna's fists were clenched. Her shaking magnified. "I won't accept this."

"Careful child," her father whispered fast as he once again took his throne. "And know who his mother is."

Augustus raised his hands before him, signaling for peace. "It's all right. And I have long taken care of my own battles."

Relief filled the king. "Very good, I'm pleased to know that."

"She is a scary broad, though." Augustus gave an awkward laugh, watching his princess, hoping she'd look at him in a different way. "Isn't she?"

"That she is."

"I will not marry," Vienna spoke without realizing it. Her clever plan, her perfect scheme, had failed! This man, *this* sure enemy, had outsmarted her; had seen through her. This champion? No. This villain!

"Vienna!" her father warned.

But Vienna was already screaming, "I will not marry you!"

"Stop being childish!"

"I am perfectly serious."

Augustus remained calm, unswervingly calm, and he said, "You're going against your word? The word of the Princess of Highest Guard?"

"I will never marry you."

The warlock grinned. "Oh, I very much doubt that. I expected this, and though I love you, I do not love you enough to let you go. I won you. You are my princess."

"I am not yours." Vienna slapped his words away and cursed him with her piercing eyes. His emeralds held her firm, but she was beyond them. "I do not belong to anyone!"

"I never wanted to cage you. I only wanted to give you wings, and only if you should wish them."

"Then leave me in peace!" She threw the necklace and its wicked pearl, listening as it hit the wall, not looking to see where it had fallen. The king and the warlock looked, as if she had thrown it into its little grave.

"I cannot," Augustus said more firmly, more aggressively. "As I am playing by the rules that *you* yourself set. You have no right to turn me away, not without at least getting to know me."

"Let's all just calm down," the king tried.

The warlock wasn't listening. It was as if the only people in the room were the warlock and his princess. "You don't understand love or the pain of love, and until you do, you shall never love me, eternally, epically –"

"Shut up, whack-job!" Vienna screamed. She pointed to the door, forgetting her training and long life as royalty. "Get out!"

"So I hereby curse you!" The warlock raised his arms, and darkness crept over them.

"Wait just a minute–" the king tried.

"No one will believe you," Augustus told Vienna, throwing at her the full fury of the dragon in his heart, "because no one but you will see them –"

And now, Vienna was terrified. "Father!"

"Stop this!" was the king's demand.

But there was nothing to be done. The warlock set the curse. "Not just ghosts, but men, and the broken hearts of men. I curse you!"

154

The royal family jumped to their feet.

And the warlock disappeared.

Vienna stared, unmoving for some time, before turning toward her father.

"Don't look at me," the king said. "You're the one who upset him."

CHAPTER FIVE

The Stranger

The doctors were sent for at once. Even though Vienna had no ailment, she didn't mind them checking her over. The warlock had cursed her, and, unless he was a fake, he really could inflict damage on her. But, for the time being, she seemed to be in perfect health.

She changed into a silver gown that was fit for riding, and put on a large, bulky bonnet that would, if nothing else, keep the sun out of her eyes.

She walked into the dining hall, planning on waiting there a moment, before rushing off in search of an escape. The day had been a troubling one, and she needed a release.

But a man – a man she had never met – was sitting in her father's chair.

"That's the king's chair," Vienna informed him. The man jumped up and stared at her in a way that made her feel deeply troubled.

"Is it now?" he asked, looking at the seat. "I'm very sorry."

Vienna tried to look past him to see if there was anyone nearby. When she saw the guards, she breathed with ease. She had long stopped second-guessing herself on the appropriateness of being alone with a man, other than Poem. But, even if she wasn't the best judge of character, this man seemed to be harmless.

"Who are you?" she asked.

"Who are you? That's what I'm wondering."

Vienna blinked several times. "I'm Princess Vienna, daughter of King Gladness, king of all Highest Guard."

"Are you really? A princess! My word!" The man said, excitedly. "What a pleasure it is to meet you, Princess Gladness of Highest . . . Whatever."

"Weren't you listening?" Vienna tried not to laugh, but failed miserably.

"I was trying to, but something about you took over my thoughts."

"Then let me release you from your troubles. I was just leaving."

The man bowed.

"Well, at least you remembered to do that." Vienna laughed again.

"My name is Vincent." The man rushed around the table and stood in front of her to give her a proper bow of respect. "Your humble servant."

"I'm Princess Vienna," she explained, noting that he hadn't been listening the first time. He was a well-built young man. A nicely built man, actually. He wasn't overly muscled, and his long, red hair was tied back with a blue ribbon. "I'm going riding."

"Well, I have nothing to do . . ." Vincent's willingness was evident in his eyes, and in the twist of his mouth.

"You want me to accept your company?" Vienna laughed again, shaking her head. "I don't know what to think of you, sir. You have me quite puzzled."

"Please . . ."

"I suppose . . ." the princess decided. She walked past him, deciding that, if he was going to come, he had better keep up. She'd had a very difficult day. Perhaps this new person might bring her some ease.

Poem was waiting for Vienna outside and gave her a proper bow when she appeared. Vienna could hear Vincent making a verbal note about it under his breath. She decided that it was best not to glance at him, but to ignore him in front of Poem. She wouldn't be rude, not at all, but she wouldn't over esteem his character until she was sure his character was worthy of her esteem.

"Here she is, my lady." Poem led an already saddled, black-coated mare out of her stall.

"Very well." Vienna stroked the horse's shoulder. "But I'll be needing two horses today."

"Two, miss?"

"Yes, of course."

Poem's eyes showed curiosity.

"Oh, I don't ride, that's okay." Vincent waved his hands in front of him, looking up at the great beast. The horse snorted loudly, making them all jump. "Whoa, horsey!" Vincent said on reflex and the mare struck out. Poem shouted for Her Majesty to get out of the way, but the horse's hoof clipped her heel, drawing blood.

Vienna stumbled back, and the horse reared up.

"Are you all right?" Vincent ran past the horse, toward the fallen princess, and the horse shot backward, eyes wild, breathing heavily.

Vienna didn't pay attention to Vincent. "Poem," she whispered, watching as the boy calmed the trembling animal before putting her back into her stall.

157

"My lady!" Poem rushed to her. "I'm so sorry. I don't know what happened!"

"I've ridden her hundreds of times, Poem." Vienna assured her friend that he wasn't going to get into trouble for this. "It's not your fault. I don't quite know what happened either. Nothing's changed, except . . ." She looked over at Vincent.

"Oh, come on!" Vincent defended himself. Then he huffed. "Sure, it's got to be Vincent. Of course, it was all my fault."

"You're the only thing different . . ." Vienna said to him.

"What is, my lady?" Poem asked, choosing his words carefully.

"Him . . ." Vienna gestured toward the man shaking his head.

Poem looked at Vincent for some time before looking back at the princess. "My lady . . . Are you to say someone is there? That . . . You see someone there?"

"Of course." Vienna watched as Poem paled. He didn't explain. He just acted. He scooped her into his strong arms and ran. He ran as fast as he could with a dainty princess in his arms, rushing back into the palace and toward the remaining doctors.

Vienna didn't object.

As Poem rushed her out of the barn, Vincent stayed, waving sadly as he watched them go.

And then, finding transparency, he completely disappeared from sight.

CHAPTER SIX

The Ghosts of Men

She was ordered to stay in bed for a week, and when nothing else happened, she was allowed to leave, under the supervision of an escort. She performed what you might call a 'hissy-fit' and would only agree to be supervised by Poem.

Poem didn't mind.

Neither did Vienna.

Fresh air was part of her treatment, commissioned by her many doctors. Poem and the princess went on their first walk together through the royal gardens. She was about to suggest that they interest themselves in the swings hanging from the flowering trees, when Vincent walked up to her.

"Oh my god," she whispered. Poem stopped, attentively asking her questions she couldn't hear.

"We've got a problem," Vincent informed her. His hands were nervously concerned with a fine piece of cloth that looked to be a woman's handkerchief.

"I'd say we do," Vienna whispered. She whispered as if she were trying to keep Poem from hearing, even though he was right beside her. "You're not real, are you?"

"Well —" Vincent finally stuffed the cloth into his pocket, "neither is that guy." He pointed to one of the swings, occupied by a forty-year-old man who was crying into his hands.

"What?"

"Yeah." Vincent cleared his throat. "Try not to act like you can see him. If word gets around, you'll have dozens of dead dudes on your doorstep. I, for one, haven't told anyone you can see me."

"You're dead?" *I think I'm going to have a panic attack.*

"Yes, and keep your voice down." Vincent removed himself from her path, and said, "In fact, pretend you don't see me."

Panic attack . . . Coming . . . Now!

Her hands clasped her sides as she fought to breathe. Tears arrived in her eyes, and she began to choke. Poem was calling for help and trying to calm her down. She gripped his golden-brown tunic, desperately hanging onto him as if by doing so, she could hold on to her sanity.

"Hey, girl, are you okay?" the crying man came up to ask her.

"Oh shit," she heard Vincent say.

And then she screamed so much and so wildly that the doctors had her sedated.

Vienna awoke from a bad dream. She had dreamed that a warlock had put a curse on her and now she was seeing people who weren't really there. No. Not people. Men. She was seeing men who no longer existed.

She pulled her covers closer to her face and felt more comforted that way. Her mind was barely coherent with the world, until she heard chattering. At first, she told herself that the whispering didn't exist. It wasn't there; it couldn't be. She wrapped herself tighter in her covers, trying to cover her ears, but the whispering didn't stop.

When she heard Vincent's voice, she opened her eyes, her long brown hair circling her head like a halo.

"What do you all think you're doing in my room?" Vienna screeched, watching the color leave Vincent's dead cheeks. "Get out!"

"She's awake!" they all rejoiced instead. Vincent threw himself into the many dead dudes' paths so that they wouldn't dog pile on the princess.

"Seamus!" Vincent shouted to a guy sprawled out in the princess's bedside chair, reading a book. He was reading one of *her* books. "Give me a hand!"

"You look like you've got it under control," Seamus, a rough-looking guy (even for a dead guy) said. His dark eyes matched the rest of him. "Hey! Watch it!" he scowled, shouting at the princess as she ripped the book out of his creepy, dead hands.

"She left me!" one of the dead guys shouted at Vienna, his dead eyes streaming with tears, and the princess was too stunned to look away. "She left me there! I was sick, dying, and she left me! I thought she loved me!"

"No one cares!" Seamus yelled at him, reaching over to take the book back, and then settled into the chair again, and flipped the pages to where he'd left off. "Does it look like she cares, idiot?"

160

"She killed me!" another man cried at her. "She hit me with her car and killed me! I thought we were going to be together forever!"

Seamus just laughed at that one.

Vincent couldn't hold them all back, and they broke past him. Vienna threw her covers over her head, shielding herself from them, but their dead hands tried to grab at her. Their cries for her to listen to their stories came fast, and she was stranded in a mess of confusion and tears and fifteen men, all talking at once.

Vienna screamed. She screamed for her father to help her. She screamed for Poem. She screamed for guards, but whether they came, she couldn't be sure. She only remembered the many voices and then nothing at all.

When Vienna awoke, it was to silence. She kept hold of her covers, hiding her face, until she was sure she was alone. When she opened her eyes, turning herself over to the day, she saw her father and three doctors watching her, discussing her situation.

"Daddy?" Vienna wiped her eyes sleepily.

"I'm here, my angel." Her father took her into his arms, stroking her hair, and she nestled herself against him as if she could make a nest atop his shoulders. "How are you feeling?"

She was about to tell him she was better – fine, perfectly fine now because the nightmare seemed to have past – when someone else spoke, making her head jerk up.

"Angel, huh?" Seamus flipped the pages of a new book. "You ever have kids, Vincent? Have I asked you that before?"

"No," Vincent told him, "and no."

Vienna swallowed hard.

"Vienna?" her father asked, nervously, seeing that *nothing* had caught her attention.

"He cursed me." Vienna swallowed down her grief once more. "He said no one else would be able to see them. He was right. I'm being haunted by really sad, dead guys!"

"Did you hear that, Vincent?" Seamus smacked his lips together. "We're really sad, dead guys."

"I knew you were." Vincent snickered.

"Are you sure . . . ?" The king hesitated and then sighed. "That was a stupid question. Where are they? Can you see them now?"

Vienna nodded and then pointed to Seamus and Vincent. "There are only two of them right now."

"It's rude to point." Seamus inhaled aggressively, sounding vulgar and then spat on her floor.

"That's enough, Seamus," Vincent warned him. "Sorry, Princess Vienna. You can tell your father, the king . . . Oh my, I'm in the same room as the king!"

"Save it, loopy." Seamus spat again. "And get to the point."

Vincent collected himself. "You can tell your father that we seem to have sorted out things for now, but you're going to have to stay here and talk to them one at a time."

"What?" Vienna demanded.

Vincent flinched.

Seamus looked up from his book, impressed with the authority in her voice. "Very sexy," he told her.

"What is it?" her father pressed.

"What do you mean I've got to talk to them one at a time?" Vienna asked Vincent.

"Vienna." Her father's voice got sterner.

"There's a line-up, just outside your door. Got it?" Seamus offered no sympathy as if it were her own fault she was in this mess, and it certainly was not.

"Oh my god." Vienna hid her face with her hands.

Gently – so very gently – her father removed them from her face. "My daughter, tell me what's happening. I can't see what you're seeing. You're going to have to explain it to me. Take your time. I'm not going anywhere. I won't leave your side if you don't want me to."

"Wow," Seamus observed. "He's a pretty good dad."

Vincent nodded.

Vienna closed her eyes, inhaling several times before answering. "Yesterday, when I woke up, my room was full of men. They were crying and unhappy, and they were trying to talk to me all at once." She paused, and then pointed at Seamus and Vincent; although Seamus had told her that it was rude. She knew it was rude. She was raised as a princess. She

162

knew what rude was, but she didn't care, not at this point. "Those two guys over there . . . There are two guys over there, and their names are Vincent and Seamus, and it seems they've organized the dead guys. They're lined up in the hall, waiting to have one-on-one conversations with me to talk about . . ." She had no idea what they wanted to talk about. "Vincent? What do they want?"

"Well, what every dead person wants," Vincent explained. "To tell someone they're still here, to let someone know why they died, to have someone care about them . . ."

"'Cause god knows a dead dude don't care about another dead dude's problems," Seamus agreed. He assessed Vincent's reaction before saying, "No offence, man."

"None taken, dead dude," he agreed.

"But why you can't see her, or her, or that dead guy –" Seamus pointed to nothing around the room, "I have no idea."

"There are other dead people here, and I can't see them?" Vienna asked. She was more relieved than anything else.

"They're trying to see if you can see them, but nope. Looks like you can only see really sad, crying, pathetic dead guys," Seamus muttered, flipping another page of one of her books. "Strange."

"Does that make you a really sad, crying, pathetic dead guy?" Vienna baited.

Seamus got to his feet.

But so did Vienna. She wasn't sure why. She'd never gotten into a fight with anyone before, least of all a dead guy.

"Vienna . . ." Her father put a hand on her shoulder. "Just because they're dead, doesn't mean you should be discourteous. It's not ladylike."

Vienna nodded and let him lead her back to the bed.

Seamus smirked, thinking he'd clearly won something.

"She was the bigger man." Vincent put him straight.

"Don't start with me!" Seamus scowled.

"Vienna . . ." Her father focused her back onto him, taking her face in his hands so that she would look at him. "What's going on? What do you want me to do?"

"Vincent . . . ?" the princess asked for his advice.

"There's only one thing you can do, I'm afraid," he said, pained by her burden and confusion.

"Send them in!" Seamus said, throwing up his hands and knocking the book away.

CHAPTER SEVEN

The Curse

and

What It has Taken from Her

The doctors were sent out of the room, looking thrilled to have received such an order. Vincent opened the door and called in the first man while Seamus worked as a kind of bouncer. He punched anyone who tried to sneak in and tossed men out the window if they tried to stay longer than they were supposed to. This made Vienna anxious. She had never seen anyone punch another person before, let alone toss a person (even a dead one) out a window.

The days went on like this. All the while, her father stayed by her side. Afraid to leave her, he had provisions brought to her. She was afraid to leave her bed for fear that a strange, alarming dead man might follow her into the bathroom.

So far that hadn't happened. Still, the line grew every day.

Vincent let in another man. The dead guy, draped in purple cloth, knelt by her bedside. "I'm not like them, okay? I'm not going to cry all over you," he began.

"She'll believe that when she sees it." Seamus warned the guy by continually flexing his hands and then forming fists.

"My name is Henry," he continued. "And I fell in love. She was ridiculously hot. I mean, ridiculously."

Vienna shifted in her bed. "I am a princess, you know? That's not really appropriate."

Her father boiled over. "Is that dead man insulting you?"

"No, he just made me a little uncomfortable," Vienna assured him, instructing the man to keep a suitable tongue.

"You're dealing with men and their *feelings* now, princess," Seamus mocked her. "You're going to have to toughen those ears up if you want to survive now."

Vienna ignored him, bidding the man to continue.

"She married me. We were so happy, the happiest I'd been in my whole life!"

"And she died?" Vienna asked. "She hurt you?"

"What? No. She didn't hurt me. She died in childbirth, giving birth to my son, John, who still lives. I'm trying to find her in the scramble of things. Actually, I was hoping that talking to you about it all would make it possible for me to cross over or something. You know? To finally have the light shine on me, and have heaven open its doors. To see her waiting and we could finally be together again."

Seamus was pretending to hang himself, and Vincent slapped him.

"Maybe if I talk some more about her, you know? She had blond hair and these passionate blue eyes, like yours. I wish she was looking at me right now. I really do. It was true love, you know? Still is . . ." He started to tear up.

Now both Vincent and Seamus were pretending to hang themselves.

"God, I miss her!" he blubbered, although he had promised he wouldn't. The dead man grasped Vienna's hands and cried all over her.

"That's it!" Seamus grabbed him by the shoulders, slapped him twice in the face, and then chucked him out the window. "And don't come back, jerk!"

"What just happened?" the king asked her.

"Seamus sent another man out the window."

"Seamus." Her father spoke to his own hands since he couldn't see Seamus. "That's not how we deal with people in this kingdom, even if they're dead."

Seamus wasn't convinced. "If you saw what he was doing to your daughter, you'd be telling a different story."

"Did Seamus answer me?"

Vienna nodded. "He said he's sorry, and he'll try not to do it again."

"I don't remember saying that." Seamus sat down, and all of them looked up as someone knocked on the door. So far, the dead hadn't knocked.

"Enter," the king ordered, and one of his advisers stepped into the room. Unknowingly, he let in a crying man, but since Vincent hadn't sent for him, Seamus immediately sent him flying.

The adviser whispered something in the king's ear, and the king nodded, sending him away. Once the adviser left, the king stood. "Are you perfectly safe with Vincent and Seamus?"

"You can count on us, Your Majesty!" Vincent said, even though the king could not hear him.

"More or less. Probably less," was Seamus's answer.

"I think so," Vienna told her father.

"I have to go and be a king now," he told her. "I'm not sure when I'll be finished."

"It's all right. I'm sure we're almost done." She looked at Vincent, who tried to look encouraging, but failed in his mission. She watched her father exit, and then told her companions in the horrid, never-ending scene that they might as well send in the next dead person.

She chugged her goblet of coffee, set it down on her bedside table, and then gave a slight flick of her wrist, telling the man to begin.

But he just started crying.

"That's it!" Seamus lost his patience. He grabbed the man by the shoulder, dragged him across the room, opened the door, and chucked him out. "Listen you wimpy, dried up corpses! That's enough! Fuck off! If I see anyone of you bastards anywhere near this cracked palace again, I'll kick the shit out of you!"

They scattered.

Seamus stood at the door, trying to calm himself down. Vincent headed to his friend, speaking low, and then both of them turned to the princess.

"Princess Vienna." Vincent gave Seamus a quick, shameful glance. "I'm sorry if that frightened you."

"Are you kidding? Why didn't you do that sooner?" Vienna asked, irate. If she had been able to slap either of them, she just might have.

Finally, a day dawned when Vienna was able to carry on with normal palace life. She had breakfast, drinking a substantial amount of coffee, and eating whatever the chefs had prepared for her. Today it was crème brûlée and chocolate breads.

Vienna then dressed for riding and ran to the stable. She now had to bribe Poem to let her ride, even in the daylight hours. And the price was high: two handfuls of chocolates and a caramel.

Poem brought her father's grey stallion. It was clear he was wondering if Vienna would start to panic again.

The horse began to prance. His snorting was loud and terrifying.

Vienna glanced behind her. Vincent and Seamus had their arms crossed as they leaned against the barn wall.

"My lady . . ." Poem decided this probably wasn't the best idea, no matter how many sweets were involved.

"I know," Vienna said and then tried to calm the animal with a soothing voice. But, just then, a desperate dead man burst through the stable doors and charged at the princess. "Crap," was her reaction to that.

Poem raised his eyebrows in disbelief.

Seamus and Vincent moved to tackle the man.

The stallion bolted, fleeing to the back of the barn. Poem, still on his feet, was dragged away.

Vienna's hands were clamped to her ears, and her nails dug into them. That warlock had cursed her, making her see ghosts. As if that wasn't bad enough, now they wouldn't leave her alone, making it impossible for her to ride. She had to live with the fact that as things stood, it was dangerous for her to be in the stables. The horses were terrified of the ghosts. Soon they would learn to associate her with them and would begin to flee from her.

She would have to give up riding.

Infuriated, she marched over to the three brawling dead men.

She held her riding whip firmly in hand, and then pounded the crop on the intruder's head. She didn't wonder if he could feel it, although it seemed like he could. That made it all the more cathartic. She whipped him so much that, if he were a human, his head would have been surely severed from his body.

Straightening up, Vienna looked behind her to see Poem standing, mystified, wondering if she had completely lost her mind. She felt sure she had. She pushed her bonnet into place and straightened her tangle of brown hair before throwing her nose in the air and walking out of the barn.

But she wanted to run. She wanted to escape. If she couldn't ride, she decided, she would hide in her favorite blue-and-white-colored room and enrapture herself in a novel. In her purple summer dress, she took her place in her favorite window seat, and tried to read.

Tried to read because Vincent and Seamus wouldn't stop talking!

"Would you shut up?" Vienna threw them the most withering look she could master. "I'm trying to read!"

"We'll gladly leave," Seamus said, lazily. "Just say the word."

"Seamus," Vincent warned.

"Yes! Please!" Vienna snapped her book shut, her hands shaking with anger. "Go away, *Seamus.*"

Seamus smirked, silencing the other man when he tried to speak. "Come on, Vincent, and let us see how the 'Miss Learn to Appreciate Us Pageant' carries on without us."

As soon as they left, dead men swarmed in. They pulled at her hands and begged her to hear their stories. She couldn't take it any longer and screamed bloody murder for Vincent and Seamus to come back.

She knew now as she watched the scramble in the room, that the warlock hadn't just cursed her. He had taken everything she loved away from her. She couldn't read. She couldn't ride. She could barely sleep and had to drink massive amounts of coffee to remain standing because she was so exhausted. Everyone thought she was crazy, and her present appearance didn't discourage that thought.

That warlock . . .

He's taken everything I love from me.

CHAPTER EIGHT
The Magic-Man

She tried to watch television, but when she tried to turn the volume up, it seemed that the dead people just talked louder. She tried blaring music, but that made them dance and continually ask the only living girl who could see them if she wanted to dance with them. She contemplated her many failed attempts to ignore the curse as she put her feet up on the dashboard of her father's blue Camaro. Horses were afraid of her now, so they couldn't journey on horseback, and her father endlessly complained about this. The gas prices were really too high for them to drive anywhere, let alone all around the countryside.

Seamus and Vincent were in the backseat.

They'd been to three different witch doctors and five different voodoo men so far, and all of them had told her that she was either faking it or simply crazy. She didn't take kindly to any of that.

"Make a right," Vincent told the king, even though he wasn't able to hear him.

"Idiot, he's supposed to go left," Seamus corrected.

"Did that goblin say we should turn up here . . . ?" her father whispered, trying not to get them lost. He had stopped for directions, and then he had done so again when those directions had brought them to a dead end.

"They're arguing about that." Vienna shrugged. She wasn't any help when it came to directions. "Vincent says to go left. I trust him more than Seamus."

"I think I'm going to go straight," the king declared, to the annoyance of the dead backseat drivers. They were certain that their knowledge on the subject was superior to the king's royal instincts. However, his instincts proved hardy because they passed a shop called 'Lifey's Magic Shop.'

"Shit, dad, there it is! We just went by it!" Vienna twisted around in her seat to get a better look. It was nicer than the other places they'd been to. White daisies filled the gardens that circled the shop. Although the building looked like it needed a new paint job, and a new roof.

"What does chipped paint and a leaky roof say about the quality of a magic-man's magic?" Seamus asked Vincent.

"The mechanic we employed had a car, and it always broke down. I often wondered what that said about him, but he was the best mechanic in the country at the time," was Vincent's answer.

"Vienna, don't say that word. It's not fit for royal lips. And put your seatbelt on," her father directed her.

"You've said 'shit' five times so far today," the princess mumbled under her breath as her father turned the car around and drove into the shop's parking lot.

All four of them exited the car and walked inside.

At once, Seamus saw something shiny and told Vincent, "Sweet! Come take a look at this!"

"Welcome!" A man stood behind the counter, his hands clasped behind his back. "I'm Lifey, and this —" He was suddenly in front of their faces. He held cards above his head and they turned into lively butterflies as he exhaled. Coming together, the butterflies turned into a single pink rose. "Is my magic shop," he said, winking at the princess as he handed her the rose.

He was an overly thin man with black eyes that had evident red specks. He bowed to his guests, playfully, almost mockingly. He had silver-streaked, short, red hair.

Vienna let the rose hang at her side, the bloom facing the floor. "Are you a fake?"

The magic-man blinked several times. "No."

"My name is Gladness." Her father gave a slight tip of his head. "And this is my daughter, Vienna."

"Gladness and Vienna? Royal family Gladness and Vienna?" The man looked from child to man.

"As in *king*?" Vienna sized Lifey up. "Yeah, you're looking at him."

Lifey performed a real bow this time. "To what do I owe?"

"We seek help," the king began, but Vienna interrupted. She couldn't help herself. She was rather unhappy about her situation, and she was more than willing to let it show.

"Some douchebag of a warlock named Augustus cursed me, and now I can see ghosts, and not just ghosts, really weepy ones!" The princess watched Lifey's eyes widen.

171

"Augustus?" he asked calmly, a hint of a smile playing on his lips. "You mean the Dragon Witch's son?"

"Yes," the king said, thinking back and longing for the good old days. "He was a wonderful adviser at the palace. His magic came in handy on more than one occasion. He was always polite and well-tempered. Always liked him –"

"Dad!" Vienna said, outraged.

"He cursed you?" Lifey wasn't convinced. "Well, I can't see that. I know him. He's a great guy."

"You know him?" The king encouraged him to go on.

"We were childhood friends. I can't remember a time when he wasn't healing wounded animals or the sick or bringing food to the poor. Even when we were kids. He's the most upstanding guy I know. Don't get me wrong. He's only twenty-three. He's young. He's made one or two mistakes in his life. Like, swimming naked in the creek of death. That wasn't our brightest moment. But hey, we were twenty and high on mushroom dust, and we made it out alive, thanks to his quick thinking." He tilted his head back, admiring his past. "Good times."

For the first time on this bizarre road trip, Vienna felt hopeful. "Can you break the spell?"

"If Augustus cast it, no. I've got no chance. None of the magic-men around here do. I hate to admit it, but he's in an entirely different league." The magic-man paused, thinking as he watched Vienna. "Vienna? Princess Vienna? V?"

"Excuse me?"

"You're V, I take it?" He rocked back on his heels, letting loose a saddened, barking laugh. "That poor shmuck! If I had known all this time that he was in love with a princess, I never would have spent years convincing him to finally make a move. He gave you that heart necklace, didn't he? Damn. He's been carrying that thing around with him since he was sixteen." He stopped again, closing his eyes, as if he should have known all along. "Since he started working at the palace!"

"What is this guy talking about?" Seamus walked to Vienna's side. "If I punch him, do you think he will feel it?"

"Don't be mean," Vienna hissed at him.

Lifey stared at her.

172

"Sorry." Vienna blushed. She had forgotten that no one else could see Seamus or Vincent, who was laughing while he looked at objects around the store. "You were talking about how you could break my curse."

"Weren't you listening?" Lifey then turned to the king, looking for an explanation. He didn't find one. "I *can't* lift the curse. I can't even tell you anything about it or about what you might do to nullify it. Like I said, he's on a completely different level than me." He walked to the side of the store, standing for a moment beside Vincent, who gave him a respectful greeting. The greeting went unnoticed, of course. Lifey came back with a handful of objects. "I can make clever things and cast B level spells. If you were bald, I could bring your hair back. Broken bones? No problem. I can even turn you into a mouse if I wanted to, or maybe a violin. But you said you can see dead people? That's way beyond A level magic."

"So you'd call that an A plus?" Seamus smirked.

Vincent walked over to them. "Nifty."

"No, *Vincent,* it's not *nifty*! It's my life and I want it back!" Vienna screamed at him and stormed out of the store, tossing the pink rose into the trash.

CHAPTER NINE
The Witch of the Falling Stars

Lifey told them about a place that might be able to help.

Outside Highest Guard, was a small town framed with sunflower fields and blue skies. Farmers were outside, working their land. A horse farm was busy training horses, and a cattle farm was busy milking cattle. Goatherders crossed roads, guiding their herds to new fields. And sheep followed their shepherds to new fields, doing the same thing in other parts of the town. There was a white chapel in the center of the town, as well as dozens of little bakeshops and butcher stores and a wonderful flower market. And there was also a magic shop called 'Bicker and Brooms.'

When Vienna walked up to the front door she read the sign, 'No Toads Allowed.'

"What do you think? It's wonderful here, isn't it?" the king took in big, gulping breaths, delighting in the country air.

Seamus had his eyes on something. "I'll be back."

"Me too," Vincent agreed, heading in a different direction. He admired the tempting bakeshops and looked at food he was no longer able to taste.

The Camaro was parked crookedly, and the pink rose that Vienna's father had picked out of the trash was lying on the dashboard. The king opened the entrance door, and she stepped inside.

The store was fresh with the smell of vanilla and cinnamon. A calico cat twitched its tail at them and then jumped onto a shelf of potion bottles. Vienna walked over to the feline and scratched the top of its head before reading some of the labels. 'True Love' potion, 'Get out of Work' potion, 'Skip Class – No Fail' potion, and 'Sexy Prom Night' potion were some of the most popular.

"Halloween, get off those shelves!" A woman whose hair matched the cat's black, white and orange fur, walked in carrying a large cardboard box. She set it on a table and then addressed her customers. "You look too rich to be from this town, and, since I know everyone here, I can say for sure that you're not." She picked bottles out of the box she'd hauled in and put them on the shelves. "What's your pleasure, kids? Can I interest you in some father-daughter outfits? They're sparkly!"

"No thanks." The king tried to keep his laughter at bay. It worked. He was the king, after all.

He had supreme control.

"Lifey said you might be able to help us?" Vienna redirected the conversation to her immediate need.

That caught the witch's attention. "So that's you, is it? Yes. Lifey's owl arrived with his letter this morning." She wiped her hands on her orange dress. "You're shorter than I imagined you to be."

Vienna huffed. How dare she talk to the princess like that! "Can you help me?"

"Help?" The witch cackled. "No. He's thinking I might be able to tell you where Augustus is. Well, I can't. I haven't heard from him in three years. Not since I proposed to him, and he turned me down. Me? Emily Tempest? Witch of the Falling Stars?" She occupied herself with stocking shelves once again. The cat came over to rub itself against her legs and purred comfortably. "Go catch a mouse, Halloween!" she hissed at it, and the cat ran off.

"Can you at least try examining her? Look over the magic? Anything?" the king asked. He was unsure of how to word any of this properly. At this point, he felt like he was close to losing his sanity as well. "I don't know."

"Sure. Fine." The witch wiped her hands on her dress again, walking toward Vienna. She circled her and then took her hands. The witch closed her eyes. When nothing happened, she spoke a few select words in Latin, keeping her eyes closed. "Huh . . ."

"What is it?" Vienna whispered. Had she seen something?

"If this wasn't Augustus's curse," she said, throwing the princess's hands back to her, "I'd say you were faking it."

Not again! "Faking it?"

"Can you point to any ghosts in here? That's what you claim you can see, right?"

"No, I can't point any out!"

"Ha!"

"I mean, not here, in this store, because they're off looking at baked goods!"

The king sighed. "Where are those dead fellows when you need them?"

175

"That's it, we're leaving!" Vienna fumed, marching to the front door. She grabbed the doorknob.

"About those father-daughter outfits . . ." the king said to the witch.

"I can give you twenty-five percent off for being the king of the land," the witch said.

"Really?" the king was delighted at the idea.

Vienna shrieked and ran out of the store.

Maple trees lined the dirt road, as did lamp posts, making Vienna wish that she could wander about in the dark once again. There were yellow bows on every door, reminding her of happier times when she, too, lovingly embraced the fall. Pumpkins were everywhere, their carved faces not so mysterious during the daylight. They seemed to be mocking her as she made her way down the street, looking for Vincent. Sure enough, there he was, drooling over homemade peach pies and warm cinnamon buns.

"I could really have used your help in there," Vienna informed him, unkindly. She straightened her gloves, trying not to delight too much in the homey smell of bread from the bakery. She had to maintain her indifferent appearance. She couldn't let Vincent see that she was anything less than furious with him.

He pulled himself away from the Halloween cakes. "You've never required my help."

True. She had never needed it until that Emily witch told her to point out a dead guy.

"Where's Seamus? We're leaving."

"If he's not with you . . ." He thought for a moment and then looked around. "There's only one place he could be." He wiggled his nose and bunched up his lips before letting a full-toothed smile take over his face. "You had better get him, then. I'll head to the car. Don't you think I'll look dashing leaning against that blue Camaro?" He didn't wait for her answer. "You'll find him in the flower shop. If he's not there, then look for the town's garden. He'll be there. Always by the roses."

Vincent walked away from her, leaving her to reflect on Seamus and his words about him. She found herself walking, but she was also caught up in her memory of an old-looking man crying over the rose bushes in the palace garden. He'd been sitting on a swing, hadn't he? She had been walking with Poem on that day . . . Had that been Seamus crying? Was Seamus even capable of crying?

She wandered back until she found the flower store they had passed on their way to 'Bicker and Brooms,' where no toads were allowed. Seamus was standing there, a white rose in his hands, his eyes closed as he lost himself in the smell of roses.

"Seamus . . . ?" Vienna approached him cautiously. She'd always been a little afraid of him. He was different from Vincent. She could yell at Vincent, knowing he wouldn't take offense. But she couldn't yell at Seamus without knowing whether he'd see through her. That was scarier.

He opened his eyes.

"You were that man, weren't you?" she said, well aware that people were curious as to why she was talking to herself. She picked up a rose and then set it down again. "In the garden. Back at the palace." He didn't answer. He closed his eyes again and leaned his head back against the wall. "Did she hurt you, Seamus? Are you just like them?" she dared to ask.

Just like them . . . . All those men dying inside because they had loved . . .

"All those guys have been dead for a very long time. Their tears are mostly the result of their relief that you can see them," Seamus informed her. He did not look at her. "And, mostly, they're just whiny bastards. You're getting the wrong idea about love, kiddo. You think this curse is so that you can see how you hurt this warlock jerk or something. But that's not it. I think he wanted you to see what love is. To have someone tell you that love is the only thing worth dying for."

Then why were you in the garden? Why are you here now? "Then why were you crying?"

"Because I miss her that much."

When she didn't say anything, he took a few steps to leave. "Don't go!" Vienna pleaded. In their time together, he had become something like a friend. If he needed to say something . . . If he needed her to listen . . . "Wait. Seamus . . . What was she like?"

He came back to her. His movements were slow and cautious as he held the flower safely in his hands. "She grew white roses," he said. "Her hair, even when I knew her in her teens, was white and reached down to her hips. We'd make love under the trees in her family's orchard."

He wasn't crying, not like the other guys who had told her their stories. All this time, she had thought that the ghosts regretted loving those girls. They were all dead now; how could they not? But Seamus was different. His words were different.

"Was she a nobleman's daughter?" our princess asked him.

Seamus shook his head, letting the rose he held in his hand fall to the ground. "I was a nobleman's son."

He tried to walk away again, but this time she didn't plead. She cut in front of him. Her hands out to stop him from pushing past her. "Do you know how old you looked in that garden? What are you, thirty-years-old? You looked twenty years older!" He listened, and she continued. She'd be lying to herself if she said he wasn't a nuisance, but he wasn't a bad nuisance. She'd be lying to herself if she said she hadn't grown to care for him, and for Vincent. Although, becoming friends with two emotional ghosts seemed crazy. "How can you say love's worth dying for, when you clearly wish you hadn't? All you're doing is going through existence trying to be strong. And it doesn't matter because she's not here, is she? You hold on to those roses like that's all that matters. Well, it's not. There's so much more. You shouldn't have to make yourself about that one thing and then never stop crying about it, you weepy bastard! Grow up!"

"Vienna?" he said coolly, effectively.

"What?"

"Where's your mother?"

"I . . ." This time, he walked past her, and this time, she wasn't about to stop him. He didn't wait for an answer, but somehow she knew that he wasn't done talking about this.

She followed him back to the car. Vincent was leaning on the car door, eyeing the people who walked by, projecting a 'that's right, this is my car, dig it man' attitude.

"What a nice, nice lady," Vienna's father murmured as he walked out of the store.

A nice, nice lady? A nice, nice lady!

"We've been everywhere!" Vienna raged, getting into the passenger's seat and slamming the car door. "They all tell us the same thing. *I don't see anything. You must be crazy.* Bloody fakes!"

Seamus and Vincent piled into the backseat, and her father took the wheel. The pink rose still lay on the dash. The king pushed back his daughter's hair as she tried to hide her red-stained eyes.

"I can't stay like this forever!" she cried.

178

The king nodded, contemplating before turning the key and starting the engine. He listened to it hum before he nodded. "We've only one place left to go then."

Vienna's father pulled away as she asked, "Where?"

"To the Dragon Witch."

CHAPTER TEN
The Dragon Witch

They drove through the night and throughout the next day and the next night. Finally, they reached ominous mountains and the entrance of a dark, portentous cave. A chill passed through Vienna as she stepped out of the car. She held her forearms, trying to warm herself, but the cool morning air was inescapable.

Her father came up behind her, wrapping a black, velvet cape around her, but she pushed it away. He put it on the car's hood.

"This is where she lives?" Vienna asked. "I didn't take it literally when you said she dwelled in the mountains' caves."

"It is a bit dodgy, isn't it?" Vincent agreed.

"Yeah."

The king eyed his daughter.

"Sorry." Vienna nodded toward the ghost at her side. "I was talking to him. The dead guy."

Exhausted, the king took the first steps forward, entering the cave. Both of them were engulfed by the damp, murky effect. There wasn't any light, so the king switched on the flashlight he was carrying.

There was nothing in the cave, but a long walk through the dark emptiness.

Then smoke traveled along the bottoms of the walls. Candles suddenly lit up, showing the way forward. The royal family followed all the way to a carpeted room with a jeweled ceiling and walls made of skulls. A dragon lay on a bed of gold. The massive, sickly grey-green dragon stared at them expressively, tilting her head one way and then another. Vienna set her shoulders and raised her head, trying to look unafraid.

"It's good to see you again, Dragon Witch," the king greeted the dragon. Her claws began to knead the gold. "We have come here seeking your help."

The dragon sat upright, and rings of smoke flew out of her mouth before she looked at them with a new level of seriousness. Her giant wings spread out and she took flight. When she landed, she was a woman, wearing an elegant gold dress.

"A king shouldn't need help from me," the dragon said.

"Oh, but I do, good witch."

Good witch? Was there such a thing?

The king continued, "My daughter . . ."

"Yes, I can already see. She is haunted. Someone cursed you," the Dragon Witch told Vienna. The princess hid behind her father like a small child.

"Not just anyone," the king explained. "Your son."

The Dragon Witch laughed. Vincent's ghostly elbow continually attempted to strike Vienna.

He mouthed his criticism, telling her to face the witch.

The last time I faced a witch I was cursed . . .

"My son?" the dragon said in disbelief, the force of her laughter apparent on her face. "My son? I don't think so."

"And why is that?" the king asked.

"Well, please, you've met my son."

"I have."

"And what did you think of him?"

"I thought him a very splendid young man."

"Exactly. Why would he go around cursing young girls, and a princess for that matter?"

The king gave a long, hard look at his daughter before sighing. He explained, "I take it you know of the task my daughter set for her suitors?" He watched the witch nod before he said, "Well, he was my daughter's champion."

The witch stood for a moment, amazed. "My son? King?"

"Well..."

"He's really a great guy."

"I thought so. I really liked him, but . . ."

He didn't have to say another word. The witch cast a long stare at the princess. "You turned him away?"

"Now you can run," Vincent told her.

But Vienna raised her head high. "Not every girl wants a prince. He shouldn't have felt discriminated against. I don't want anyone."

The witch considered her, almost liking her. But she couldn't, of course. It was *her* son whom she had cast away. "And yet you managed to find the one decent man on the planet and rip him to shreds? Badly done, Little Majesty. If he hadn't already cursed you, I might have done so myself."

"How can you say that?"

"He's my son."

"I mean that he's a nice guy. He cursed me!"

"You denied him. He cursed you because you cursed him first."

I did no such thing! And yet . . . She thought about how she had thrown the necklace with the wooden heart and the pearl – just thrown it to its grave. Had her eyes cursed him first?

Well, if she cursed him, she had every right to. She was the princess after all, for bloody sake.

"I did no such thing. I only wanted him, all of them, to leave me alone." Vienna took that moment to compare herself to the Dragon Witch. She was wearing a gown of peach-colored lace, and the witch was clad in gold. Although Vienna was a princess, the witch's presence overpowered her.

"Well, I was quite happy," the king said, wistfully. "I thought he'd make me a very sweet son."

"Oh, he would have," the witch agreed. "He sings to the weeping willows when their weeping reaches its heights, and if the daisies are scared, he'll kiss them goodnight –"

"Does he really?" the king inquired. "What a sweet boy!"

"Hello?" Vienna interrupted. "I'm still cursed here!"

The king cleared his throat. "Right . . ."

"Can you break the curse?" Vienna asked the witch.

The woman looked over the princess, eyeing her, and then circling her. She examined her son's spell work and admired his craftsmanship before answering. "I know I am the Dragon Witch. I should be able to break anything my son casts, but, alas, I cannot. He is my son as well as his father's son, and that makes him much more powerful than I am. That is as it should be. I am sorry, little princess. I admire your confidence and conviction. There's not many a woman in this world who can stand before a man and tell him to his face that she doesn't need him. Of course, I wish you hadn't done it to my son, but no matter. I like you. However, this spell, I cannot break. Only he who cast it can uncast it."

Vienna looked up at her father. "You still think he's a nice guy?"

182

Her father shrugged. Obviously, yes.

"For cursing me? Strange way you brought him up to show his affection!" she yelled at the witch, who swelled with anger. "If he wanted me to get to know him, he didn't leave much to be desired!"

She turned on her heels, storming out of the cave.

"What are you going to do, little princess?" the witch called after her, a great deal of mockery in her tone.

"It's no use yelling at you, you're not the one who cursed me!" Vienna marched to the car with Vincent hot on her heels. She sat, fuming. Her father joined her, started the car, and drove away.

Seamus didn't ask how it went.

CHAPTER ELEVEN
The Witch's Broken, Scornful Heart

"What do we do now?" Vienna inquired, although she'd already decided. No one had said a word for two and a half days, not even the usually chatty ones in the back. The leather seats weren't all that comfortable. Vienna wrapped her blanket around herself.

"We're going back to the palace," her father informed her. "I need to make sure my kingdom is still alive. From there, I'll commission search parties to find Augustus. I'll imprison him if I have to, if that's what it takes for him to lift the curse."

She had to hand it to her father. He had formulated a better plan than she had. She was determined to find Augustus, yes, but she had planned on going alone. Maybe hopping a train . . . She looked out her window, as she rested her head on the fluffy pillow she had brought along.

Maybe it had belonged to her mother once . . .

"Vienna . . ." Her father didn't finish. They sat in silence, watching the nightscape of this nowhere land roll by. There weren't trees, houses, or hills – just plains, leveled land for miles and miles. Finally, after another mile, he spoke. "Vienna . . . You know I don't have any regrets, don't you? I mean about your mother. Even though it didn't work out –"

"Dad, look out!" Vienna screamed.

There was a person in the middle of the road!

The king swerved, and the car ran off the road and into the ditch.

King Gladness had Vienna in his arms. He had to make sure she was all right.

"I'm okay," she assured him.

"Well, I'm not!" Seamus hissed, floating out of the car door.

Vienna and King Gladness held each other's gazes, then rushed out of the car.

"I didn't hit anyone, did I?" the king asked, but it seemed that everyone was fine.

Yes. Indeed. Everyone, but them.

A woman stood on the dirt road, her black dress flapping like wings in the wind she was summoning forth. The sky began to rumble with thunder and web with lightning. A calico cat sat at her feet, its tail twitching playfully.

"She a nice, nice lady now?" Vienna muttered.

Emily Tempest, Witch of the Falling Stars, pointed at Vienna. Halloween hunched her back and hissed at the princess as the witch spoke, hissing her words like the angry feline. "Vienna, Princess of Highest Guard, you are unworthy of your title!" The thunder roared so loudly that both the princess and the king covered their ears. Halloween's hissing sounded like laughter. "We will not have lying, loveless frauds in our realm!"

"That's enough, witch," the king demanded. "As the king of the land —"

"Silence!" the witch's other hand shot up and the king fell to the ground, onto a bed of white feathers.

Vienna watched, bewildered.

"Vienna!" Vincent was rushing toward her. "Run!"

It was like watching a movie in slow motion. His words were drawn out and his actions played out bit by bit. Seamus was running for her too, both of them fighting to get to her.

Vienna wasn't sure if she was still breathing. She was trying to count her breaths, trying to draw back into herself, but it was hopeless. Fear had made her stupid. She was paralyzed as the witch's fingers moved upon the air, sending spiders and spider webs rushing toward her.

"You are banished for what you did to him!" The witch's words clawed at the princess's mind, and she told her, "For your cruelty, may you never know love. You are unworthy of it!"

Vincent and Seamus were fighting to get to her before it was too late.

The spider webs wrapped around her, black spiders biting her flesh, and Vienna screamed and fought and kicked and slapped the spiders away, wrestling out of the webs. She jumped up and around, grabbing spiders one after another and throwing them away from her.

"Vincent?" She didn't look up as she got the last insect out of her hair. "Seamus?" She listened to the calls of owls and the howling of wolves. "Father?" The trees were thick, and when she took a step, she sank deep into a mud pit. Struggling out, she threw her hands over her mouth to keep her shrieks in.

She had no idea where she was.

She was alone.

CHAPTER TWELVE
The Wild Wolf in the Wild Forest

There was nothing more to think about. She had only one choice. She had to keep moving in search of civilization. Of course, if she found anyone, there was no reason for them to help her. There was nothing to suggest that she was a princess. As it was, she had brought nothing with her. She was in pink bunny pajama pants and a white top. She removed the hair elastic from her wrist and put up her hair as she swatted mosquitoes away. That was all she had: pajamas and one hair elastic.

The stars were visible through the treetops, but the princess tried not to look at them. After all, it was the Witch of Fallen Stars who had forced her to end up here in the middle of, well, wherever she was. The moon gave very little light. It was enough to find her way in the endless darkness, in the endless clutter of forest life.

Twice, she tripped over the same log, falling to her knees and getting wet muck on her pajamas. Everything seemed hopeless, and yet she continued to make her way, traveling in any direction. As long as she kept moving there might be a hope of discovering something other than mud and darkness and more mud.

A tree branch slapped her in the face, and she cursed loudly and in a very unladylike manner.

"Is anyone there?" she screamed. A part of her knew that shouting in a forbidden forest was a very stupid thing to do. She'd read enough books to know that. But she couldn't help it. She was, in fact, helpless, and she wanted – wanted beyond measurement – to scream. "Anyone!" And then she said something very stupid, something she couldn't believe was coming out of her mouth. "Augustus!"

A man stood in her path.

"A-Augustus?" Vienna stuttered, straining her eyes to see the figure. No. It wasn't the warlock that sent the princess through feelings of relief and bitter dread. If the warlock *had* shown himself, she might have been able to get rid of the curse *tonight*.

But, instead . . .

"You can see me?" the figure spoke, coming closer.

"Oh no, not another dead guy!" Vienna yelled, despite her inner-self's proposal of a state of calm.

"I died here," the man whispered, starting to cry like they all did. "There was an attack . . ."

"I don't care if you cry, just don't cry *at* me!" Vienna ran away from him, against his objections. He was shouting for her to come back, but she ran until his voice was nothing more than a memory, and then she ran until it wasn't even that.

She held on to a tree to keep herself standing. She ran all night, and the morning sun was starting to rise, turning the forest into a foggy blue cloud. She slid to the ground, panting and gasping, sucking in air until she no longer felt sick. The spider bites covering her arms and stomach were wretched and horribly itchy things. She was desperate to scratch them, but begged for courage not to rip herself apart doing so.

A black snake slithered up her arm. Vienna jumped up and grabbed the creature by the head before it shot up to bite her face. She pitched it into the forest and then turned back around.

A grizzly bear was watching her from the trees. Walking forward, it assessed the girl accordingly.

And then the grizzly roared.

Vienna's inner- self was screaming. She could hear the screams and feel them in her throat although her mouth never opened to release them.

Were these her last moments? Was she going to die here – wherever *here* was?

"Oh please, please momma bear," Vienna whispered, slowly walking backward, "tell me you don't have cubs nearby."

The grizzly rose to her feet, towering over her, and roared again. Screaming, Vienna toppled to the ground. She crawled until her back hit one of the trees. She could taste her fear: a horrible sandy taste before it became sweet, like rotten raspberries, and panic sank in.

I can't die. My father needs me. I have a whole kingdom that needs me.

The grizzly landed with impressive force and lunged after her through the trees. Her mouth was open as if she could already taste the intruder's blood. Her eyes were fierce with her fear for her family. She had to protect them from the ambiguous threat posed by this being.

Vienna hid her face with her hands.

Noise. Suddenly there was so much noise that Vienna had to uncover her eyes. A wolf was fighting the bear, both of them raging with wild cries and curses, both of them wild-eyed and snarling. The grizzly's muzzle was bleeding as she swatted at the wolf, but the wolf was fast and agile and ran straight up the bear, latching onto her throat.

The creature roared, and Vienna screamed as she watched her grab hold of the sandy brown wolf and toss him against a tree. The wolf yelped as he landed. He lay motionless on the ground.

The grizzly turned back for Vienna.

Panicking, she grabbed the only thing there was to grab. She held a fallen tree branch in her hands as something inside her mocked her for thinking that a tree branch might hold up against a bear.

She had nothing else.

She had to try.

The creature bellowed, and the princess bellowed back. She lifted the branch above her head, trying to make herself seem more terrifying than she actually was.

The grizzly paused, studying her, and the wolf ran up the bear's back and hooked himself to her, biting her head. The grizzly cried, trying to grab the wolf, but he had already moved, hitting the ground and thundering for her neck.

With one last terrible surge, the bear fought. Then, with one last trembling cry, she ran back into the trees, away from the wolf and the pink-bunny pajama-wearing girl.

Then the wolf turned on the princess. She guessed that saying, "I'm the Princess of Highest Guard," wouldn't make a difference to the massive wolf who seemed to be leering at her with his large, expressive teeth.

He growled, and Vienna fell back. Pointing the stick at the creature, she braced her shoulders and narrowed her eyes. If she was going to die today, she would at least die a death worthy of her royal blood. She would put up some kind of fight.

But then the sandy brown wolf whimpered, his ears going down, and he crawled closer to her. Slowly, she extended her hand to him, and he licked it. She dropped the tree branch and flung her arms around the animal. At first, he was startled. He even tried to get away, but she wouldn't let him. She was so grateful!

"Thank you!" she said to the wolf, feeling his soft fur against her neck and cheeks. "Thank you!"

The wolf pulled back a little and started licking her.

She slapped him away. "Gross! Knock it off!" She got to her feet and wiped her face. The wolf watched her, tilting his head to one side and then to the other. He had very curious eyes for a wolf, and they kept changing color. One was blue and the other brown, and then one was green and the other gold. "Anyway, thanks."

The wolf turned and started walking away.

"Where are you going?" Vienna demanded, but the creature didn't stop. "If you think you're leaving me here, you had better think again!"

The wolf kept walking, although he seemed to realize she was following after him.

CHAPTER THIRTEEN
The Girl and Her Wolf

Days went by and the wolf stayed with her. She attempted to make fires, but they never worked. She cuddled close to the wolf and, like a blanket, his fur kept her warm through the cold autumn nights. She wasn't sure if it was a coincidence, but he would lead her by nuts and berries. Starving, she would gulp them down and collect as many as she could carry. She followed him, day and night, wherever he led her. She had nowhere else to go, nothing else to do, and no idea how to get anywhere. When he found water, she drank. When he found food, she ate, and she was grateful. She thanked him constantly, knowing perfectly well she would die without him, although she continually wondered why he was putting up with her.

Wherever he was going, surely she was slowing him down.

She walked by his side, sometimes keeping her hand on his back, sometimes stroking his noble head. She wondered where her father was right now, and if he had people looking for her. She wondered if they had captured the witch who had banished her. She hoped they had. She hoped she had been imprisoned, and maybe even been tortured. Those thoughts, at least, made it easier for her to look up at the stars again.

Now she walked with an apple in one hand, and she rested her other hand on the wolf's head. Seamus had said that he and the woman he loved would sleep together under the trees in her family's orchard. She wondered what kind of orchard it had been, if there was more to his story, and if she'd ever see him again.

She wanted to ask the wolf questions, but she knew how silly that was. As far as she knew, he couldn't talk back, and, if he could, he'd chosen not to. So she didn't speak much. She just wondered. She wondered about Vincent and Poem and if she'd ever get back. She wondered if anyone would find her.

The days went by and eventually, by following a stream, the wolf led Vienna out of the forest. The stream turned into a river, and in the middle of the river, a young man with sandy brown hair stood fishing.

"Maybe we should go this way, Hero," Vienna whispered to the wolf. She'd named him something appropriate. But the wolf continued on, his eyes changing colors and watching the young man with consideration.

Vienna prayed that they wouldn't be noticed. The pattern on her clothing was not visible now. They were covered in mud and stains. Moreover, her long hair was an awful mess, and her blue eyes weren't pretty things anymore. They were wild things, watching the predator's every move.

However, there was still enough 'princess' left in her to make her want to avoid the first person she stumbled upon. She could not be seen like this.

Of course he looked up, and of course he held her gaze. He was older than she was. Unlike her long lines of suitors, he wasn't perfectly muscled or sculpted from knighthood. He didn't have a pompous, prince-bred air about him, and it was clear he'd never lifted a sword in his life. He didn't seem to have the same eyes as the money hunters who had made their way to her either. He just looked like a boy fly fishing and not a dead boy fly fishing either.

"Can we run?" she urged Hero, but the wolf seemed unconcerned. She looked back at the young man. He was trying to speak to her. He moved forward, trying to catch up before the wolf led her away completely.

"Wait!" he cried, and his voice filled Vienna with emotion. To hear another human's voice again was something magical in itself. His voice felt like sunlight and smelt of honey. "Please! Please, wait!"

Hero stood between them as the young man caught up. He was walking in the water, too close for Vienna's comfort. She really wished her wolf had run with her, and yet a piece of her soul was thankful to him, as always. She couldn't stop staring at the young man with his sandy brown hair. His green eyes seemed to breathe into her, and she inhaled those breaths as though she'd never inhaled before.

"Can you speak?" he asked and Vienna felt sunlight on her skin again. She smelt honey. It was as if she were holding a jar right in front of her nose, plunging her hand into it, and watching the honey drip off her fingers. "Can you speak?" he asked again.

She said nothing, deciding that she must really look like a creature, a forest child, if he was wondering if she knew how to speak.

Hero growled at him, warning him to keep his distance.

"Thank you, Hero," she said on reflex.

"So you can speak," said the boy. There was something peculiar about him. There was something drawing and alluring, attracting her to him all the more.

"Not to you," she snapped, causing him to feel the alpha that Seamus had once noted in her voice. "Hero, let us run," she begged him.

"No, please," the young man begged as well. "Please don't run. I..."

But stride for stride, the wolf and the wolf girl ran. Hero bounded, and Vienna bounded after him. They ran along the river's edge, leaving the young man and his natural sunlight and honey behind.

"Thank you, Hero," she repeated continually. "Thank you. Thank you!"

CHAPTER FOURTEEN
The Boy Bloom

Together, they entered the village with Hero showing her the way. He led her to a clothesline on which someone with a daughter had hung up simple peasant gowns to dry. At this point, anything would do. While Hero turned away, Vienna put on the tan-colored dress, thrilled to be wearing something *clean*. She basked in the remembrance of cleanliness, not caring that the gown was still a little damp.

She left her clothing there.

They were expensive pajamas. All they needed was a wash.

Her hair elastic was long broken. So she snatched a few strips of yellow ribbon from someone else's clothesline and tied up her hair. She was thrilled to finally be able to keep the wretched mess out of her face.

"What?" she asked as Hero's judging eyes questioned her. She tied the other ribbon around her waist, fastening a delicate bow at her right hip. "You started it. If I become a master thief, it's all your fault."

The wolf yawned, showing his indifference.

Around town, in shops and houses, there were pictures of her father, and she looked at his smiling face and his elaborate embroidered clothing with longing. So far, she couldn't tell whether anyone owned a television. She wanted to know if anyone was looking for her, spreading the word through mass media.

Fall decorations were still out. This community was as festive as that of the last town she had been in. She was eyeing the purple and black bows on the mailboxes, the leafless trees, the pumpkins, and the haunting decorations in the windows when a police officer walked up to her.

"There are leash laws in this town, missy. If you don't want that animal caged, you had better put him on a leash."

Vienna studied the officer. If she told him she was the princess of Highest Guard, would he believe her? To be honest, she wasn't sure they were in Highest Guard anymore, or if the people here knew where it was. "Oh, yes," she said, deciding to keep quiet. "Yes, sir."

For the present, the officer let them pass.

Vienna looked at Hero. He looked at her. They both understood that there was no way he was going to wear a collar.

The dirt road they wanted to cross was in need of a steady rainfall. The dust flew up as their feet hit its surface and dragged along it. Hero was leading her into a tavern.

"Hero, we can't go in there. You don't have a leash and I don't have any money."

He didn't care. He was going in.

People rode their horses by them or tied their beasts to posts so that they could enter the shops, houses, or tavern. All the while, they eyed Vienna and her wolf. That didn't trouble her much. Typically, she would be talking to herself, yelling at men whom no one else could see. But now that she thought about it, she hadn't come across a single ghost.

They walked into the dimly lit tavern. The drinking, laughing, and eating all came to a halt as the wolf pushed through the door.

"Hey," the barkeep barked, his voice rough, "no animals! Keep your mutt outside, or out with the both of ye!"

But then he looked into Hero's eyes and saw them change color, and he suddenly fell silent. He took a step back, as if to steady himself, and then said very kindly, "Welcome to Frank's Tavern. That's the name of the guy I shot to claim this bar. It was murder, yes, but no one knows. I'd appreciate it if you kept that quiet. Follow me to your table."

"Hero, I don't know if this is such a good idea," Vienna whispered, but Hero followed the barkeep to a table.

The barkeep pulled Vienna's chair out for her and came back with menus. "Do you need a moment to look over the menu?"

"Um . . ." Vienna noticed that everyone in the room was staring at her, and Hero sat down beside her feet. "Yes, please, thank you."

"No, thank you!" the barkeep said happily, somehow a changed man. He hadn't seemed like the cheerful type when they'd walked in.

Vienna opened the menu. "Hero, I'm thinking you're a steak with a side of steak kind of guy." He watched her closely, both of his eyes turning gold like they always did when she was on to something. "Steak with a side of steak it is."

Giggling, she glanced up from the menu as someone walked into the tavern. It was the young man with the honey-flavored voice.

"Shit!" she whispered. Hero's eyes changed again as Vienna hid behind the menu. She peeked over it.

"Afternoon, Sam," the young man greeted the barkeep.

"Welcome!" Sam was joyful to have another customer. "Please be seated! Our special today is lamb pie!"

The young man stared in horror, and then decided on mockery. "You all right there, Sam? I was expecting a 'You again, huh?' or an 'If you want to eat in my tavern you'd better pay first' ordeal."

Sam's smile never faltered. He tilted his head as if he had no idea what the man was talking about.

"Okay, yeah, Sam. I'll seat myself." The fly fisher nodded. "Don't come near me. You've obviously caught the Black Death and it's messing with your mind."

He chose a table in front of Vienna. Settling down, he removed the straw hat he was wearing and placed it on the table. Sam brought him a whiskey and a coffee, and the young man took the shot before taking the coffee goblet in his hands and glanced around the room.

He looked at Vienna, who was peeking over her menu. She quickly hid, but then realized that the wolf at her feet was clearly visible. The wolf had his eyes on the fly fisher as well. He watched him inquisitively.

"May I sit down?" the young man asked.

Vienna really didn't want him to. But if anyone found out that she was a princess, and if her father found out that she'd refused to sit with a respectable civilian, she'd be hanged.

"I don't want you to."

He sat down. "You know," he whispered intently, and she felt consumed with his eyes and his voice and that wonderful smell of honey. It had to be his cologne. "I thought I'd be telling stories about you for the rest of my life," he continued. "Telling everyone how I saw this enchanting girl with a wolf walking through the trees. I thought I was going crazy."

"Maybe you're imagining things now."

Bloom reached over and lightly touched her hand. He swallowed nervously, but so did she. "You're real."

Sam stood in front of them, his giant smile interrupting. "Ready to order? Bloom, how's the coffee?"

The young man choked. "What did you say?"

"Five steaks please." Vienna handed back the menus.

"Bloom?" Sam asked, taking the menus.

"I'll . . . It would be really cool to say, 'I'll have what she's having.'" He chuckled tensely. "But I'll just have the coffee."

Sam left, and Vienna decided that she might as well get something out of this awkward seating arrangement. "Are we in Highest Guard?"

Bloom choked on his coffee. He set the goblet down and wiped his shirt with a napkin. "No, Highest Guard is an entirely different country. Why?"

"Then where are we?"

"We're in White Minstrel."

"You're telling me we're in the country Highest Guard has warred with the most?" Now she was relieved she hadn't confided in that officer. "That's just great."

"Is it? There are only four countries on this planet, and I'm not sure White Minstrel is everyone's first choice." Bloom paused, looking confused, but willing to aid her. "Are you needing to get to Highest Guard?"

Vienna tried to steady herself. That witch really was something else. Vienna would have taken Blood Port over White Minstrel, but at least, at the very least, she now knew where she was. She put her hand on Hero's head. She didn't know what would have happened if Hero hadn't found her. That witch had really meant to kill her.

"Are you in trouble?" Bloom whispered. He leaned across the table, then reclaimed his seat when Sam came back with her order. Sam set five plates down on the table. Five tender steaks smothered in gravy. Each one was sided with mashed potatoes, a wide array of vegetables, and two biscuits.

Vienna kept one plate and put the other four down for Hero. It didn't take long before the two of them were snarling over who was entitled to her last biscuit.

"What's your name?" Bloom changed his question.

She wondered whether she should lie, but decided against it. "Vienna."

"Are you in trouble, Vienna?"

"I don't see what business that is of yours."

He watched his hands, silenced by the authority in her tone. "I guess it's not, but I guess it is. If you need help . . ." He braved it. He stole her gaze, keeping it for himself for a few undying seconds. "I could help you."

"Why would you do that?"

197

"Do you think gentlemen only live in Highest Guard? White Minstrel's got them too."

Vienna blushed.

So did Bloom.

"If you helped me . . ." Vienna began, noticing Hero's gold eyes. "How would you help me?"

The bar had thinned. Lunch hour was over, but Bloom and Vienna remained. Hero sat on Vienna's feet, leaning into her. Surprisingly, the wooden chairs weren't as uncomfortable as they had first seemed. Bloom set his clasped hands on the table, which was stained by the dim light of the tavern. It seemed to Vienna that Bloom would be better suited to a golden field with the sun at its highest point in the sky, blazing down on him. She could imagine him opening his arms wide to welcome the radiance, and then, as that sweet smell maintained its hold on her, she imagined running into his open arms.

"I'd —"

Vienna jumped to her feet, but Hero was already ahead of her. She couldn't stay here any longer. This boy was trouble. "I've got to go!"

"Wait —" He reached out and a part of her wanted to reach out to him. But the stronger part of her was already out the door, running to catch up with Hero.

The officer watched in shock.

"Don't stop!" she ordered, although Hero wasn't planning to. "Don't stop running, Hero!"

CHAPTER FIFTEEN
The Way to Highest Guard

When they were back at the river, they stopped. She felt like an idiot for running away because she *needed* him. Bloom had agreed to help her, and she needed to get to Highest Guard. She needed to find Augustus, and she needed to get her life back. But she couldn't help but wonder – she couldn't help but notice – that she hadn't seen one ghost in that village, not one.

Hero watched her with two gold-colored eyes.

Bloom's green gems took over Vienna's mind and she cursed. "What was with that guy?"

Hero didn't say anything. He just sat there, staring at her like always.

Kicking the grass, Vienna swung herself around a few dozen trees, trying to understand how she had gotten to this point in her life. She couldn't tell anyone here that she was Princess Vienna of Highest Guard. Her life would surely be in danger. Just as it had been endangered in the forest. Hero had found her then. Bloom had found her now.

Vienna felt like she was missing something that was right in front of her face, and she needed glasses to see it. Feeling far too stressed to function, she clasped her head in her arms. Then she did the only thing she could do, the only thing that was left to do.

She threw herself into the river.

It wasn't deep where she jumped in, and she stretched her arms and legs out. Letting the water bear her weight, she watched the sky and felt as if she were flying up above the trees, like an angel.

Hero sat at the water's edge, watching her as his eyes changed color furiously.

Vienna smiled at him. Warmth filled her, and she soaked up his presence. Then she turned away, gazed into the trees, and thought of the first time she'd met Vincent.

There was a fishing pole against one of the trees, and two baskets had been left there with a blanket over them.

Oh god . . . Bloom only stopped for lunch . . . Bloom was coming back here!

Vienna tried to hurry. The water seemed to be dragging her down instead of giving her wings, and she found herself at the bottom of the river. She pushed herself up, trying to run, but she slipped and fell to the bottom again. Her mouth was full of water, and she was choking, taking more river water into her mouth.

Am I going to drown?

She pushed herself up, and her mind fought to find something solid. She counted to three, trying to sew her thoughts back together long enough for her to take charge of her actions. She hoisted herself up and found firm footing in the river.

Spitting out water, she raised her head, and there was Bloom. He was so close that, if she just leaned forward, she'd be pressed against him. He was drenched, and his green eyes were frightened, blinded by his fear. His sandy brown hair was hugging his head and the water was dripping down his face. He blinked it away as it fell into his eyes.

Bloom grabbed Vienna by the shoulders. "Are you out of your mind? I thought you were drowning!"

"Unhand me!" She was released and then slapped him as hard as she could. She turned and began running away, but it was dreadfully hard to run in water, and she wasn't going very fast.

He was right beside her. He was hardly finished talking yet. "Why would you go swimming if you can't swim? What are you doing here anyway? Who are you? I want to know." He took her arm, spinning her around to face him. "Why do you keep running from me?"

That honey smell was at its height, pouring out with his fear. Vienna wanted to cry. He was so concerned, but he didn't even know her. It also kind of pissed her off. "You said you'd help me!"

Baffled, he let her go. "I want to help you!"

"I need to get to Highest Guard!" she yelled at him.

"Fine!" he yelled back. "I'll take you. Don't worry about it!"

"Thank you!"

"You're welcome!"

They stopped yelling and stared at each other, both breathing heavily, both red in the face from their passionate encounter. Bloom slammed his fists into the water, his chest rising and falling, and then he started laughing. His laugh made Vienna laugh.

Hero had watched all of this without moving.

200

"Do you wear cologne?" Vienna asked after taking large, obvious breaths.

"No." Bloom shied away. "I can't afford it. Why?"

"So you smell like that naturally?"

He raised his eyebrows. "Smell like what?"

Vienna blushed. She couldn't tell him. "Nothing." She started to run again.

Bloom caught her by the hand, drawing her back. "No, no, no, no," he sang, smiling too playfully, his voice too effective. "You've got to tell me. Do I smell like cheese?"

Vienna giggled. "No!"

"Do I smell like old cheese?"

"No!" Vienna twirled as he twirled her in the water, as if music had started to play and that was the beginning of the dance. She stripped her hand away, feeling his fingers brush against her wrist, and her entire body tingled in response. Stepping back, she couldn't hold back the little sigh that escaped from her lips.

Bloom stopped, watching her, and when nothing happened, he asked seriously, "Do I smell like fish?"

Vienna filled her cupped hands with water and sprayed him. "No!"

"Do I smell good?"

Giggling, Vienna set her hands on Bloom's chest and pushed him so that he fell backward.

She was already rushing away, her legs straining against the water's force when he hit the water.

"No!" she sang, turning back once she reached Hero, watching as Bloom shook the water off.

All the while, Hero was watching.

CHAPTER SIXTEEN
The Princess of Highest Guard

Five days went by before Bloom got passes for them to leave the country. He even got one for Hero. Vienna asked the wolf if he was sure he wanted to go with her, but he said nothing. His irises remained that clear gold color.

Bloom lived alone in a log cabin in the woods. She had wondered if she'd adapt well to the change, but she found the log cabin to be wonderfully cozy. It wasn't because she'd spent the recent days sleeping on the forest floor. It was because of the homemade quilts and the stew waiting in the evening and the bacon and baked eggs in the mornings. It was because the bath was large enough to accommodate three of her, much like the bath she had at home. It was because they would all sit together in the evenings, the fire going, while Bloom read books out loud. And it was because she was starting to recognize that honey smell, almost as if it were her own.

She was waiting in the little country kitchen for Bloom to come home, and she heard his footsteps on the woodland path before she saw him. She wanted to meet him with giggles and smiles. She wanted to jump up and down like a little schoolgirl with a crush, but, instead, she pretended not to notice him entering the room.

"I picked up the three travel-passes," he told her, putting his good hat on its hanger before handing the papers to her.

Bloom's description was very accurate. "It says Hero is a state official," Vienna said, continuing to read through the papers. But she found as much pleasure in Hero's new bow tie as Bloom did when he bought it. She flipped the page, reading on to find out who her own travel-pass claimed her to be. "I'm a boy?"

Bloom set a box in front of her, and Vienna freed the red ribbon and removed the lid. There was a bowler hat inside. There were also trousers, suspenders, and a button up shirt.

"Apparently, the only 'Vienna' in White Minstrel is a twelve-year-old boy . . ." Bloom explained. White Minstrel had lists of all the people living there. If you weren't on the list, you weren't getting a travel- pass. Bloom had to find the 'Heros' and 'Viennas' who were living in White Minstrel before he could have Hero and Vienna pose as them.

And the only 'Hero' is a state official . . . Vienna thought. *This could be potentially disastrous.*

She wasn't thrilled that she'd have to pretend to be a boy, but anything was better than nothing. "I guess I'll have to grin and bear it."

"Besides, I figured it might be safer." He went to take her hand and then thought better of it. "You still haven't told me why you need to go to Highest Guard or why you keep running. So, I thought that maybe someone out there was looking for a girl like you, someone you didn't want to find you."

"It's quite the opposite, actually," Vienna admitted.

Hero walked into the kitchen and rested his head on the princess's knee.

Clearing his throat, Bloom walked out of the room. When he came back, he was carrying two traveling packs. He handed one to Vienna, who had used the time to change into her new clothing in the washroom.

Vienna judged the heavy looking pack in his hand. "Am I supposed to carry that myself?"

Bloom shook his head at her, like he always did when he thought she was joking but she wasn't. "What are you? A princess?"

Vienna took the leather backpack and swung it on. "Of course not." Trying to remain confident, she took the bow tie off the table and put it around Hero's neck, who wasn't particularly thrilled.

Together, they walked out of the log cabin and began their journey to the station. At first they were quiet, Bloom kicking rocks out of his way, more irritated than usual.

"You don't have to come with me to Highest Guard," Vienna said, deciding Bloom's odd behavior was due to the thought of leaving his home behind. "You can leave me at the station and stay in White Minstrel if you'd like."

"You've got a lover at home, don't you? And you don't want me to know."

"What's brought this on?"

"Why else would you tell me to stay in White Minstrel?"

Were they all the same? She tried not to think that her dear friend Bloom could be the kind of guy who would bring a diamond to a princess in the hope of winning her hand in marriage. "You misunderstand me completely, not my words, but my character. A lover? Perhaps, if that were permitted and I wasn't so proper."

"A husband then?"

"No."

"Never?"

"Why should I have a husband?"

"To be loved eternally . . ." Bloom was unwilling to look at her while his sentiments on this topic were written so clearly upon his face, exposing what she might consider to be weakness. He looked away.

"Is that all?"

"I think you're braver than me, wanting to walk this world alone."

Why did everyone always say things like this to her? "I'm not alone. I have my father, Vincent, and Seamus, Poem, my horses, and all my books. Hell, I have an entire realm to see to. It's impossible for me to walk alone."

Bloom slid to a stop. "What? What do you mean *realm*?" And then pieces started to string themselves together. "Vienna? *Princess* Vienna of Highest Guard?" He knew it was true. Her manners gave her away.

"Everyone thinks, unless you fall in love, you've failed and that's the end. But I've fallen in love with hundreds of different things, with hundreds of different heroes from a hundred different stories. I just don't want to get married. And that has nothing to do with being alone."

"Falling in love and getting married are two different things."

"*Really?* Well, I'm glad to hear you say that because I wasn't going to be given a choice."

Bloom took a moment to let all this sink in, and then he took another moment before continuing, "So what happened?"

"Some jerk told me I was a pearl and not a diamond." Now that she'd started talking about everything that had happened, she wasn't sure if she could stop.

"Don't you like pearls?"

"I love them. That's all I like to wear."

"So what's the problem?"

"Are you serious?" He lived in a cabin, but he wasn't out of touch with the rest of the world. Even in White Minstrel, they'd know the basics of her predicament. Although, hopefully, that would exclude the part about being cursed. Either way, a 'What's the problem?' question deserved an 'Are you serious?' response.

"No. I know. You didn't know him. You probably never even talked to him before."

Vienna wandered back through her mind. "I did. Once. Maybe twice."

"If he had any sort of sense, he'd at least have had an entire conversation with you. I'm sure he's sorry about that."

"I hope he is!" Vienna's fists dug into her sides. "I hope he's as unhappy that he cursed me as I am about being cursed!"

"What?"

And yet she hadn't seen one ghost in White Minstrel . . . "I refused him, and he cursed me."

"Sore loser, huh? It's not something disgusting, is it, the curse?"

"No, you're perfectly safe."

"This warlock, I take it . . ."

"Yes?"

"You really hate him, don't you?"

As the three travelers went on, the last of the falling leaves rained down on them. A few colored leaves remained in her hair and Bloom reached over to pick them off. He had done that: treating her like a princess without knowing she was one. Now that he knew, he wasn't acting differently.

The sky was greying and rain was sure to be coming. Or maybe snow. She wondered what White Minstrel was like in the winter. She could picture the trees, covered in a layer of snow. Everything would be hidden, like secrets that the snow promised to keep, keeping them until spring.

"I need to find him." Vienna shifted her pack onto one shoulder.

"What if I were a prince? Would you love me if I gave you a pearl?" Bloom wanted to know.

"Certainly much less!" Vienna laughed.

"What if I were a warlock? Would you love me if I gave you a pearl?" Bloom wanted to know still.

"Certainly not at all!"

"What if I were me, would you love me if I gave you a pearl?"

He was serious, and Vienna found herself quite out of breath. She had taken this for a joke. But now that he'd put the question to her... She couldn't answer, and yet she could not shy away from it either.

It was because she stayed still that he braved what came next. Carefully, he took her hand in his. And because it was his hand, because she had no words, she let him.

CHAPTER SEVENTEEN
The Soldiers

The road was long and painted with autumn leaves. The odd one turned in the wind, capturing the most glorious of yellows and oranges and reds on this canvas of waking life.

They spent their nights just off the side of the road, surrounded by purple and red flowers that would glisten in the early morning. Bloom had packed blankets, and they used Hero as a pillow. Enjoying the full use of those entitlements now – with Bloom and Hero still in dreamland – Vienna welcomed the new day.

She watched Bloom sleep for a measured amount of time. Any other day she would have remained with Hero while Bloom collected nuts or berries, hunted rabbits, or fished for minnows.

But how wonderful it would be if *he* should wake up to a breakfast that *she* had provided for him!

Against the breath of morning, Vienna set out. Away from the safety of the road, she wondered about the watchfulness of the trees.

Deeper and deeper she ventured, chasing fairies and admiring shimmering seedlings, kissing unsure daisies good morning, and running with the deer of this White Minstrel wood.

At last, she stood below a hazelnut tree. Gathering hazelnuts worth her weight in gold, she thought about how silly she'd been to leave her pack behind. She ripped apart the sleeves of her buttoned shirt, stuffed and then tied them; turning them into handy pouches.

Of course, that's when she saw the 'Caution' signs and the 'Beware Ogre Territory' warnings. Arrows pinned portraits of ogres wanted for murder and suspicion of murder to the trees.

Vienna had made it this far unnoticed. She was certain she could return safely. She began her journey back to her heroes, picturing their sleeping forms as she went.

That was until a man stood in front of her.

"I know what I'm doing in ogre territory, but what are you doing in ogre territory?" Vienna addressed the stranger. He looked to be a bounty hunter of some kind. Perhaps he was here to slay a few prized ogres. She decided he might be able to help her safely back to her kin, but to her horror he stared, unbelieving.

"You can see *me?*" he asked like so many ghosts before him had asked her.

So there were ghosts in White Minstrel . . .

"No," she said without much thought about it. "No, I can't see you."

"But you're talking to me."

"You'll find you're mistaken. I'll find I'm talking to myself." She was already on her way before she said, "Excuse me," and was visited once more by her immense hatred for the warlock who had cursed her.

"Wait!" the man beseeched her, but Vienna would not wait. She only stopped when the great pounding of hooves thundered in her ears.

She fell to her hands and knees and crawled, her wooly scarf pulling at her neck while its excess dragged along the ground. She crawled until she came to a different road, one that she knew well. She had traveled it before with her father. Their carriage had been pulled by galloping horses, crossing through the highway-transport in Highest Guard and entering White Minstrel without the guards, horses, or their carriage missing a stride. But that was the highway-transport, and one needed travel-passes to get onto it. Just like Bloom needed to get travel-passes to use the station to enter Highest Guard on foot. Vienna knew that you could turn on to the very road she could see now from White Minstrel's highway-transport. It was the quickest path to the palace, which meant that the lines of men and galloping grey stallions she was seeing now were a royal fleet.

No. She was not rescued. If anything, her life was in greater danger. White Minstrel and Highest Guard only tolerated each other, and if the steward of White Minstrel were presented with the opportunity, he would betray Highest Guard without hesitation.

Vienna tried to creep away, but her ambition failed. A hawk-eyed soldier swung his silver stallion around, sounding the slim trumpet that was slung around his neck. The fleet followed him, sliding their horses to a stop and drawing their swords.

The hawk-eyed soldier pointed his sword at Vienna while the others carefully surveyed their surroundings, ready for ogres or thieves and their fiery arrows.

"Come out, little thief, and you may win my tolerance."

Vienna straightened herself and walked out from her hiding place as she said, "I'm no thief, sir. I'm trying to make my way to the station."

"Then I'll have to ask to see your travel-pass."

Luckily, she had it in her back pocket, unspoiled by her new found life as a vagabond. She unfolded the paper and handed it to him.

The soldier dismounted, his loyal steed following him as he came to inspect her fake travel-pass.

He considered the paper and then considered her. "It says here you're a shoemaker, on your way to Highest Guard. Purpose?"

"Visiting family."

He folded the paper and handed it back to her. "You got enough money to be making it through Highest Guard, son?"

"In fact, I've no money at all."

The kind-hearted soldier let his pity sit for a while. He had sympathy for the lowly, twelve-year-old boy. "Can you sing or dance or read cards, boy?"

"I can sing."

"If you sing us a song, every man here will give you one silver coin. Are you willing?"

Vienna knew that Bloom had very little money. What he had, he was using to get her home.

There were over a hundred men here to sing for, and a hundred silver coins would pay Bloom back and more. Vienna made her decision. "If you find you like my song, then we have an accord."

The soldier chuckled as he mounted his horse. "Then be sure we do. A fortune's on the line."

Bloom was right. There were gentlemen in White Minstrel. The gentle soldier, his hard build and war-marked face, waited for Vienna to begin. Most of his body was hidden beneath steel and armored layers.

The hazelnuts still in hand, Vienna began to sing. She sang about knights slaying dragons and saving maidens. She sang a song about a man's paradise. It was a silly thing, but she'd heard the knights singing it back at the palace. As she sang, she thought of home, until someone interrupted her.

"Vienna!" A man was rushing through the trees. "Vienna!"

Not now, Bloom. She'd found herself thrown into a good thing, and someone else's presence would only bring about questions and suspicions.

But it wasn't Bloom.

209

"Vienna!" a ghost called her name.

"Vincent!" Her feet moved on their own. The spastic jerk of her abrupt movement sent her boy's hat tumbling off and she flung herself at him. "Vincent!" She embedded herself into his ghostly form, his sturdy chin resting on her head. "How did you find me? How are you here?"

"We figured if she didn't send you to a different planet, you'd be in White Minstrel. Seamus and I hopped the transport out of Highest Guard's station in search of you. We split up. We listened for news, but no one had seen you. Until today. Someone sent in a report that a girl had *seen* him."

"A report?"

"The dead don't live in an uncivilized manner either, you know? We have laws, law enforcers, and a communication office that we're all kind of connected to."

Nope. She wasn't even going to try to figure that one out.

"I came straight away, but Vienna —"

"Vincent, I'm so relieved!"

"Vienna?"

"What could possibly ruin this moment?"

"You're talking to a dead guy, and they can't see me."

She looked into over a hundred stunned faces. "Oh no . . ."

"Run," Vincent whispered.

"Seize her!" the gentleman soldier ordered, and horses took flight, sending ropes to contain her. But he was already there. His hawk-eyes were aflame as his hand hooked onto the back of her shirt and hoisted her up and over the saddle. He turned his horse. Freed from her boy's hat, Vienna's long hair was wild. Her cheeks were rosy from the force of the wind, as he led the fleet, storming into the palace.

CHAPTER EIGHTEEN
The Start of Dungeon Days

White Minstrel had gotten part of its name from its white needled evergreens and the white feathered wings of the fairies who nested in them. They would come out during the witching hour to play their flutes. Vienna could see the city as she looked out her dungeon window. The houses and shops gave the impression that they were made out of icing and gingerbread. Baby blue roses were scattered about the gardens that lined every shop. Dozens of skyscrapers circled the palace, as if to make a protective barrier. But, apart from a massive cathedral, the palace was the most artistically Gothic building in the city. 'Wanted' ogre posters hung in stores. They were a reminder of the nation's most pressing threat. And 'Highest Guard Sucks' slogans were tolerated on vandalized school property, where they encouraged children to get away with what their elders could not.

From her little dungeon window, bars and all, Vienna could see swings and benches and statues of winged lions and commemoration stones. A statue of the Minstrel (the founder of White Minstrel) was in the town square, and she felt as if the bookshops were pointing and laughing at her because she wanted so much to enter them and was unable to do so. She was alone in the dungeon except for eleven dead men, all of whom wanted a piece of her. Especially Vincent.

"Are you listening to me?" he was saying.

"I prefer imprisonment to be a solitary activity."

"Princess . . ." he objected as kindly as he could.

"Vincent, you want me to be a therapist for the dead."

"That's practically what you are now," he said, his pen and notepad securely in hand.

This was all his idea, of course.

"But you want to make it official, and, judging by your extraordinarily long appointment list, you *have* made it official!"

"Don't yell at me. I'm not the one who cursed you," he reminded her, holding up the appointment book. "I've organized the dead. In order to speak to you, they have to make an appointment with me. And yes. We have a waiting list."

Vienna knew that Vincent was onto something. If he didn't have them make appointments, she'd be overrun with ghosts again. They'd all try to speak at once, each one convinced that his story was worth her time more than another's story. Vincent had taken chaos and forced it to work. He had forced it into a system that would let her keep her sanity. She should have been grateful. She knew that.

"I don't think so, Vincent. I don't even want to talk to *these guys,*" she said in reference to the ten male ghosts who were listening to their conversation.

"What you mean to say is that you don't have *time* to talk to them because you have a schedule to keep. We're already behind. I started taking appointments days ago, hoping I'd found you by then. I'm calling the first gentleman in, and you *are* going to be polite." He watched her cross her arms and turn up her nose. "Vienna . . . ?"

She knew she had a choice. It was either this way or the old way. Sighing, Vienna said, "Send him in."

Vincent's lips flicked up encouragingly. However, both of them wondered what they would do without Seamus when someone needed a forceful exit. Regardless, Vincent read the first name on the list. "Carol Seymour."

A man appeared in front of Vienna. He was wearing a full sailor's uniform and comically took in his new surroundings. "What are we doing in White Minstrel?" he asked. "What are we doing in a dungeon?"

"Welcome." Vienna politely gestured to the stool in front of her, and the ghost took a seat. Vincent sat at her side. "You may begin your troubled story, and, no, I'm not ready to talk about mine, so no questions. A dungeon's a dungeon, and this one's as good as any."

"Vienna . . ." Vincent warned. She was a princess, his gaze was telling her, and she should act like one.

She shifted in her seat.

Carol studied his hands before letting them witness the extreme anguish of his trial of love. "This is a story about a boy who fell in love with a girl."

"They all are." Vienna hung her head. She wondered whether anyone would notice if she were to fall asleep.

"And I'm not sorry." Carol lit up. "I'll never be sorry. I didn't know how much one could have in this life until I knew her."

He wasn't crying. It was actually quite shocking.

"Did she hurt you?" Vienna asked.

"No." Carol shook his head. He looked like a man who had marched into battle and won a war. Triumphant and glowing, he said, "She married me. We met when I was eighteen. Two years after she ran away from home. I was a sea captain, and she didn't mind the sea." He basked in the remembrance of her. "She didn't mind at all."

"You're not crying . . ."

"Why would I cry?" Carol asked. "I'm just so happy to tell someone. I didn't waste my life, but I would have wasted it, if I hadn't lived it with her."

"But you're dead . . ."

"So?"

"But she's not with you . . ."

Carol looked out the barred window with longing. "No. But we will be. I know it. She'll fight to get to me, as hard as I'm fighting to get back to her. It's a wide world out there, child. Do you know how hard we had to fight to finally get to know each other when we were alive? I didn't expect death to be any different. It will take some time, but I'll hold her in my arms again." He looked down at himself. "Even if I am a ghost."

"He didn't cry once," she told Vincent although Carol was still in the room. "Seamus will never believe us."

Carol placed his hands on his legs, ready to venture off. "Thank you for listening. You have no idea how many times I've screamed at the living, telling them they're making mistakes, and they don't listen. You have no idea how many times I tell them not to wait, that that's all that matters, but they just walk away. All I wanted to do was tell someone that I'm one man who doesn't know regret."

"Well, thank you for not yelling that at me." Vienna smoothed her lips with her index finger, not quite knowing what to make of this guy. But if she didn't know now, she never would because he disappeared, satisfied.

"My wife had me imprisoned here," the man in the cell across from Vienna's huffed. "I can't *believe* I still love her."

"See." Vienna pointed to the ratty looking prisoner. "Those are the kinds of stories I'm used to."

"Ross Owen," Vincent read from the list.

Just then, the dungeon door opened.

The gentleman soldier with the hawk-eyes walked up to Vienna's cell door, and Ross Owen turned around, confused as to where he was. The soldier was no longer in his suit of armor. Rather, he carried his helmet under his arm and was dressed in a green tunic, breeches, and black, knee-high riding boots.

"I've been sent here to question you," he began. His features were sharp and bird-like, and his hair was like feathers atop his head. "We need to get a few things squared up before we can start talking about your release."

Ross Owen sized the soldier up, snorting while holding his beer-gut. "That's some tactic, isn't it? Don't you tell them nothing, honey."

"Please," Vincent urged the man. "Have a seat."

"Don't mind if I do!" Ross sat on the stool. He was unsuited for the tiny object.

The soldier clicked his front teeth together before continuing. "Let's start with an easy question. What's your name?"

Vienna wondered about this knight. She wondered about the man underneath the mask, the man who had been willing to aid a poor boy, offering over a hundred silver coins for a silly song. "Is there such a thing as an easy question?"

"It's impolite to answer a question with a question. I asked you about your name."

"What's yours?"

Ross howled in approval. "That a girl! You keep him on his toes!"

The soldier smiled lightly, placing his helmet on the floor. "I'll tell you what, little lady. I'll tell you my name, my title too, if you wish it. But you have to answer my question first."

Vienna measured his words, knowing she couldn't give him her real name. He already knew she was trying to get to Highest Guard. He'd soon make the connection that she was much, much more than she'd first made herself out to be.

"V. Just V," Vienna told him. "A bargain's a bargain."

"So it is." The soldier leaned on the cell bars. "Sir James Spear, Captain of the Royal Fleet and Second Platoon, Champion of White Minstrel."

"Show off." Ross puffed out his chest.

"It's a pleasure to make your acquaintance, Captain." Vienna tipped the imaginary hat on her head.

"Where did you get your fake travel-pass?" James asked. He continued to lean against the bars. His hands were moving above his head as they traveled along the iron, and his gaze became ominous, for he was a mass of a man, and she was a dainty beauty.

"I don't know where," Vienna replied strongly. She wasn't intimidated by him. Although, perhaps she should have been. "It was given to me."

"Who gave it to you?"

Bloom . . . She had to protect him. She couldn't involve him in this. "I can't tell you that."

James's face took on a strange expression, like a bird of prey anticipating the tasting of the mouse it was diving for. "Recently, a man transported into this country illegally. Are you in any way connected to that?"

"I hardly know. Depends upon the man, I suppose. Who is he?"

"There's only one sort of man who can jump from place to place without being publicly transported. But to come into a country legally, he has to show his warlock permit."

Augustus? No way. That was too much of a coincidence, she thought. But, if it was him, then that was *swell.* She'd somehow break out of here and give him a piece of her mind. "I can assure you I am in no way connected to that."

"I believe you," he said seriously.

"Careful, Captain," Vienna teased. "It's easier to believe lies than to believe the truth." She realized then that she was perhaps taking too much liberty, so she confirmed his thoughts, saying, "But I'm not lying."

"I believe you because you have the sort of look of someone running away." His arms came down, gripping the bars, keeping his hands level with his chest. "Why are you trying to get to Highest Guard?"

She had known that very soon he would start asking questions she could not answer. They came sooner than she had expected, and she was forced to say nothing.

"Who's Vincent?" he changed the course of his interrogation.

Vincent coughed in the background.

"You believe there was a man?" Vienna looked away from her interrogator.

215

"I believe you believed there was a man," James corrected her and Vienna said nothing. "I'm trying to help you, V. But you need to start trying to help yourself." He shoved himself away from the bars, knowing he wasn't going to get much further with her than that, and picked up his helmet. "Don't push my patience, little one. I'm still a soldier. I'll do what it takes to get results."

Vienna turned back to match his stare, folding her hands on her lap. "Are you suggesting you'll torture me for something I may or may not be able to tell you?"

"A little bird like you?" Sir James Spear walked out of the prison, leaving her with menacing last words. "There's no knowing what you might know."

For the first time since her arrival, there was silence in the dungeon. The ghosts who haunted it, some still secured to the walls by chains, didn't know what to say.

Vincent was going to say something encouraging, but Ross spoke first.

"I'm proud of you, honey." Ross set his hands as if he were about to lift a ridiculously large boulder. "You held your own. I didn't want to interfere. You were doing so well yourself."

"I appreciate that," Vienna said, adapting a calm, graceful mien and steadying her adrenalin. "Now that he's gone, I'm here to listen as you tell me about the girl you used to love."

Ross had to correct her. "The girl I love!"

CHAPTER NINETEEN
The Hour

There was little life in the prison, but there was more than anyone knew. Ghosts came and went, and since they were called one at a time, there was no competition among them. Thus far, Seamus's assistance hadn't been required.

Vienna had spent the night sleeping on the worst, most vulgar surface yet. She would have preferred the forest floor and her long ago spider bites to this cold stone. The guards cared for her to the littlest possible extent, and, in the morning, when the city came to life outside her cage, she was brought a goblet of water and one green apple. The forgetful guard left the dungeon door open, and she was able to see the odd person passing by.

Not two hours after sunrise, Seamus appeared outside her prison cell.

"Where have you been?" Vincent demanded.

A harsh-looking Seamus passed through the cell bars. "Iron Hand."

"How did you end up in that country?"

"Don't ask!"

Vienna wanted to hug him and kiss his cheeks. The last time she had seen him they had been in a car accident. Vincent told her that, last he knew, her father had been back at the palace, searching for her, and Seamus had been searching as well. That, in itself, warranted a kiss on his cheek. But due to his apparent bitterness, she wasn't sure how to act, and he seemed to be pretending that they hadn't spent any time apart.

"Vincent filled you in on this sideshow of his?" Seamus decided to lounge at the back of the cell.

"Twenty souls last night." Vincent consulted his notebook. "Five so far this morning."

Seamus narrowed his eyes at them. "You're behind schedule."

Vienna looked out of the open door, which suggested a way out of the prison. Her jail mates had their priorities wrong. She needed to find a way out of here. She couldn't see much, but she tried to soak in all that she might learn from the hall, its red-carpeted walls, and the stories that its gold thread told. She'd been taken through the palace with a hood over her head, so she didn't have much to go on. But it looked like there were stairs at the end of the hall . . .

"Princess Vienna . . ." Vincent warmly attempted to redirect her back to her current situation. "Are you ready to talk to the next ghost?"

But Vienna wasn't paying attention. A group of people had come down the staircase. They were huddled together, speaking much too fast for her to catch pieces of the conversation. They were dressed in elaborate clothing and adorned with colored necklaces. However, there was one man she recognized. His hands were clasped behind his back. His silver hair stood out and his grey eyes were as sharp as his words.

He was an adviser to the King of Highest Guard.

"Just bring in the next bastard," Seamus told Vincent, cracking his knuckles. "I'll deal with him. I'm fired up. Got my ass handed to me for losing the princess. Like I could know a crazed loon was going to go postal, huh?"

Vincent's voice was light as he read the next name on the list.

But Vienna was beyond either of them. "Hour!" she screamed. Her arms thrashed against the bars, trying to make him notice her. She watched him stop and look around, as if someone had breathed his name on the wind. Fear touched her heart, a light wisp in the heat of things, as James came down the hall behind the bickering advisers. Her arms reached out desperately for him. "Hour!" And this time, he looked right at her. "Hour!"

Startled when Hour set off at a run, the escorts forced themselves against the walls. He hit the solid door to the dungeon with his shoulder. His black traveler's cape followed behind him, and his riding boots thundered against the stone floor. When he saw the monstrous state that his beloved princess was in, his face grew paler and paler.

"Oh my god!" He reached her cell, taking her hands and pressing them to his chest so that she could feel the pounding of his heart.

"Do you know this girl?" James asked, standing behind him. He led a group of guards and the advisers of White Minstrel behind him. Hour, although frantic, was forced to drop Vienna's hands.

"She's —" But Hour knew, as well as Vienna did, how dangerous it would be for them to know that she was the daughter of King Gladness, ruler of all the land. White Minstrel was managed by a steward, but it was ruled by the king of The Four Countries. If they knew they had the king's daughter in their grasp, they'd try to force him to grant them independence. "She's my wife."

Vincent choked.

Seamus laughed.

And the ghost whom Vincent had called, took a seat and asked, "What the hell kind of lives are you *modern* people living? In my day, we didn't have parties in dungeons. That was considered bad taste."

"Your wife?" James seemed to be watching this all from above, soaring in the air over their heads. A slick expression held his lips and his attentive stare.

"Your wife?" Another soldier, in full uniform, asked. He chose to believe him simply so that he could mock him. "Well, we found your wife in the forest going on and on while no one was there."

"Yeah . . . She does that," Hour admitted awkwardly. "But it's hardly cause for imprisonment."

"No," James challenged. He looked as if he held their lives, shrewdly kept, in his hands. "But a fake travel-pass does."

"Oh . . ." Hour paused, observing James and James fervently observed him. "Yes, that would warrant it."

"Let's get out of the dungeon, gentlemen," one of the advisers pleaded. "We do have work that needs your attention, Hour."

Reluctant to leave her, Hour stood. He was unsure of what to do until the princess's mouth formed one word: 'Go.'

"Yes, of course," Hour replied to the advisers of White Minstrel. "Darling," he told Vienna, nervously. "You really get into far too much trouble. You're just that kind of girl, as your father always told me. He and I shall have to see what we can do with this."

"Tell him V loves him!" she cried, warning him not to use her real name.

"Yes, V, of course." Hour caught on. He lingered at the dungeon door, unwilling to leave her in such a place.

James gave her one last glance before closing the prison door. The lock sounded through the lonely prison.

Gripping the prison bars, Vienna slid to the floor.

"Whoa," the ghost, who had been lucky enough to be called to the

219

prison, muttered. "I expect tea at events such as this, but I think this occasion calls for a much stronger substance."

"You're dead, pal," Seamus barked at him. "That's all the substance you got."

CHAPTER TWENTY

The Truth

"I'm dead," Cole, the dead man, said.

"Um . . ." Vienna contemplated the ghost. "Assumedly for quite some time now."

"You're not listening to me!" the ghost shouted. "I died. And I went nowhere. I'm still stuck in my same crappy mind, except there's no perks. I'm perkless!"

"Generally," Vienna hesitated, "when people come to me, they talk about their love lives."

"Who the hell wants to talk about that? That was the only good part. If you're going to complain to the living, at least make it worth everyone's time. I'm dead. I died! I don't know how I feel about that. I'm not sure I should be expected to accept this."

"You're having a problem with death?"

"Doesn't everyone? I had a problem with it when I was living," the dead man went on, looking around the room. He began talking to ghosts Vienna couldn't see. "Do you not have a problem with it?" he asked them. "And you?" His anger increased, and he promised Vienna: "I've got years of bottled rage; prepare yourself."

"Sir, I'm going to stop you right there. You said you're not sure how you should feel about death. Is it because you feel alone? Have you not found your, um, earthly partner in the, um, world of ghosts . . . ?"

"Actually, now that you mention it, I haven't. But that's really kind of understandable. I had to chase her all over the place when we were alive. It's only right I should have to do the same thing when we're dead – now that we're dead."

"And, um, how does that make you feel?" Vienna encouraged him to stay on topic. "Are you going to cry about it?"

"Are you mocking me?"

"It wasn't my intention." She supposed she should stop asking that question. It was just that they all seemed to start and finish with tears.

He seemed to have also bewildered Vincent and Seamus.

"I think your anger is rooted in the real problem. Why is your death so unsatisfying to you? Surely you couldn't have had any expectations: like dying should automatically suggest that god grant you a cool car. Was your life really so unsatisfying that you have become so unhappy in death?"

"No." He took a moment to decide. "I mean, sure, I wish we had settled down like she originally wanted. It was me who kept the band going, and that was the reason for the fights and the drugs. We couldn't bring kids into that, and it wasn't cool to want a white picket fence. *Now* I wonder *why* she stayed with me. I guess, yeah, I wonder if that's the reason I can't find her out here. Because she doesn't want me to find her."

"I think you need to come to terms with yourself before you can come to terms with your death." Vienna carefully proceeded, hoping that everything she was saying was making sense. "I can see you because you loved so eternally. I don't know if that means it was the same for her, but if it makes any difference, I haven't yet come across one man that's found his soul mate in death."

"Really? I wonder what that's all about . . ."

She leaned back, startled.

James was there, sitting on a stool in front of her prison cell. He was listening to her as she had a conversation with herself. Her legs were crossed, and she promptly set both feet on the floor, clamping them together. Her chest was rising and falling rapidly. She folded her hands on her lap, fighting to regain composer.

"Don't stop on my account." James tilted his body to the right, his head moving up and down. "It's absolutely fascinating."

"Holy shit!" Cole exclaimed. "When the hell did he come in?"

"Vincent, why didn't you say something?" Seamus was furious.

"I didn't notice him," Vincent defended himself. "I was too mesmerized. Vienna was really making an impression."

"You really are a curious creature. Does your *husband* support your profession, being a counselor for the dead?" When Vienna said nothing, he tapped the side of his nose, signifying that he already knew she was lying. "It does interest me, seeing how loyal a king's adviser can be. I ran your picture and your prints against White Minstrel's travel database and came across nothing, which means we have a second illegal immigrant. How did you get into White Minstrel?" Vienna said nothing, which only encouraged him. "If I send your picture to Highest Guard's database, what am I going to find?" He leaned forward, his hand rubbing his chin, excited for the challenge. "Who are you?"

This was very bad. If he found out who she was, he would tell the steward, and the steward would hold her for ransom. Yes, this soldier was an interrogator, and he was assuming that she was some kind of terrorist, but there was also more to him. She had seen it on that day when he had caught her eye on the roadside. He was a knight. His heart was noble and true, and perhaps if he knew she was royalty, the good knight would show her mercy.

She had to make a decision now. But if she was unable to convince him to keep her identity a secret, she would have to escape from this prison tonight, at all costs.

"You were kind to me," she reminded him, hoping that he would consider kindness once again, "that day you found me in the woods."

She watched as he replayed the memory in his mind. It was evident on his face, and she could almost hear the song she had sung for him. But as soon as the value of that moment played out, her betrayal, which he considered very grave, grew fangs at the end of his stare and sank into her. "You lied to me," he said. "I'm not a fan of liars."

"I didn't lie about everything." Gripping her hands tightly in her lap, she made her decision. She prayed for his mercy before she admitted, "My name is Vienna and I am trying to get home, back to my family."

James leaned back, scratching the side of his face before crossing his arms. "By all means, continue."

"I was driving with my father, and we almost hit a witch who was standing with her cat in the middle of the road. She banished me here. Since then, I've been attacked by a bear, have been imprisoned, and now I am being interrogated by you."

"Why would a witch banish you to White Minstrel?"

"Because it's the one place – regardless of where I go or who I meet – where my life is in danger."

"And why is that?"

"You mean you haven't connected the dots? It comes to as a relief, actually, that rumors of my failing sanity have yet to reach White Minstrel. I'm not crazy, by the way. Just because you can't see something doesn't mean it doesn't exist for someone else, especially if that someone else doesn't particularly want it to exist for them." She watched him for a moment as he considered her. "Yes, there is a man named Vincent in here. And yes, I was talking to a ghost just now."

"But not Vincent," Vincent corrected.

"Right," Vienna agreed. "But not Vincent."

James raised his eyebrows, shifting in his seat.

"Think about it, James. Why would someone so close to the king care about me? It's because it's expected of him. If he didn't, he'd surely be imprisoned for treason. Do you not hear the authority in my voice from my upbringing? My name is Vienna of Highest Guard."

The soldier paled as the truth sank in.

"You're a knight, sworn to protect royalty and you take your position most sincerely. My life is in danger, sir. You can't let anyone know what I've told you. Will you help me?"

"Princess . . ." His voice took a different tone, that of a true knight.

"James . . . Please . . ."

"I will protect you."

"You can't tell the steward."

"He can help."

"No, and you know that. I know I've put you in a terrible situation. If you help me, you'll feel as though you're betraying White Minstrel, and if you fulfill your duty to White Minstrel, you'll be betraying me. But you didn't leave me with a choice."

"You misjudge the steward. He'll be loyal to the king."

"Not everyone is as noble as you are! Please, James!"

He rose to his feet. "I'll have to form a plan. I . . . I don't know what I'm going to do yet. But please be at ease; whatever I choose, I'll choose it because I believe it is best for you, to protect you and your royal title." He left the prison.

Vienna's heart fell. "He's going to tell the steward."

Cole got to his feet. "What do we do?"

Seamus pointed to him. "You aren't going to do anything. Bye, Bye."

"Wait —" He started to fade away. "I can help!"

"Vienna . . . ?" Vincent awaited orders.

But she hardly knew what to say.

CHAPTER TWENTY-ONE
The Steward

A day past and no one came for her. No one threatened to drag her out of the dungeon by her hair or offered to send her back to her father in pieces if she didn't consent to the will of malcontents. It seemed that James was true to his word. He was taking time to think things over, giving the three jailbirds the opportunity to converse and bicker about their best course of action. However, not one of them formed an acceptable plan of escape.

And then, at ten minutes past midnight, while our princess dreamed of flying out the window and listened to the ghost of a sniper speak about a girl from the Bronx, the steward did come. The jolt of the lock and the forceful swing of the door sent all the ghosts to their feet. But Vienna continued to watch the city sleep, ashamed that she was still here, that she hadn't yet won her salvation.

Two guards stood beside the lanky man as he leered at our princess, trying to imagine her through the misery. He attempted to imagine her with flowing lace and styled hair. "Yes," he finally declared. "It is you, isn't it, Princess Vienna?" When she said nothing, he gestured to the door. "Leave us," he commanded the guards.

"Who's this punk?" the sniper asked, pausing his story, but Vienna didn't look up.

"I can't imagine why you'd keep yourself hidden and locked away when we are all the most *loyal* of subjects," the steward began, his long legs gliding him closer to her cage.

"You weren't kidding," Seamus agreed. "He is a punk."

"We'll treat you fairly, of course." He smoothed his fingers over his antenna-like eyebrows, peering at her with his bug-like eyes. It was as if he had many eyes to see her with. "There's no reason why you should remain in the dungeon. I'm going to have you moved to my private chambers, for your own safety of course."

Vincent walked to the bars and stood before the steward, ready to throw the first punch.

"You're dead, remember?" Seamus informed him.

"Just what is *he* implying?" Vincent asked, outraged.

"I think you'll be happy in White Minstrel," the steward told her, believing they were completely alone.

Vienna had to hand it to him. This wasn't what she had expected. It seemed his ambition was far greater than she had anticipated. "Forget about taking the throne through me." Vienna shifted her sights onto the menacing villain before her. "I will not marry you."

"But who will have you?" The steward ran his hand over the bars, flirtatiously. "Once you have been defiled by me? Who will have you if it should be that you conceive my child? Wouldn't your father be overjoyed if I should write him a letter saying you've found happiness in White Minstrel?"

"He'll never believe it," Vienna warned him.

"I wish I had my gun!" the sniper raged through clenched teeth.

"Even if I have a magic-man forge your handwriting?" He waited to see if Vienna would flinch. She didn't, and he pressed on. "You should rejoice, *princess*. I have every intention of being most gracious." He turned to the prison door. "Guards!"

Seamus and the sniper jumped to their feet, standing with Vincent, their fists at the ready. Vienna gripped the bars on her window desperately, and, in her desperation, something caught her attention. In the darkness, a figure stood, looking up at the palace. His fearless green eyes had the intensity of knives. At first, Vienna thought he was somebody else. But when he took a step forward, and the night released his lovely form, her heart wanted to soar out of her chest.

It was Bloom.

The guards threw open her cell door. Her three friends fought bravely, attacking the intruders with everything they had, and if they had been human, they would have been the heroes of her heart.

But the guards moved forward, trying to get Vienna to walk on her own. When her shaky voice cried out a name, they swatted her hands, wrenching her from the window's bars.

"Bloom!" she screamed before a guard threw her over his shoulder and carried her out of the dungeon.

They locked the door behind them.

"Unhand me at once, swine. I'm perfectly capable of walking without the assistance of an invalid!" She let her voice rage with all her fury. The

226

steward confirmed her order, telling the guard to set her on her feet. Vienna brushed herself off and glared at them all as her three ghost friends circled her, trying to create a shield.

"By all means, princess." The steward bid them forward, insisting that they proceed. "In fact, it would be fortunate for you to be willing on all accounts."

They led her through the palace, making their way to the top floor and to the steward's chambers. Suits of armor and dashing paintings and portraits lined the walls. There were tables with flowers and trinkets, placed along the black-carpeted floor. The walls were adorned with expensive carpeted designs: strings of gold and red thread depicting stories of dragons, kings, queens and destruction. It was all very Gothic and cold. There were statues of demon-faced creatures and winged monsters, followed by memorabilia of the Minstrel, dancing a wicked, black-spelled dance while playing his fiddle.

It occurred to her that she was very selfish. She couldn't expect Bloom to come rushing in here to save her. He was a lowly fisherman and would be against dozens and dozens of professional soldiers. It wouldn't do anyone any good if he died today because she'd been too much of a princess to save herself. She wasn't planning on waiting for anyone. She'd take the first opportunity that presented itself, even if that meant jumping out of a window.

The guards led her into the middle of a well-furnished and well-designed room. The Victorian style was something she was accustomed to. The steward walked to his bedside table, where he removed his leather gloves. "Leave us," he insisted, and then locked the door.

Vienna ran to the window, flung it open and then paused. It was a ludicrously long way down. The fall would surely kill her. Was this really a choice between life and death?

The steward chuckled and clapped his hands while Vienna stuck her head out the window, trying to see if she could climb down. He walked toward her, handing her a white dress with a clutter of blue roses embroidered down the side. "Why don't you go into the bath and then put this on?" he offered, and Vienna crawled back into the room away from the window. She pushed her hair behind her ears. She was wondering whether there was a window in the bathroom, or a trap door in here somewhere. All crooked men had trapdoors, didn't they?

She took the dress and shut the door to the bath, locking it from the inside. Vincent and Seamus had followed her, along with their sniper friend.

"What do we do?" Vincent whispered, although there was no risk of anyone overhearing him.

Vienna shook her head, trying to come up with something – anything.

"What are you still doing here?" Seamus asked the sniper.

"What do you mean?" He was outraged at the thought. "I want to help!"

"Everyone wants to *help*." Seamus growled. "If Vincent and I are forced to be useless, then we'll be useless without your help. Goodbye." And, cursing, the sniper faded away at Seamus's order. He turned to Vienna. "Anyone thought up anything yet?"

"You've got quite a lot of authority over the dead, don't you?" Vienna whispered. She was impressed that whenever he told someone to get lost, they did.

"He should," Vincent mumbled. "He's an officer."

"You were an officer?"

"No," Seamus corrected her. "I was a nobleman. Now I'm an officer."

"You became an officer after you died?"

"Yeah."

She wasn't even going to try to figure that one out. Besides, she had much more pressing concerns at present.

The bathroom was elegant and welcoming despite belonging to a villain. Someone had already drawn her a bath and it was still steaming. Sighing, she said, "I'm going to bathe, change into that dress, and –"

Seamus was shaking his head, his face reddening with fury. "You're not going to –"

"No, I most certainly am not going to do anything of *that* sort." Vienna looked down at her hands, wondering if Bloom was really here somewhere or if her desire to see him again had caused her to imagine him. "But my bathing will buy us some time, and one of you had better find the answer before I'm finished. Now go out there and keep an eye on him. I'm going to get undressed now and your eyes are unworthy to witness me in such a state."

Vincent lingered, before asking gently, "What if the worst happens?"

Vienna suppressed her fear and looked into the mirror on the wall. There wasn't a window, just a mirror. Her reflection was that of a girl she'd never seen before. "Then your eyes will be unfit to see me in such a state, and I'd appreciate it if you made yourself scarce." She turned her back on them, waited five seconds, and then turned around.

They were gone.

Only then did she begin to cry.

CHAPTER TWENTY-TWO
The Fight

The water was hot, and it made her frail body turn pink. Her long hair folded over her naked body as she sank to the bottom. She tried to decide what options she had left. Ultimately, she realized that she had to ready herself for the worst. She was not planning on losing without a fight, and she remembered seeing a letter opener on one of the tables near the bed. If she could get to it without being caught, she might be able to wound the steward and make an attempt to flee from the palace.

Maybe Bloom was outside, waiting for her . . .

And, unless Vincent and Seamus had come up with something better, that was all she had. Leaving a blackened pool behind her, she dried herself off and slid into the dress he had picked out for her. It fit perfectly. With her wet hair loose behind her back, she stood in front of the mirror, trying to encourage herself. She looked like a princess again.

She turned her nose up and placed one hand on the doorknob and one on the lock. Her heart was hammering against her chest, fluttering furiously. She promised herself that, no matter what happened tonight, she wouldn't cry.

Abruptly, she let herself back into the serpent's den.

The steward sat on a gold-colored chair with his legs crossed and watched her close the bathroom door behind her. His navy-blue hair was short and fell into his eyes as he stood. He began to stride toward her.

"Vienna," Vincent and Seamus said simultaneously.

The princess shook her head. There was nothing they could do. "Just leave," she commanded, and the two ghosts stared at each other, broken-hearted because they knew they were powerless.

"I'm afraid that's impossible while you stand, a vision, in that dress," the steward commented. He assumed that she was talking to him.

Vienna didn't turn her back on him as she slowly made her way to the bed and the table. Her hands searched for the letter opener and found it. She held it at the ready in front of her.

The steward smiled and held back his laughter. "There's no need for that." He came closer, so close that she could see his darkening soul. He was like a devil with his sinful expression, and Vienna fought the desire to hide herself with her hands.

It seemed like he watched her for an eternity before he launched himself forward. He was too close for her to stab him in the chest, but she raised her arm, preparing to send the knife into his back. He caught her hand, and then threw her onto the bed.

Vienna fought and kicked and struggled while he held her arms above her head. The knife fell to the floor. But he couldn't contain her, and she tried to crawl away. He dug his claws into her ankles and dragged her back to him. She kicked him in the face and he tumbled off the bed.

She threw herself at the knife.

The steward cursed and got to his feet.

And that's when something started growling.

Moving through the closed door, a massive, sandy brown wolf crept into the room, his eyes a horrifying gold. His teeth were set in a murderous response, and he snarled at the steward. Vienna took a step back and watched as the creature bared its fangs at her, snarling, to force her behind him. He slinked toward the steward, ready to kill him.

"You . . ." the steward whispered, watching the wolf in absolute terror.

"Thank god," Seamus whispered, watching the wolf in absolute relief. But the wolf unleashed a series of barks at Seamus and Vincent. He barked so wildly – like a rabid animal – that Vienna screamed and Seamus and Vincent were blasted away. And then the wolf leapt at the man. Blood already filled the wolf's set stare.

"Stop!" Vienna screamed, and the wolf paused, pinning the man underneath him. His teeth were at the man's eyes, promising death.

"He'll be punished," she told the wolf. "I promise you. I swear it. But I've met a hundred different souls, all filled with regret, and, if you kill him, surely you'll never be able to let it go. Come here, Hero, let's just run. Please," she begged her wolf, "let us run."

The wolf's growls rippled through his throat in one final warning before he jumped away from the man and landed at Vienna's side.

They turned their backs and started for the door.

The steward launched himself at them, but the wolf turned. His eyes were solid green emeralds as he stared at the coward of a man, and the steward fell to the floor with a gay smile on his face. After a moment, he got to his feet and declared: "You know, I think I'm going to give up politics and open a bakeshop." His joyous smile never left his face. "I do so love cookies! Don't you?" And he skipped out the door, humming to himself about his epic love for cookies. The steward turned down the hall while Hero cocked his head to the side, admiring his new found ambition.

Vienna looked down at Hero, but the wolf just yawned and walked through the hall. She rested her hand on his back, walking past shocked guards and whispering officials. In bewilderment, they asked each other whether pets were allowed within the palace walls.

Hero led her out of the palace and, stride for stride, they took off at a run. Vienna held her dress up at first, but then let it fall. Her thin legs wished for the freedom of her old trousers. The air was cold. It was cold enough for snow to start falling at any moment. Hero howled as he ran, and a hand grasped Vienna's as she dashed after him. Running beside her, he matched her stride for stride.

Bloom led her forward, following Hero back into the wild and the falling snow.

CHAPTER TWENTY-THREE
The Beginning of What Would End

In the early morning, triumphant and free, Vienna tumbled to the forest floor. Hero leaped around her, barking joyfully. But Bloom was furious and took hold of her shoulders.

"Are you insane?" he shouted, his voice booming against the silent trees. "I woke up, and you were gone! Do you have any idea how hard I've been searching for you?"

"Unhand me this instant!" she demanded and slapped his hands away before slapping him in the face. Their breath was visible on the winter air. "I wanted to bring you breakfast!"

"Breakfast?"

"Yes!" she screamed back at him.

"I told you I would take care of all that!"

"I wanted to do something nice for *you!*" she bellowed.

"Whenever you get a thought like that, think again!"

"You came for me!"

"Of course I did!"

"Thank you!"

"You're welcome!"

They sat, panting. Their faces were red from their passionate argument. His fear for her was evident in his features, and the heavy scent of honey that she'd come to expect whenever he spoke washed over her. As she gulped the air, she took in his shouted words. He was so close to her, and her heart was fluttering. She was relieved and excited to see him. He had come for her. Bloom and Hero had saved her life.

Snow danced in the air, and then fell all around them.

Bloom forced her against him, taking her into his arms before she could object. As he whispered her name in relief, she felt herself glowing. Even in the winter air, she felt his voice on her skin like full, radiant sunlight and it called her home in a way she had never been called before.

She found herself back in trousers and baggy boy clothing, for that was all Bloom had, taking her and Hero back to his log cabin. The fire roared against the chill of winter, and Vienna waited at the windowsill. A part of her wished that she was home and on a midnight ride, but her fragile heart was also glad she was here.

She hadn't seen Vincent or Seamus since she had left the palace, twelve days ago, and she decided that it had been Hero who had repelled the ghosts all along. It made sense, thinking about it now. It was when she met Hero that she stopped seeing ghosts, and it was when she left his side that they promptly came back.

But she missed Vincent and Seamus. She would have liked to have them here with her while she waited for Bloom to return. Hero was sprawled out on the living room floor by the fire. The house was a medley of oil paintings, well-crafted furniture, and honest comforts.

Vienna saw Bloom coming up the woodland path and rushed to the door to greet him. He carried a basket of freshly caught fish, which fell out of his hands when she threw her arms around him.

"Oh, no." He laughed, shrugging her off, and throwing the basket on the kitchen table. Luckily, the lid hadn't come off when it had dropped from his hands. "You only do that when you want something."

"I have to do something." There was a bowl of nuts in the middle of the table, and she pulled them toward her. She picked up the nutcracker and began shoving hazelnuts into her mouth as she watched Bloom's shoulders stiffen. She knew that he was happy. But she couldn't stay in the paradise that he had created for her forever. She had a home to get back to, and a kingdom that was looking for her.

As he cleaned the fish, his voice became agitated. He knew what she was going to say. "You need to get to Highest Guard."

"Yes."

He wrapped the fish in paper and placed them, one at a time, in the freezer. "We can't go through the station, not with only two travel-passes. How do you suppose we'll get there?" He cleaned the mess and set three fish aside, ready to be cooked for dinner. Setting the knife on the cutting board, he seemed to understand. "You want to find the warlock?"

"I told you." Vienna found herself pleading, although the thought of leaving here was a torturous one. The inside of the log cabin consisted of grey stone, hardwood, and accommodating fireplaces. This log cabin was of the greatest value to her. But so was home, her real home, Highest Guard. "The knight said a warlock transported into White Minstrel illegally. He's got to be here still. If we find him, he can take us to Highest Guard."

Bloom huffed and sighed. "Is that all?"

"I'm not saying it won't be difficult," Vienna whispered. By now, those in White Minstrel knew that the princess was wandering around. They knew that she had escaped from the prison and that she was somehow connected to the steward's sudden decision to quit his job and start a bakeshop. Traveling would be much more difficult than it had been.

"You want to find a warlock?"

"Is that a 'you're going to help me' or is that a 'you're going to be a jerk and not help me?' Huh?"

"And say we find this warlock? He's just supposed to help us, just like that?"

"Hello!" She motioned to herself. "I'm a princess!" Fiddling with the nutcracker, she added, "And if he happens to be the warlock who cursed me, we can have a good long argument about that too."

Bloom didn't say anything. He seemed unsure on how to proceed.

Vienna came up beside him, taking the three fish and tossing them into a pan to fry. "I know you wish we could stay like this forever . . ."

"You're going to burn that," Bloom told her as he lowered the heat to medium-low on the stove.

"What did I do now?" She laughed, watching him take the clutter of meat off the burner. He transferred it to a plate, and then let each one cook evenly at a time.

"What do you think you're doing?" He chuckled when she started throwing odds and ends into the pan.

"Cooking," she explained.

He picked out everything she had thrown in. Half of it wasn't edible.

"Remember what I told you? When you get thoughts like that, think again?" He took the spatula out of her hands.

"Hey!" She made a grab for it. "Give that back!"

"Not if you insist on frying the nutcracker." He lifted his arm as high as it could go, keeping the spatula away from her, and she jumped to retrieve it.

"That's not fair." She clutched onto his shirt, looking into his darling green eyes that seemed to belong to her now. Tears formed, but she tried to hide them. What would happen to them if they did get to Highest Guard together? He was from White Minstrel. Her father wouldn't approve. And if he did? She wasn't sure their time together warranted marriage. Either way, she didn't want to lose him.

He dropped the spatula, folded his arms around her, and breathed her in. "Yes," he whispered, closing his eyes, and trying to hide himself in her. "I do wish we could stay like this forever."

CHAPTER TWENTY-FOUR
The Shattered Trust

Basket in one hand and a fishing pole in the other, Bloom tipped his hat to her before he headed out the door to go ice fishing. Vienna beamed from the chair she'd commandeered. She had a quilt around her and an open book in her lap. Hero slept on the couch, too heavy to move and too long to make room for another creature.

She counted to twenty before she headed to the window and watched Bloom disappear. Carefully, so not to wake Hero, she swung the red velvet cape Bloom had bought her around her shoulders. She fastened her wooly scarf and mittens, and then headed out the door. Looking through the window, she made sure Hero was still asleep.

He was.

Bloom had agreed to go looking for the warlock, and they were scheduled to depart in three days' time. She knew that once they found the warlock (if they could find him) and were able to get to Highest Guard, things would change. It was important to enjoy the time they had together. So she was taking it upon herself to set him in a trap. She would follow him to the river, and then jump out and startle him, telling him how silly it was that he hadn't noticed her until then.

It was an excellent winter's morning, silent and glittering, with snow falling from the trees. The sky was opening up, signifying a vast day ahead. She had only to follow his footsteps in the snow. She crept in them, quickly and quietly moving along. She was keen to play her little prank.

Her cheeks succumbed to a winter's blush, but her boots were good boots and kept her feet snug as she sank into the drifts. She watched a white owl calling from high in a tree. It swooped down past her and flew away. She kept moving, catching glimpses of Bloom's distant figure.

Vienna continued more carefully until Bloom stopped and scanned the woods. It was as if he could sense that she was following him. She hid behind some bushes, hoping her plan hadn't failed wretchedly.

"Come out," he demanded. "I can feel your presence."

Honestly . . . But she was far too impressed by him to be very angry.

To her great surprise, a figure appeared, leaning against one of the trees.

"It's a dangerous game you're playing," Seamus said to Bloom.

Vienna covered her mouth with her hands. How was this possible? Bloom could see Seamus? And what the hell was Seamus doing here?

"You shouldn't be here," Bloom told the ghost, eyeing his surroundings. "It's too risky for me to have you coming and going as you please."

"I'm here because I'm worried about her," Seamus said.

"I have things relatively under control."

"You have things wrapped in lies."

"I love her."

"I know. That's why this has to end."

"I love her, and the more I'm with her, the more I want to be. The more time goes on, the harder it is to tell the truth. You think she'll forgive me, Seamus? I can't take that chance."

"So what now? You're going to find a warlock?"

"I was thinking of summoning Lifey here; pretending he's the one she's looking for and having him transport us back."

"Is Lifey capable of transporting anywhere?"

"No. I'll have to bring him here and then transport us all to Highest Guard. She won't know the difference."

"And what about when you get to Highest Guard? You going to be Bloom the fisherman for the rest of your life? *You?*"

Bloom blushed. "Why not?"

"You're spinning more lies."

"It's none of your business."

"Correction: it wasn't my business until I faced thick and thin with that girl. And now it's my only business, and I don't like the game you're playing."

"I'm not playing a game, and if you don't watch your tongue, I'll send it to a different dimension. Don't forget who commissioned you, who still holds you responsible for protecting her from the souls of men." Bloom's words were hard, but as he took Seamus's loyalty for her in, his expression softened. "I didn't have a choice. I rushed to White Minstrel as soon as the king told me what Emily had done. She would never have trusted me."

"My *job* is to protect her from the souls of men. That includes your soul."

238

"I didn't mean for things to go this far . . ." Bloom shook his head, looking away. "It's just so easy, wanting to be with her . . ." Speaking to the ground, Bloom said, "I can't lose her, Seamus."

"*Bloom* can say that. *You* can't. *Bloom* has earned her trust. *You* haven't."

"That's enough, Seamus. Hurry up and go before I make you."

Seamus disappeared.

She let her footsteps mark the silence with strings of sounds as she came to stand behind him. He slowly turned around, his expression falling.

She stared at him like he was a monster, a creature, and the fraud that he was. Her voice was poison on the air, scornful, and ugly. Her heart shattered with his betrayal.

"Who are you?" she whispered.

CHAPTER TWENTY-FIVE
The Betrayal

In the cold winter's morning, the wind bit into them. They hadn't noticed it until now, how cold everything was. But now that they stood, living this nightmare, it was freezing as their hearts began to crack and splinter, unable to tolerate the cold. "Please," Bloom whispered in a frenzied chant, begging because he couldn't believe things had come to this. "Please, Vienna."

"Don't come near me!" she shrieked although he hadn't moved.

"I won't. I promise I won't. Please, Vienna . . ." Bloom's gaze was reaching out to her, begging her, but she was too wrapped in confusion and his treachery to understand his reaching.

"Who are you? How can you see Seamus?" She started shaking. All she wanted to do was call out his name. She knew Bloom. He was honey and sunlight, and she knew his eyes so well now that it was like they belonged to her. She had thought to own those eyes forever.

She heard footsteps behind her, and her sandy brown wolf walked up to meet her and then headed for Bloom.

"No, Hero!" Vienna gripped into his fur. "We have to run! We have to go!"

"Vienna . . ." Bloom whispered.

"Stay where you are!" she ordered, and his hands reached forward, begging for an easy explanation for all of this. Hero tried to move forward, but Vienna threw her arms around him. "Hero, stay back! He's not who he says he is!"

Before her eyes and those of the wolf, Bloom began to change. His wounded expression remained on his face, showing on the outside the distress he was feeling on the inside.

Bloom's height changed first, and then his age followed. He'd only been a few inches taller than her before, and of the same age. But now his features were becoming more dominant, more mature, and more dragon-like. His hair and eyes darkened. His lips became fuller. His character became more interesting and handsome. He was less boyish, as if Bloom was introducing his remarkable cousin, instead of his true form.

"I'm still Bloom," he assured her as his appearance changed. "Everything he was is real. I'm still Bloom." He closed his eyes, haunted by her reaction. "Please, Vienna . . ."

"Augustus . . ." Vienna stepped back, horrified. "Run, Hero!" she screamed, ready to run and never stop running. "We have to run!"

But Hero stepped forward as the warlock reached his arms out to him. The warlock's fingers were moving in the open air. His fingernails were missing. Hero walked with quickened steps. Vienna was paralyzed with fear as Hero leapt forward. Within the air he grew more and more transparent, until his foggy form reached Augustus's hand, forming a long, clear rod that the warlock now held. Augustus took a step forward. The rod disappeared, weaving into him effortlessly. His fingernails grew back and the swirls of his eyes returned to their true state.

"Hero?" Vienna choked. All this time . . . Everything . . . The beings she'd come to care about . . . It had all been a lie. All of it. Bloom was Augustus. Hero was Augustus. "Oh my god."

"Your father sent my mother a message, telling her what Emily had done, and I came straight away. But I knew you'd never accept my help. Not if I looked like this," Augustus explained. He walked toward her, and the princess took a step back for every step he took. "Please, Vienna."

"You have no right to call me by my name," Vienna hissed. Her back hit a tree, reminding her of the first time she met Hero, when he saved her from the bear attack. She wasn't sure how she should act. A part of her wanted to run away, and never stop, not ever. A part of her wanted to cry, and another wanted to scream. But, instead, she acted like the princess she was, strong and forceful. "You may address me as the Princess of Highest Guard. And I demand that you take me back to my kingdom!"

"Vienna . . ."

"You are not Bloom," she whispered, making sure to send her words at him like knives. "You have no right to speak to me."

Augustus bowed his head, looking like he was either going to cry or be sick. "Of course, Your Majesty."

"I demand that you take me back to Highest Guard."

"That's all I've wanted to do. I just wanted to protect you."

"You want to protect me?" Vienna spat on the ground. "Then take back the curse!"

He shied away. "I can't do that."

"Why not?"

He couldn't meet her eyes. It seemed as though he would lose his balance and fall to the ground. "Because it's the only thing still connecting me to you."

"Do you have any idea what you've put me through?"

"Yes," he whispered. His being was clearly full of regret. "That's why I sent Vincent and Seamus to aid you."

Vienna held her breath and let it out sharply. "And Vincent?" Both of them were working for Augustus. "You can see them?"

"I can see even the ones you can't," the warlock admitted.

Her hands dug into her chest. Her heart was burning as if it were trying to claw its way out of her, as if her body was no longer a safe place and it needed to flee. "Why did you do this to me?"

"I wanted you to see me, to know me," he said, his words summoned into one perceptive hope and what he honestly saw. "And you fell in love."

"No." She stood amazed – mesmerized – by her own suffering. "You've stolen everything from me," she answered frankly. Torturing them both, she asked, "How could I ever love you?"

Within his storm of endless agony, breathing in this conscious pain, tasting his regrets as she tasted hers, he lifted his arm. His fingers moved as if he were pushing the numbers on a telephone, calling the correct number, opening the air, and waiting for the spell to respond. The woods began to fade, and Vienna felt like she was falling back. The last thing she saw were the tears in his eyes, before she found herself in her room, inside the Palace of Highest Guard.

CHAPTER TWENTY-SIX
The Return of the Princess

In the safety of her bedroom, Vienna fell to her knees. Her whole body – her entire being – had felt an eruption, the gargantuan eruption of emotion. Now, stripped from everything, she found herself quite empty.

For that single moment, her sworn emptiness came as a relief. It was a relief to have felt so much, and then not to feel anything at all.

Her chambers filled her mind with comfort and old, treasured memories, and they helped to lift her to her feet. She looked into her vanity mirror. She still wore the red cape and wooly scarf and mittens that Bloom had bought her. She removed them now, tucking them away in a bottom drawer. The winter's gown she let drop to the floor was something given by Bloom as well, and she quickly bunched it up, put it in a box, and stuffed it in the back of her wardrobe.

Changing into one of her own gowns, she sat on her vanity chair and began brushing her hair. Her room smelt like her, and there was so much enjoyment in being able to smell like herself again.

Standing up, her heavy yellow dress made ruffles around her feet. Vienna made her way through the palace, and toward the dining hall. She could hear voices, and she paused at the door to listen.

"His cardinal comes every morning." Hour paced the hall. "What's keeping it?"

"Patience, Hour," King Gladness said with effort, and Vienna let the eruption of emotion once again rush over her. She hadn't seen her father in so long. He looked weary, having suffered many sleepless nights. Two guards stood at the wall, and one adviser paced the floor. "His letter won't differ much from yesterday's letter. She's safe."

Hour halted. "How can you remain so calm, Majesty?"

"I can't." King Gladness swirled the untouched eggs on his breakfast plate. "This is just a front. In reality, my insides are wrestling, tearing themselves apart."

Hour blushed, pushing back his silver hair. "Forgive me, Majesty."

"You're a son of Highest Guard. Your reaction is only to be expected." He pushed away his plate, picked up his goblet of coffee, wrinkled his nose at it, and set it back down. "In the meantime, we need to prepare the elections for the new steward of White Minstrel."

With one more peek out the window, Hour asked, "Did you get the cookies he sent you?" He took a seat at the table and began spreading out papers for the king to inspect.

"Yes, remarkable," King Gladness commented.

"May I make a suggestion?" Vienna entered the room and both men rose to their feet, admiring her as if she were an apparition. "Appoint Sir James Spear as steward. It's true. I made at least one worthy friend in White Minstrel."

Hour was at a loss for words, but her father took his first easy breaths since she'd left his side. "Is he loyal?" the king asked.

"So loyal he should be living in Highest Guard," Vienna declared. "He did everything in his power for me without going against the steward. He's the kind of man we want sitting at the head table, managing our country while we manage it from afar. We'd be lucky if we had two more of him, one in Blood Port and one in Iron Hand. What a thought! Jobs would actually get done!"

The king took in his daughter. He found that his legs still knew how to walk, and took her up in his arms, lifting her, giving the impression that she had angel wings. She soared in the soft, feathered clouds of happiness.

"You've aged . . ." She examined her father's face. He seemed to have more wrinkles, and bags hung under his eyes. His sleeplessness made him look as if he were wearing black eyeshadow.

But the king didn't mind now.

"Signal the trumpets," King Gladness ordered to his men. "Princess Vienna of Highest Guard has returned!"

A celebration ball was being prepared to signify her homecoming. The grand affair was to take place in three days' time. She was looking forward to it as she walked to the stable, a groveling Vincent at her heels.

She paused at the stable's entrance, giving Vincent a hard look. He held his pen and appointment book in his hands. Even now, he was convinced that she was the best 'ghost therapist' to ever walk the earth. "I'm still not speaking to you," she told him. "Stay here. Your presence upsets the horses, almost as much as it upsets me these days."

In truth, she'd long forgiven him for being connected to Augustus. But, in truth, she wasn't above making him suffer for it.

He nodded, holding up the appointment book.

"Yes, yes," she assured him. "I promise, after I ride. But the dead are dead, you know? The living still need a moment to live."

Vienna stalked away from him, listening to the familiar sound of her boots on the stone floor of the stable. She delighted in the familiar smell and the jolt of her heart, begging, as the horses were begging, to go galloping.

It was a busy place today, and ladies in riding clothes walked by her. They giggled to themselves for flirting scandalously with one of the stable boys after their ride. They noticed Vienna and curtsied honorably, but they could not fool the princess. They were scandal-girls, and she was obliged to smile after them.

Poem was brushing a bay mare in her stall and didn't notice her until she let herself in and began stroking the creature's neck, cooing sweetly. Poem blushed and looked away. He turned back for another enchanted glance at his princess.

Swaying closer to him, her dress swinging back and forth like a bell chiming, she brought a caramel heart to her lips and then offered it to him. He took it gladly and knew what to do. He shifted the bridle he was carrying off his shoulder, and bridled the horse, tossing the reins over its head. He came around the side where Vienna was waiting, holding the reins. She offered him her leg, and he hoisted her up. He kept hold of her until he took the chance and kissed her knee. The folds of fabric kept his lips from her flesh. And then he opened the stall door.

"That's a good lad, Poem," Vienna whispered and pushed the horse forward with her legs. They walked out of the stable, listening to the 'click' of the mare's shoes on the hard stone. The winter air called to them both and they breathed in. Vienna looked down at her gloved hands as she breathed out. The beast responded to the beast of Vienna's burning soul, and they galloped, bareback, across the palace grounds.

CHAPTER TWENTY-SEVEN
The Ghost Therapist

They decided that it would be best to have their session in the dining hall. Vincent had his notebook and pen, and Vienna had hers. She scribbled away as she listened to a retired car salesman tell her about his first kiss, performed in the back of a pink limo.

"Man —" the car salesman thought back. "I was so into him. I always felt like I was the woman in the relationship, but you said you can only see 'weepy' (thanks for that) gentlemen, so I guess that makes me the pants instead of the skirt . . . Awesome. I was a little insecure back then."

"Do you feel better now that you've talked about it?" Vienna asked, taking a moment away from her scribbling to observe their guest.

"Yeah." He stretched his arms above his head. "I feel great!"

"Good." Vienna went back to her scribbling. "Try not to spread the word. I'm swamped as it is."

He saluted her and said, "You got it," before he disappeared.

Vincent made a grab for her notebook, but she pulled it out of his dead hands. "Where's Seamus? He must be avoiding me." She hadn't seen him since his argument with Bloom in the wood.

Vincent sat back, examining her. "You haven't seen him? Oh my, princess, you're smarter than that. If Seamus isn't with us, where would he be?"

"Hmm . . ." She sighed, pressing her notebook against herself. "How many more troubled ghosts do you have planned for the day, Vincent?"

He looked down at the list and counted. "Just three more. Then, I've scheduled time for you to read or ride, whichever you feel up to."

"Really?"

"A living girl still needs a moment to live. Isn't that right, princess?"

"I'm glad you've realized that." She strolled over to the window, stretching her legs. Her mind flashed back to her time in the dungeon, holding onto the window's bars, and screaming Bloom's name. What if he hadn't come for her? She promptly sat back down and looked at Vincent expectantly. "Next."

"What are you hiding from me?"

"Excuse me?"

"That book in your hands, or are you that bored with the dead?"

Vienna passed it to him, and he gazed over the drawing with admirable interest. "It's just a rough." Vienna wiped her hands on her dress, drying her palms. She was actually nervous to discover what Vincent thought of it.

"You're going to make an office." He traced the sketches with his fingertips. The page remained unmarked by his ghostly hands. "You've given yourself a title. Something important too."

"Why do you say that?"

"Because all important titles have the word 'the' before them." He handed her back the notebook. "I think it's superb."

"I'd like to get started on it right away," she admitted. Now that Vincent was fully in charge of her time, he'd somehow made time for everything. She remained active in her studies and realm affairs, had time for reading, and rode constantly. The brilliant thing was, she wasn't tired and that was without a single drop of coffee. "We need a place to work, don't you think?"

"Since you seem to be stuck with this, yes, I suppose."

Vienna hadn't meant it like that. For some time now she hadn't considered her curse to be much of a curse. Not with Vincent, and not when she had Hero and Bloom . . . "How about you call the next ghost in?"

Since I am The Ghost Therapist.

Vincent nodded, looking down at the list, and reading: "Scott Summons."

They spent the rest of the afternoon learning to square dance with an old-time cowboy after listening to him talk about his days working the plains with his wife, Jane. The next man told the princess how to properly dry herbs and prepare spices, having owned a shop with his girlfriend. And the last man cried at first, but then began to recite quotes from his favorite television shows. Then, at last, Vincent informed her that she had three free hours before dinner. She tried to read, but all the stories she loved, and all the heroes she'd opened herself up to, now reminded her of Bloom.

She put down the books and found Vincent. She informed him that, if he was up for it, they could call in the next tortured soul.

247

CHAPTER TWENTY-EIGHT
The Story of Seamus

Vienna closed the book, rested her hand on the cover, and took in the moment when night becomes morning. In the candlelight, the vibrant colors of her room seemed washed-out and the detailed designs became faded, darkened aspects in the romantic Victorian style setting, attracting a mischievous feeling.

Her gown for the ball was hanging by her mirror. Her father bought it and presented it to her. It was an elegant piece, with lace, ruffles, and flowing sleeves. It had a corset top and it flared at the bottom. She would wear it with fake fairy wings, designed and fitted to complement her without overpowering the ensemble.

The creation was very different from the clothes she was wearing right now. She walked to the mirror in her white pajamas, which were imprinted with red apples. Her hair was loose and messy. Staring at herself now, her blue eyes were black in the darkness.

Vienna leaned over to the dresser beside her vanity and pulled open the bottom drawer. She took out the mittens and scarf she'd been hiding from herself. She slid the mittens on, bringing her hands to her face and breathing in.

But they didn't carry the scent of honey.

Wearing them didn't give the impression of sunlight.

She'd never be able to fall asleep like this – with her mind amok with distressing thoughts. She folded up the scarf and placed it back in the drawer. Leaving the mittens on, she fetched her fur-lined, long trained, blue winter coat and matching hat, and hurried through the palace and out the door.

The palace never slept, but that wasn't what it seemed to be doing this morning. The servants had finished up and wouldn't be ready for the new day for some hours. And the ladies and gentlemen, staff, and stable hands were nowhere to be found.

Princess Vienna wandered the snow-covered path, observing the quiet trees, the enduring gateways, and the birdbaths that appeared to be wishing for spring. Everything was bathed in the blue light of winter as the moon whispered down, still owning the sky. Vienna walked about the gardens, along the same road she had strolled along with Poem one fine day. She headed for the same swings that she had been heading for then.

Sure enough, a man had commandeered one. His head was turned down and his face was turned away. He sat where roses would bloom once they tasted spring.

"Seamus." Vienna sat down on the swing beside him, swaying slightly in the cool air. Vincent had told her once before that if she wasn't sure where Seamus was, she should look for him in a garden. He'd be the one by the roses. "This is where I first saw you," Vienna continued. "Did you know who I was then? Had the warlock already chosen you to aid me through the curse?"

"I didn't expect anyone to find me here that day. I was going to come barging into your life when those other blokes did, when you actually needed me." Seamus raised his head. He stared up into the maze of tree branches above him. "I've known Augustus for a long time. He's a good guy. Just stupid in love."

"I've met a lot of interesting people lately," Vienna said, changing the subject and snuggling into her winter coat, "while you've been hiding out in the garden." When he didn't respond, Vienna asked, "What was her name?"

"Eleanora."

Did he want to talk about this? Vienna wasn't sure, except that they seemed to need to. "What were you when you were alive?"

"A nobleman."

"I mean, what was your profession?"

"What every nobleman's profession is: being a nobleman."

"Was she a great lady?"

"She was a very poor one. Not suited for a gentleman like me."

It was difficult to imagine that Vincent and Seamus were similar (if not exactly the same) to the ghosts who booked her time. "And you haven't found her in death, have you?"

"She died a long time before I did. I don't expect to find her."

"You weren't married?"

"I never married."

"I don't understand. What happened to her?"

"A tyrant set a fire. I didn't make it in time to save her."

She was murdered . . . "You lived on. I'm proud of you," Vienna said, forgetting that he was a ghost and that she had no idea how he had died. "I can imagine your suffering. You're the strongest man I've ever met."

Seamus shook his head. "I died in an opium den."

Oh . . . She nodded, understanding. "You were destroyed."

"Not all of us are lucky enough to have a life like yours."

"You mean a cursed life?"

"You just listened to *my* story," Seamus said, scornfully. "Now tell me *your* life is cursed."

She turned away.

"The man you loved made it in time. There are women out there who never received that luxury."

"I'm sorry."

"Sometimes I look at you and wonder . . ." Seamus held her gaze. "My life would have been different if I had a father like yours."

His father was the tyrant? His father killed the woman he loved? "It's not fair what happened to you, Seamus. It's not fair that two good people had to suffer so, when they didn't do anything wrong. You're blaming yourself. I can imagine you are. But I hope – no, I know – that when you find her, and I know you will, she'll tell you the same thing I'm telling you now. That knowing you has been worth all the pain."

"Vienna?"

She was waiting for him to start crying. "What?"

"Where's your mother?"

No one else had asked. No one else had thought it mattered. Shocked, Vienna replied, "I'm not accustomed to speaking about myself to ghosts."

"But you always do, when you speak to me. It's hidden in the words you use to try to bring me comfort. She must have hurt you terribly. So why do you sit and read in the one room where her portraits still hang?"

"I can't say I know what you're talking about."

"When you were in White Minstrel, I stayed behind with your father for a while, waiting to see if anyone had gotten news of you. He wrote to the Dragon Witch, knowing she'd tell Augustus and he'd rush off to find you. In those days, do you know what I saw?"

"What?"

"Letters. Letters carried in by your mother's blue jay, asking her ex-husband to send her more money. And do you know what your father did?"

"Yes. You don't have to say it out loud."

"I believe I do. He still loves her enough that he sent it to her."

Vienna got to her feet, walking behind the tree so that she wouldn't have to look at Seamus. "If my father were a ghost, I'd be able to see him, and he'd tell me tales about a woman he loved. A woman who married him for money, had a child, stole millions from the kingdom, and then ran off to Blood Port. Sending divorce papers so that she could marry the steward there, she bore my half-brother, and moved on to the next gentleman, leaving both her daughter and her son behind to be raised by the men who truly did love her."

"Are you afraid you'll be like your mother?"

"I'm not my mother. I couldn't make her mistakes. I'm not my father either, so I can't make his." She wrapped her arms around herself. "I'm surprised you've never heard this tale. The story is historic. She's known as 'Queen Lustless, the Green Queen.' It's a play on words, signifying her greed and selfishness."

"But now you're afraid to fall in love."

"And you? Could you fall in love again?"

"I don't consider loving her my mistake."

"Neither does my father. And that's his mistake."

Seamus appeared in front of her, his hand slamming on the tree's bark beside her. He leaned in so that she could feel the full force of his words. He was dead, but his actions still made her jump. He was dead, but his words still dug into her.

"You're Princess Vienna of Highest Guard," Seamus said, "and you're a very frightened little girl, pretending to be strong, telling yourself to grow up because she's not coming back. You're telling me how the events of your life haven't shaped you, that you're not an inch like your mother, and that you're not an inch like your father. But you can't fight away the pieces of your life. Just like I couldn't fight away the pieces I bear of my father. It's how you overcome those pieces, Vienna. It's how you rise above, not how you endure. You see your father's pain, and you hide from it and from your own pain. It's the same as dying in an opium den. One day you're going to overdose."

251

"I don't understand a word you're saying. But, if you're arguing her case, may I remind you that she abandoned me."

"I'm not arguing for her. I'm arguing for *you*. If someone had thrown it in my face – if someone had warned me that she was a ghost, watching me kill myself, finally leaving my side because she'd seen that I wasn't the man she had thought I was because I wasn't strong and she had seen enough – then perhaps I wouldn't have betrayed her eyes. I wouldn't have made her watch my suffering."

He thinks he can't find her in death because her ghost watched him die in an opium den? "You have an extensive imagination."

"I'm a ghost. Watching you kill yourself. Watching you suffer. And if you don't stop, you're going to die. And, one day, someone will be able to see you as a ghost, and they'll flinch as you cry all over them, trying to tell them about the life you should have lived, and the pain you should have let go."

"You're advocating for *him,* aren't you? You've got a secret agenda!"

"I'm not sworn to protect him. I'm sworn to protect you from the souls of men, and from yourself, for you're more *man* than many. That means you're much more stubborn and hard-hearted, and more capable of letting things pass by, that should never have been passed by."

"I knew it. You *are* advocating for him."

"I want you to tell me, to my face, that you're not your mother's mistakes, or your father's, and mean it this time."

"I already told you that."

"You're Princess Vienna of Highest Guard. You've got a few issues, and you can see ghosts, and you've made your own mistakes. But you're alive, and you'd rather not end up a weepy ghost. You'd be more suited being the kind of ghost that mocks my kind from afar, instead of crying, sitting on a swing, in the garden beside me."

"What do you want me to do? Cry on your shoulder?"

"That's what shoulders are for, and you've spent all this time shouldering the dead. Isn't it about time it shouldered you?"

"I had no intention of letting anyone shoulder me. I have perfectly fine shoulders that are perfectly able to shoulder themselves."

"Had?" Seamus said with care. "Do you know how old you look right now? Twenty to thirty years older. You keep holding on to something like that's all there is in life, and you've never stopped crying about it. You shouldn't make yourself about one thing, Vienna. There's a whole world waiting for you out there. Instead of forcing yourself away, you should make the choice on your own terms, and decide who you want to share that world with. Because you're a marvelous young woman, and knowing you has been worth the pain, even though there has been quite a lot of it."

"You're advocating for him, aren't you?"

"No. I know you'd never listen. But if you would, I would advocate for him."

CHAPTER TWENTY-NINE
The Story of Her Mother and Poison

The day of the ball came, and three ladies hurried around Vienna, dressing her, doing her hair, and lathering her in jewels and make-up. A poet recited his verses to keep them entertained, coming in only when the princess was presentable enough to be seen.

Her gown fell in layers around her, her little frame crushed by the corset top. The gold fabric flared out and flowed with her every movement as she sat down. The ladies put her hair up, letting pieces fall down her neck and turning them into snug, little curls. As they fastened on her wings, a knock came at the door. Her father entered the room. He looked dashing in his fitted tuxedo. He wore a chain with a large, gold rose that rested on his slender stomach.

"What do you think?" her father gripped the bottom of his jacket. Nervous and awkward, he moved his feet in a circle so that she could see all of him. "Do I look stupid?"

Vienna got to her feet, much to the annoyance of the maids, annoyed that she'd refused, as always, to wear heavy diamonds. She considered her father's dress. "I think you look rather splendid."

"Really?" He lit up, looking down at himself with new eyes.

"And me?" Vienna twirled, her movements flowing like the fairy princess her wings made her out to be.

"You always look splendid." Her father told her and kissed her forehead. "And today, particularly splendid."

Vienna took her seat in front of the mirror so that the maids could finish their work and her father sent the poet out.

"There's still time . . ." Her father took it upon himself to suggest. "I can send out last minute invitations, you know?"

The maids tried to hide their curiosity, but their eager ears turned pink with their keenness. Vienna pierced her lips. Had she been imagining what it might be like to have Bloom waiting for her on the dance floor? What it might be like to have Hero sitting at her feet, wearing a black bow tie?

Hardly, she thought, setting her jaw. "Seamus told me you heard from mother. Where is she this week?"

Her father waved his hand, and the maids hurried out of the room. He picked up where the maids had left off, attaching glittery objects to her dress. "Seamus told you? He's been keeping his eyes on me, has he?"

Vienna studied his reactions in the mirror. "He told me you sent her money. Again."

"Well, she's found herself in a bad way," he admitted. "She's in Iron Hand at the moment."

Vienna looked away. *And she conveniently doesn't send me her regards.* "You should let her flounder, father. She'll never see to her errors if you're always throwing money at them."

The king twitched his nose. "We all have an assortment of human traits." He kept an honest, even tone. "It wouldn't be love if we didn't love them all."

"That love cripples you, father."

He stepped away from fixing her dress and gave the subject the seriousness it required. "I suppose a part of me shall love her forever. But that doesn't mean there isn't room left in me to love again. We are all capable of moving on from the trials of our lives. That's the blessing of time. But if you think I send her money because I'm crippled by her and will never get past my love for her, you have wrongly underestimated my character. I'm not one of your weepy ghosts.

"What I love about your mother is that she gave me you, making me the happiest man in the world. I have no regrets. Not one. Even the highest of blessings can come out of some trouble. And oh yes," he tapped the side of her nose, "the trouble is always worth it."

"I thought you'd been caught up, a fish in a net."

"It's all right to be caught up once in a while."

"Don't know what you mean, father."

"You have been caught, love," he informed her, draping a necklace around her neck. "By royal law and your own." He kissed the top of her head as her fingers moved to touch the wooden heart. He studied her reaction in the mirror.

Keeping her fingers on the necklace, she said, "I thought I broke it."

"No. It's a hardy little heart."

255

She held it in her hand, opening the heart so that it was lying in her palm. A pearl shone up at her. *So the pearl had survived, too, had it?*

"There's still time."

Vienna snapped the heart shut. "No. I have no interest in speaking to him again."

Vienna avoided clocks and paid no heed to the hour as she rushed to her office. It had taken a day, ten servants, and a truckload of new stuff to make the therapist's office acceptable to her taste, but in the end, it had developed rather nicely.

She walked into the well-lit room and sat down at the extraordinarily large desk. It was big enough to allow her and Vincent to sit behind it like trained professionals. They also had a couch in the room for Seamus to sleep on. Although, he hadn't used it yet. If he wasn't in the garden, he was cracking his knuckles from the back corner or threatening to send dead people out the window.

Yes, the windows opened mainly so that he could toss ghosts out.

Today, however, he'd chosen the garden.

"Sorry I'm late, Vincent," Vienna said. Picking up her pen, she scribbled, 'Is he horrid?' on a card. She was referring to the man who was waiting to sob.

Vincent shrugged.

Vienna continued, addressing the man in a business suit, "I have to go to my own coming home party in thirty minutes, but I'd rather be fashionably late, so you have forty minutes to tell me all about how you lived and died."

The businessman adjusted his suit. "I was poisoned at my office. It was in my scotch. By my wife."

"And you still love her?" Vienna raised her eyebrows.

"No, I never married her. She was eighteen. My assistant."

"But . . ." Vienna contemplated, and the pieces started to fall into place. He was married to a woman but loved another. His wife found out and poisoned him. "Well —" She smiled at Vincent, her heart racing at the thought of the scandal. "My job's finally gotten interesting." Turning back to the businessman, she said, "Tell me all about it!"

CHAPTER THIRTY
The Celebration

The guests arrived, and Vienna came forth into the magnificent, breathtaking splendor. All eyes were on her. She glided in her fairy wings and gold dress. Her dainty feet moved her through the ballroom. The mystic effect of her was increasingly captured as she crossed the floor that was a pool of green-colored fog, created by dry-ice and green floor lamps. Elegant green fabrics were draped across the ceiling, and hammocks of flowers hung off the sides. The sparkling white walls held portrait after portrait of her. Bare trees stood beside each portrait. They were clothed in little gold lights, being the only other lighting besides candlelight.

Waiters roamed around, carrying appetizers of caviar, lobster puffs, and smoked salmon, while gentlemen talked business around the beverage tables. They sipped apple cider, eggnog, wine, and guzzled beer. There were rows and rows of dessert tables with mountains of French macaroons. And as the ladies sat at their tables, artists wandered around, constructing caricatures to the great and joyous amusement of the guests.

Dinner came after long hours of celebrating, each table centered with a fountain of orange juice. It was a party for Vienna, and her favorite foods were those of the brunch category. They started with lobster crepes. Then came the main course, Eggs Benedict, and then followed by sweet soufflés. Three courses fit her perfectly, finishing with a fruit plate and a collection of custards.

There was a great deal more talking and drinking, and then the king stood in front of them all to make a speech. Throughout the evening, Vienna had felt unsettled. She kept looking for things that she hadn't realize she'd been looking for. She had expected certain people to show up when she had known that it wasn't fair of her to expect.

She knew she was being ridiculous. She couldn't honestly be angry with him for not being here, when she knew she'd have been angry with him if he were here.

The king seemed to realize that he didn't have her full attention. However, he commenced. "Children of Highest Guard, I thank you. Your devotion to your princess has been beyond expectations. Your love for her evident by your reactions to the mere rumors of her disappearance and in your true brotherly conduct when you discovered those rumors to be true. I was made aware that rallies were held in back-alleys and in town squares, and even teenagers on school property declared a marching sweep of the world, to find her. When rumors spread that she had been spotted in White Minstrel, my sons demanded war. As father to you all, I had to cradle the nation, but it was your devotion that won the appreciation of your king.

"Now, I can't be going on like this, being too serious, addressing a bunch of drunks eating Eggs Benedict. Not that I blame you. I wouldn't want to be listening to an old, blubbering man like me either, not while there's hollandaise still on my plate. And, seeing as there is still hollandaise on my plate, I'd better make this quick.

"There have been many questions and rumors about the return of the princess. One story claims she wrestled a sea monster and won, the creature carrying her atop its head as they crossed the ocean. I'd prefer that theory, if it weren't for the truth.

"A son of Highest Guard returned Princess Vienna to us.

"I send out my appreciation to the men and women of Highest Guard and their strong hearts for coming together with equal valor in all the trials that our country has had to face. With our pearl's return, our strong nation can continue, untainted.

"Since this is the princess's welcome home ball, I may not have been the first to welcome her home. But, I trust I am the first to stand in front of a crowd to say: welcome home. I declare today, like every day, my whole-hearted, fatherly love for her. And I would like to express my love, by stealing her first dance here this evening."

Vienna was sitting beside him at the long table in front of the crowd. The king took his daughter's hand, led her onto the dance floor, and started the dance.

Green fog swirled around their ankles. The ball would begin and end with the waltz. As her father led her, Vienna tossed her head about. She was searching for something, but she couldn't admit it to herself.

"He's not here, you know?" the king whispered. "Right or wrong, I tend to yield to your every wish."

Vienna snapped out of the world of daydreams, forced to focus on the dance and what her father was suggesting. "Who?"

"That man you love," the king answered.

"I may have held someone in high esteem, father, but it wasn't held for that warlock fellow."

The king thought for a moment, humming as he did so. "How can you be so sure?"

Her father was a superb dancer and a partner whom any woman, including his daughter, would be lucky to have. But on this occasion, Vienna wanted the dance to end. "Simply because I hold ownership over my own thoughts and mind. It's for me to know."

"I wonder about that, child. Are we really the owners of our thoughts when even thoughts can lie? Humans often find themselves skillful liars. Imagine how skillful we can become when lying to ourselves."

"What a scoundrel you are, calling your own daughter a liar."

"It's quite far from being gentlemanly, I admit, but not far from being fatherly." The king fixed her with a stare beyond the authority he'd use on a subject because his daughter was rather harder to handle and was accustomed to having the last words in an argument. But he had to admit that it would be quite some time before she defeated him in a quarrel.

She said nothing more, and the dance ended. They bowed to each other, and the band started up again, and the guests took wing now to the floor.

She tried to sneak away, but it was difficult. Many young gentlemen had their eyes on her, but by dodging around chairs, hiding under tables, and wandering among the shadows, she was able to make a wild, successful dash for the exit.

She wandered through the empty halls, listening to the music from the ballroom. The music was so loud that it sounded like the party was in the halls. She found herself in one of the drawing-rooms, where they'd received company on lesser occasions than this. There was a piano, instead of a full orchestra, and more comfortable furniture than the many tables and chairs that had been set up for tonight's guests. She expected to be alone in the darkened room, but Seamus stood at the window, hidden within the curtains.

"I was wondering about Vincent and yourself," Vienna informed him, coming to stand beside him. There were two servants walking a pack of husky dogs in the palace grounds. "Are you not going to welcome me at my own welcome home party?"

Seamus wasn't watching the royal dogs. He was admiring the stars. "We decided that one night without ghosts was probably the nicest gift you could receive tonight."

Vienna flushed. Vincent and Seamus weren't mere ghosts to her anymore. They were like family. "Why do the best of friends always seem to get things wrong?"

Seamus's eyes took her in, framed against the window's curtains. "Were we?"

"Nevertheless . . ." She glided to the middle of the room, curtsying low. "It seems I was kind enough to save you a dance."

Seamus thought that over. "You sure that's proper?"

"What do you mean?"

"You're a young, impressionable princess." Seamus smirked. "And I'm a ghost."

"Have you forgotten how?" Vienna mocked, and he crossed the floor toward her. She hadn't risen from her curtsy, and he came over, taking her hand as if he really could grasp it. He lifted her to her feet.

"I wonder . . ." he said and began to dance.

Vienna's hand kept threatening to fall through his shoulder, but it was easy to follow him. If he were alive, he'd likely be the best dancer at the ball. He began to hum a tune that Vienna had never heard before. When the song came to an end, he took the princess's hand and kissed it, and for a moment she thought she actually felt his lips on her hand.

"See," Vienna told him, "that wasn't so improper."

He stepped away, walking back to the window. "I'm sorry that I'm not him."

Vienna blushed. "Who?"

The stars sketched themselves in his eyes. "He's still Bloom, you know? The same man: just a different face."

The princess growled. "Do I look like I'm pining? Why do the best of friends always get things wrong?" She threw the question with force. If it had been a solid thing, it would have shattered the window. She stormed out of the room, and Seamus didn't call after her. Instead, he looked up at the stars, soaking them in with a curious expression on his face. He was distressed to see her in pain because he knew he wasn't wrong.

261

CHAPTER THIRTY-ONE
The Battle

She intended to go back to the party, but ended up in her bedroom. She was planning to go back, surely. It was *her* party, after all. And though everyone seemed to think she was a big, walking mess, haunted by a broken heart and the pieces of a broken heart, she would not give them the satisfaction of believing they were right. She'd dance and laugh and spin around in the eyes of men, thrashing their thoughts of her misery away.

But, in the meantime, she took a moment before tossing those thoughts away. She walked to her dresser and opened the bottom drawer. Standing before her mirror, she slipped them onto her dainty hands. They'd long-lost their smell of a life somewhere else. Now they smelt as though they lived in a bottom drawer, kept away: a lonely secret.

She admired herself in the vanity mirror, wearing the wooly mittens and the wooden heart that harbored a pearl.

She looked away, disgusted with herself.

"I didn't think we'd have our final meeting so soon." A woman walked out of the shadows, and Vienna watched her reflection emerge in the mirror. She was too stunned to turn around. "I'm glad you didn't keep me waiting long."

"Emily Tempest . . .?" Vienna blinked several times, wondering whether she was having a nightmare.

"That's 'Witch of the Falling Stars' to you." Emily hissed. Her calico cat jumped onto Vienna's bed, purring madly. Emily, whose hair was the same color as her cat's coat, was outlined in the moonlight.

"Are you serious with this?" Vienna asked, speaking to the mirror. She knew that yelling at the witch wasn't the wisest choice. But she couldn't help herself. "Are all witches this emotionally twisted? Isn't there some kind of law saying you can't spew magic every time you want to spew it? I'm asking because you might have an ounce of intelligence left in your head (but I already know the answer to that). There *are* laws. It doesn't matter what you do tonight. You're a wanted criminal because you banished me unfairly. You *will* lose your witch's permit." She slowly took off her mittens, tossing them onto the vanity, and turned around to face the witch. "If you come to your senses, you might not have to face life in the dungeon."

"Unfair banishment, you say?" Emily cackled, running her hand over the bed before letting it rest on the cat. "I gave you a life sentence and forbade love from ever knowing your heart. It's aggravating when my spells are overthrown by higher magic, especially *his*."

"Yes," Vienna fumed, not taking kindly to the thought of being banished again. "You love him. So why aren't you yelling at him? Honestly," she muttered before pointing out, "I told him to go away!"

"A friend of mine fell in love and earned his right as king." Emily threw the tale at the princess. "He was refused, even though he occupied himself with her rules. A witch banished her, and he became the paladin of her heart in a different form. And once again, he was cast away." She paused, removing her hand from her cat's back. "Yes, I love him. But he is also my friend, and you have deeply wounded him. You call yourself Princess of the Land, when you so easily throw hearts aside. What kind of queen will you make: daughter of the Green Queen?" Her voice rose and the palace shook. The wind blasted the window open, letting in the great, screaming wind. "You are unfit to rule! You: who rejects love!"

Thunder rolled, and lightning struck the palace.

Vienna jumped.

"Tell me once and for all!" The witch was glowing. She had turned a fiery red. "Do you have a selfless heart?"

Vienna couldn't breathe. She was scared, that if she stopped holding her breath, she would scream. Finally, as she watched the witch's arm come up to cast a spell, Vienna looked into her heart and cast the lies out of her mind. She found her own weepy honesty. "Maybe I love him . . ."

The witch sneered. "Good." Her arm came back as she worked the spell. "Then I can do this!"

Vienna ducked as Emily threw the spell. A ball of electricity flew through the air and smashed into the mirror. Glass fell around Vienna before she flung herself to the door. She could hear someone screaming for her.

"Vincent!" Vienna cried. She dodged another blue ball as it flew through the air toward her. She heard the witch's crackling laughter in the background. Another ball came fast, blasting a hole in the wall. It sent off sparks until the wall succumbed to flames.

Smoke filled Vienna's lungs as she called for the ghost, but she could no longer hear his voice. There was nothing but the insufferable heat, the smoke in her lungs, and the witch's laughter in her ears. She crawled along the floor, trying to figure out how she would survive this.

And then it became clear to her. There was no time to wait for whoever Vincent was calling for help. Vienna was her own knight, and if she died today, she would die like one.

Under the cover of smoke, Vienna ripped the dragon imprinted shield and sword from her wall. She rushed to her bed, where Halloween was still purring, delighting in the chaos, deciding it was long over for the princess.

Vienna assured the feline that it certainly was not!

She grabbed hold of the cat, picking it up by the scruff of its neck, and pointed her sword at its stomach. "I have my sword ready to impale your cat!" Vienna cried. Her shield had replaced Halloween on the bed. "If you do not cease your madness, I will be forced to kill it!"

Emily stepped forward, her black dress hugging her body. She looked down at Halloween and then leered at Vienna. "Go ahead, *little princess*, try."

Could she really kill a cat? Vienna's mouth curled in determination and she readied her sword. But Halloween began to grow. The cat grew and grew until she could no longer be contained by the walls. Halloween kicked at the walls, making holes in the ceiling and indents on the floor with her claws. Then she swatted at Vienna, hissing wildly.

Our princess jumped for her shield, gripping her sword as Halloween and the laughing witch stood before her. She crouched low, knowing there wasn't much hope, but she was determined to die a death worthy of her royal title.

If that was what it came down to.

Halloween prepared to spring forward, and Emily raised her arm. "Goodbye," she whispered, "*little princess*."

Halloween's mouth widened. Her teeth were hypnotizing as she lunged forward.

Vienna was blasted backward, and she slammed against what was left of the wall. She shook her head to fight off her dizziness before she looked up.

A man was standing between her and her attackers. Halloween had disappeared. The man's arms lowered to his sides and the flames around them were washed away, sizzling as they vanished.

He and the witch began to circle each other.

"I would never have guessed that one day we'd have to face each other like this," Augustus said. His dragon-like features were crisp and clear against the night's cloak.

Emily lifted her arms above her head and the space between them glowed. "It has been long since you possessed the ability to guess my actions."

"You're a childhood friend . . ." Augustus didn't move his hands from his sides. He didn't prepare to cast a spell. Instead, his features seemed to darken. His voice hit Vienna like sunlight, deepening into the break of day, and filling the room with the smell of honey. "Don't overvalue our friendship," he said. "If killing you means saving Vienna's life, I will not hesitate."

"Fool!" She sent her blue force at the warlock. The palace trembled as it streamed through the air. "You've already killed me once!"

"No!" Vienna screamed, but the warlock fixed his stare on the blue force. It lessened and lessened as it neared him, and then it was nothing but a wisp of smoke.

Augustus walked forward, and Emily's eyes widened in fear as he raised his hand. She grabbed at her throat, gasping for air, crying because, like her spell, his was set to kill. "Emily Tempest, Witch of the Falling Stars, you are unworthy to practice magic," he whispered as she fell to her knees. Her face turned blue, and her lips formed words of pleading. "You should have vanished while I still kept my patience."

His fingers began to move, and Emily struggled with her last breaths.

"Stop!" Vienna screamed. "As Princess of Highest Guard, I order you to stop!"

Emily's gulping breaths were frightening noises as he released his hold on her. "You think you can save her?" the warlock asked the princess, doubtingly. His eyes remained on the witch, monitoring her every move. "I'm afraid I can't let her live now that the dragon inside me has awoken. I can smell her hatred. She'll never stop hunting you."

"Then I'll make it easy for you!" Emily promised and an arrow flew from her hands, aiming for Vienna's heart.

265

There was a noise so terrifying that Vienna found herself screaming. The world around her disappeared. For a moment, she was trapped in ebony as a dragon cried. The sound was coming from inside the warlock. The witch had been set aflame and turned to ash. The arrow raced for Vienna. Panicked, she threw her hands up to cover her face. When she looked through the gaps of her fingers, the warlock was in front of her, holding the arrow. Unmoved from its course in the air, the arrow spun in his hands and then vanished from sight.

"You . . ." Vienna sat in amazement. The witch was gone, completely burned away, killed by the man she loved.

Grief erupted inside Vienna as she looked over all that one man had done for her . . .

Augustus turned to her. Kneeling down, he stripped her hands from her face before he bellowed in fury. "What do you think you were doing? Trying to fight a witch? You could have been killed!"

"Unhand me this instant!" Vienna snatched back her hands, her face burning with fury. "She came at me! What was I supposed to do?"

"Take up a sword and shield, of course!"

The feeling of his voice . . . And his eyes were so familiar, as if they had belonged to someone else once and that person was looking at her once again. "You weren't at the ball!" She let her temper soar.

"You didn't want me there!"

"No, I didn't!"

"Well then!"

"I think you saved my life!"

"Yes! I did!"

"I'm not thanking you!"

"No problem!"

"You're yelling at me!"

"Of course I am!"

They sat, panting, staring at each other. Her blue eyes were struck by his emeralds and swirls. The boy she used to know was so faint in his features, and yet so dominant in his actions.

There were shouts and cries from below, and Vienna knew that very soon they would be swarmed with guards and questions and assumptions.

Her eyes traveled with his. They looked to the wooden heart around her neck. With saddened movements and saddened words, he whispered,

"You wear my heart so well, my pearl." His fingers came up to push back her long hair, and for a reason she couldn't understand, she let him. He backed away, taking a few strides, and prepared to vanish.

"Wait!" Vienna demanded. Feeling too dizzy to get to her feet, she stayed seated on the floor.

With his back to her, he glanced back.

In the stillness, she found herself at a loss for words. What had she meant to say to him?

"If you're going to tell me you love me . . ." He waited, expectantly.

"I wasn't!"

He gave a nod and prepared to leave.

"Wait!"

"Quickly, love. I cannot stay here. I've used the dragon in my soul. I need to cool him before he strikes needlessly."

"Will he strike me?"

Slowly, as the choir of shouts and curses of the guards and king grew nearer, he turned. "Of course not."

In physical pain, Vienna hoisted herself to her feet and walked over to him. "Before you go, I need you to transport me to the royal gardens."

He raised his eyebrows. "Your father will be worried."

"You're a warlock," Vienna snapped. "Leave a note, won't you?"

His green eyes glowed as he considered her request, the dragon in him breathing as he breathed. He wrapped his arms around her, sending them both into the air. They vanished through thought and space. An envelope with gold writing fell from nowhere and landed on the floor where they had been.

Slowly, the dragon dominating his every action, Augustus removed his arms from her. He took in deep breaths, and then turned away. His steps sounded, the snow crunching beneath his feet, as Vienna watched him leave.

It was quiet. The leafless trees were covered in snow. The swings swayed silently in the cool wind, all while Vienna assessed the weight of her weepy heart.

"Where are you going?" she asked him, watching as he turned with a look of confusion. "You're not so bright, are you? Why else would I ask you to take us to a place where no one else would be?"

267

He stood, hopeful, but confused. It was his princess who was asking, after all. It wasn't safe to hope.

She walked up to him, shaking her head at her future husband's stupidity. She decided it would one day be an action well-mastered. "Don't you think it's about time you had an actual conversation with me?"

She shivered in the cold, and he touched the wooden heart that she carried. He looked at her with eyes that had endured a thousand heartaches, knowing a world of longing and disappointment, having had his happily ever after stripped from him when she had stripped it from him, once upon a time.

He took her in now. His voice warmed her against the winter air, giving her the impression of sunlight.

"Yes." His entire body found ease. The fierce dragon, hidden within him, fell back asleep as he whispered, "Of course."

CHAPTER THIRTY-TWO
Vienna in Love

Spring had come at last. The buds on the trees were waking up, foals trotted to-and-fro in the grassy pastures, terrorizing Poem, and Seamus spent his days in the gardens, walking on the garden path, thinking about white roses.

Vienna held a book under her arm as she strolled through the orchard, admiring the peach trees returning to life. It would be some time before she tasted a peach pie, but it was something she joyfully looked forward to.

Yes, she was strolling, but she wasn't without an agenda. She had followed him here. He was leaning against a peach tree, looking up into the tangled branches. He noticed her now as she moved toward him.

She had met Vincent first, but she knew so little about him. Each day, he sat with her, called out names, and listened to story after story of long-lost love and days of wishing and longing.

But the one name he never called out, was his own.

Vienna crossed the grounds and approached him. She leaned beside him and together they looked up into the mess and maze of tree branches. They seemed to signify more than tree branches.

Kindly, Vienna whispered, "You were in love, too, weren't you, Vincent?"

"Yes," he answered like all the other weepy ghosts as they remembered bits of their lives that still haunted them in death.

"Was it epic?" It seemed like a forbidden question. She had discussed love with hundreds and hundreds of different men, but somehow it was different when she talked about it with Vincent. Somehow it was personal.

He nodded. "It was epic."

"Did she hurt you?" Vienna asked, shyly asking the question she had asked them all.

"Several times," Vincent said, after some thought. "But I hurt her several times too." He gave the princess a knowing look. "You'll find you will. Love is about forgiveness, beyond all else."

"What was she like?"

He hummed, closing his eyes, thinking of her. "She was a real lady, with blond hair and grey eyes, wearing bonnets and clever enough to get her way without ever raising her voice. She played the piano. She played until night hid her waking world away. She would then dress in drag and take the fiddle she hid under her bed to the bar where the servants went to every night. There she would play as a man. No one found out of course. She was far too clever."

Vienna smiled, picturing Vincent with a rebel of a woman. "How did you meet?"

"I was one of the fools who'd ask for her hand in dances and doted on her when she'd play piano. She hated all that. One night, after some business with her father, I saw her climbing out of her balcony window. I followed her to the bar." He laughed to himself. "Enter a long series of events."

"I thought you said no one found out."

"Well, no one cleverer than I."

"And you fell in love?"

"Not at first. She didn't love me. She didn't trust me."

"But you kept her secret?"

"I like the fiddle much more than the piano."

"What was her name?"

"I should introduce her to you sometime."

"When you find her?"

"Hmm . . ." Vincent leaned on his elbow, propping himself up so that he could see her better. "Who's to say I haven't?"

"Do you mean to say that you *have* found her?"

He leaned back against the tree. "She's dying to meet you. But I told her it's impossible. Your *sight* is horribly misogynistic."

"I don't understand. How could you have found your love when no one else has?"

He took a woman's handkerchief out of his pocket. "I like to think it's because, quite literally, we lived happily ever after."

Vienna was at a loss for words, until another man's presence interrupted them. Vienna told Vincent that she'd be right back, and then hurried to greet him.

"Did you know Vincent found his true love in death?"

Augustus looked Vienna over before looking at the ghost under the peach tree. "His wife, Keria?"

"Keria?" She tasted the name.

With one hand Augustus cupped her face and brushed his thumb over her lips. "We can always go back to White Minstrel, you know? Spend a few hours fishing by the river. I don't think the new steward would mind a few illegal immigrants passing through. Plus, I hear there's a splendid bakeshop there."

"I've got an appointment at eleven o'clock."

"Are you sure you don't want me to remove the curse?"

"What curse?"

He raised his eyebrows.

"And lose Vincent and Seamus?" Vienna shook her head. "Besides, I think I've found my calling."

"Being a ghost therapist?"

"Every great ruler has something wonderfully peculiar about them." Vienna justified her decision. "I just so happen to be able to see dead, broken-hearted, crying men."

"What shmuck put you through that?"

"Hmm . . . I don't know. But word around is that he's a really nice guy."

"That tends to happen, once you get to know someone."

"Or once he finally strikes up a conversation with her," she argued. "In fact, I think I started that conversation."

"Yes, my pearl." He stroked back her hair, lovingly. "Yes you did. And I truly believe we will live happily ever after."

The End

Postscript
Princess Vienna of the house of Morel and Augustus East, son of the Dragon Witch, did get married. Five years later.